Jocks

A coming-of-age story

by Brock Archer

Brock Archer Arts Phoenix

JOCKS

Printed in the United States of America.

FIRST EDITION. SECOND PRINTING.

ISBN 979-8-218-50547-9

www.brockarcher.net

Acknowledgments and Disclaimers

The author wishes to thank Eduardo Suñer and Denier™ for the use of their advertising photographs (by Tarek del Moreno) in the production of the artwork used on the cover and inside this book. He also thanks them for permission to use the names Denier™, Addicted™, ES™, and AD Fetish™ in the text.

Thanks also go to Toyota™ and Lexus™ for permission to use the Lexus name and to Marriott™ for the use of that name. There are other companies and brands mentioned in this work, but these occur most frequently and most prominently.

Thanks also to Robert Milton Ingram for the use of the lyrics to "Strange Feelings."
https://youtu.be/rrQgCpUrjYo

DDICTED

jock

noun

1
athlete
especially, a school or college athlete (almost always male)

2
a person devoted to a single pursuit or interest
e.g., computer jock

3
athletic supporter

clothing designed to protect an athlete's genitals during sports (or other energetic activities);
may also be worn as a fashion statement or sex symbol

1 The Blue Bandana

I was an early bloomer, entering puberty shortly after my tenth birthday, but it was another year or so before I discovered the glories of pleasuring myself to a climax. Yeah, I heard older boys talking about it at school, but I thought it was all just talk, like their boasts about the girls they had supposedly fondled or fucked. In their dreams. Nobody really believed that anybody actually did that shit, did they? Might as well believe in the Easter Bunny or the Tooth Fairy.

Growing up on a small farm in Hilldale, Texas, between Waco and Austin, of course I knew all about sex...or so I thought. I mean, I witnessed chickens, goats, pigs, and sheep rutting until they collapsed, but who ever saw a goat jerk off? I mean, really?

My name is Patrick Murphy, but everybody calls me Rick. My brother Mike is about seven years older than me, so even though I looked up to him, I never really learned stuff from him the way that guys do with brothers who are just one or two years older than they are. Mike and I were complete opposites back then. He was tall, strong, handsome, athletic, smart, outgoing, and, consequently, very popular—

with the guys as well as the girls. I was a shy, awkward kid who didn't make friends easily. When Mike graduated from high school, he went off to the University of Texas on an athletic scholarship, so we only saw him when he would come home for holidays or school breaks.

One day when I got home from school, I set out to do my chores as usual. After I fed the chickens, pigs, and goats, I headed out to the pasture to check up on the sheep. As I broached a hill, I heard strange noises coming from the other side. At first, I thought maybe someone was hurt. As I crept closer, I saw someone leaning back against a tree with his two legs spread eagle. I knew it had to be Mike on the other side, and I almost called his name and ran to welcome him home, but at just that moment, he let out a grunt that was so loud even the sheep took notice. I saw a stream of white liquid spurt out to one side. I leaned over slightly and saw Mike with his hand on his stiff cock, jizz dripping from his right hand. Oh my god! It hit me like a ton of bricks. Guys really do jerk off! It was like that Christmas commercial when one of the animated candies discovers Santa Claus and gasps, "He really *does* exist!"

Mike was facing the other way, of course, and didn't see me, so, as he wiped the white gold from his hand with his bandana, I slipped back behind the hill and waited a few minutes for both of us to regain our composure. After a respectful pause, I crossed over the hill again, called out Mike's name, and ran to embrace him as if nothing had happened, detecting a salty sweet aroma that I have never forgotten.

The next day, Mike and I went out to the sheep pasture together and sat behind that same oak tree. Though I never mentioned the incident, my dick began to tingle as I recalled the scene. I tried to distract myself by focusing on the sheep when Mike pointed out that one of the rams had mounted a ewe and was humping hot and heavy. My dick began to inflate, and I thought I was going to die of embarrassment. I tried every maneuver I could think of to conceal my shame, but, of course, Mike noticed the bulge in my crotch and chuckled, "Bro, you better do something about that before it blows a hole in your jeans." With my face as red as a tomato, I stammered until Mike finally reached out, put his hand on my shoulder, and said, "Champ (I loved it when he called me 'champ'), it's OK. We all do it. It's no big deal. And anyway, it feels soooo good. Go for it!" With that, he squeezed my shoulder reassuringly one more time, turned, and walked back to the house.

With that license to proceed, I started rubbing my dick through my jeans until I just couldn't take it any longer. I practically tore my jeans apart trying to extract my throbbing cock. I pumped it like I had seen him do the day before, and, in no time at all, I shot off a huge load. I would love to say how good it felt, just as Mike said it would, but in all honestly, I was just shocked. I couldn't believe what I had just done. It was like a whole new world had suddenly flung open and sucked me into it.

Later, sitting across from me at the supper table, Mike threw me a slight wink, and I couldn't hold back a sparkling smile. "What are you so animated about?" asked my dad. After stammering for a couple of seconds, I found my new confidence and replied, "Oh, nothing. I'm just glad to have Mike home again." My mother said something about what a nice sentiment that was, and Mike and I just connected with our eyes. Gawd, I never loved my brother more than I did in that moment.

After supper, Mike announced that he had a date and would be home late. I went to bed prepared to jack off again, and when I reached for a rag I had tossed onto the floor, I spotted it: Mike's bandana. He had obviously left it for me. I jerked off again, but this time, there was less shock and more sensation. Man, it felt soooo good...just like Mike said it would. After I savored the moment, I wiped my hands with the rag, but then I grabbed Mike's bandana and wiped the residue off my dick. Suddenly, I realized that that bandana created a bond between my brother and me. I never washed that bandana, and I treasure it to this day.

The next morning, I woke up with another boner that just begged for relief. After I jerked off and cleaned up, I ran downstairs to see Mike. Dad was sitting in his usual spot at the kitchen table, and Mom was putting a platter of bacon and eggs in the center.

"Did Mike oversleep? I'll go get him," I volunteered.

"He's gone." My dad was a man of few words.

"What?" I asked.

"He left early. Said he had to get back to the university. Something about football duties."

Dejected, I shuffled over to my seat at the table, but before I could sit down, Mom added, "He left a note for you on the coffee table."

I started to make a mad dash for the den when Dad snapped, "Sit down! Eat your breakfast. It ain't goin' nowhere." I did as I was told, but I scarfed down my breakfast in record time.

"May I be excused?" I asked.

"Go ahead."

The note was just a single sheet of paper folded over and taped to seal it. I tore it open like a kid opening presents on Christmas morning. Mike had written just one sentence, a line from an old song, punctuated with little hand-drawn musical symbols in place of quotation marks: "Tie a yellow ribbon 'round the old oak tree." He signed it, "Your Bandana Bro." He knew.

That night, after I jerked off again, I fell asleep with Mike's note tucked under my pillow. After all these years, I still have that note, encased in a protective plastic sleeve, in a box where I keep all my condoms, lube, and sex toys. And, of course, that bandana.

From that day forward, I jerked off at least three times a day: every morning when I woke with a raging hard-on, every night when I went to bed, and every afternoon in the sheep pasture. Sometimes I even jerked off between classes in the boys' bathroom at school.

When I masturbated in the pasture, I started leaning against the oak tree with my legs spread eagle like I had seen Mike do. Each day I would try to see if I could shoot as far as he had, and afterwards I would wipe my hand clean with my bandana—mine, not the blue one he had given me—just as he had done with his.

2 Johnny

Our small-town high school, situated right in the middle of Hilldale, had only a few hundred students, and most of those lived within walking distance. A few of us were farm kids who rode the bus to and from school.

Johnny Andersen was my age and in some of the same classes my freshman year, but he and I never really associated with each other. We just weren't in the same clique. Hell, I wasn't really in anybody's clique. Johnny reminded me a lot of my brother Mike—athletic, popular, and so good-looking as to be disgusting. I hated him. With his blond/light brown hair, blue eyes, and cute little dimples, he was too handsome to be civilized. It was easy to see that in a few years he would be compared to a Norse god, but for now, I guess he was just a Norse prince. Unlike Mike, though, Johnny was just another pretty face and a dumb, stuck-up jock to me.

One night after supper, the phone rang. It was Mrs. Andersen, Johnny's mother, whom my mom knew from her garden club. Apparently, Mrs. Andersen had just learned that her aunt had died and that she and Mr. Andersen needed to leave for Shreveport first thing in the morning. She didn't want Johnny to miss the algebra test we had the next day or the football game that weekend, so she asked Mom if he could stay with us for a few days. When Mom got off the phone and told me the news, I balked, and she snapped, "Patrick!" *Oh, boy. My full given name. Here comes the hammer.* "These folks need our help."

And my dad jumped in, "And you will treat our guest like the gentleman we raised you to be."

"Yes, sir. But where's he gonna sleep?" I whined.

"You've got a double bed," my dad pointed out matter-of-factly. I fully expected him to remind me that Mike had often shared that bed with friends he had brought home from school, but, instead, Dad droned, "Or you could just sleep on the floor."

Case closed.

The next day, Johnny finished the algebra test a good 10 minutes before anyone else. *Just as I thought: another dumb jock who probably just guessed at the answers.* After the last bell, I got on the bus with an armload of textbooks and notebooks while Johnny followed me, carrying only his football, which he juggled incessantly. Though he sat beside me, he spent practically the whole time chatting with other kids around us. Feeling totally ignored, I just buried my face in one of my books.

"This is where we get off," I told him.

"Cool" was all he said.

As we walked across the field to our house, I concluded that it would be up to me to break the ice. Hell, it felt more like a glacier.

"So, how do you think you did on the algebra test?" I asked.

"OK, I guess."

Damn, you're not going to make this easy for me, are you? I decided to appeal to his interests. "Big game this weekend?"

That was the magic word. He lit up like a Roman candle. I thought I would never get him to shut up. Truth be told, though, I thought he looked really cute when he got that animated.

"Hey, wanna toss the ball around?" he asked when we approached our front porch.

"Maybe later," I said, "but first, I've gotta do my chores."

"Cool." I guess that was his signature word.

After I put my books into my room and changed into my farm clothes, I found him sitting on the front porch. I had expected to see him running around with his football, so I was shocked when he said, "Hey, if you'll let me help you with the chores, maybe we can get done faster and have more time to play afterwards."

Oh, great! He's just gonna get in my way and make it take twice as long as it should.

But it would have been rude to say no, and I was very pleasantly surprised when he really got to work. He had no qualms about getting his hands dirty, and we finished the chores in half the time.

"Wow! You're pretty good for a city boy," I exclaimed.

"I used to spend my summers helping my grandpa on his farm over in Salado," he explained.

"Cool," I quipped.

"Are you making fun of me?" he asked.

"Hell yeah," I shot back.

I thought he was going to get mad, but seeing the slight smile on my lips and in my eyes, he burst out laughing, as did I.

"You know, I had you pegged for just another stuffed-shirt nerd, but you're actually kinda—"

"Cool?" I interjected. We both laughed again.

"Actually," I confessed, "I thought you were just another stuck-up dumb jock, but you're actually not so bad."

"Cool," we chuckled in unison.

I explained that I still had to look after the sheep before we could play, and he tagged along eagerly.

It being a hot Indian Summer day, we shed our shirts as we sat under the oak tree. Soon, Johnny spotted a couple of the sheep copulating, and I noticed his crotch starting to expand.

"Dude, you'd better do something about that," I mimicked Mike, "before it blows a hole in your jeans."

I expected him to react with the same embarrassment I had felt when Mike used that line on me. Imagine my surprise when, instead, he stood up, dropped his jeans, and said, "No shit, man. You really don't mind?"

"Uh, no, I guess not," I stammered.

As I started to look away to afford him some privacy, he asked, "Well, are you just gonna sit there and make me jerk off all by myself?" I had never masturbated with another guy before, so it felt a bit awkward, but when he dropped his underwear to reveal a thick stiffie, I began to get hard too and knew that I just had to free my aching cock from my tight jeans.

"Jesus!" he exclaimed when I exposed my penis. "I thought I was big, but you're hung like a horse, man. Here I thought you were just another cute nerd. Who knew you were actually a stud in disguise?"

I had never really thought much about the size of my dick before. I mean, I had never seen another guy's dick, except Mike's, so I didn't have anything to compare to, but I guess I really was pretty big.

Then there was that other thing. Did he actually say that he thought I was cute? *Hmm.* I hadn't really thought of myself as good looking. I was still in my shy, awkward stage.

But I wasn't very shy when Johnny and I started beating off. We watched each other intensely. I was surprised at the noises that sprang involuntarily from his mouth and the various faces he made, especially when he got close to climaxing. It hadn't occurred to me until that moment, but I suddenly realized that I probably did the same thing. I made a mental note to inspect myself in a mirror the next time I jacked off.

"Oh, fuck!" he screamed as he exploded. I was usually not so demonstrative, but not to be outdone, I screamed even louder with each of my own cum bursts, "Holy fuck! Fuck! Fuck! Fuck!"

"Shit, man! Do you always shoot that far? I mean...dayum... that was twice as far as I shot."

"Practice, practice, practice," I boasted.

Johnny tried to change the subject as we reclined against the oak tree for another half hour, but our conversation quickly came back to sex. At first, we talked about girls and which ones we'd like to fuck. Somewhat to my surprise, our tastes in the opposite sex were quite similar. Eventually, we got back to the subject of masturbation. I told him about my first time, watching my brother and then following his example. He seemed surprised that I had been pleasuring myself for years since he had only jerked off for the first time last summer.

"It was at football camp," he said. "Some of the older guys had sneaked in some beer, and one night after they had gotten tipsy and uninhibited, one of them pulled out his dick and started to make like he was fucking his girlfriend. Some of the guys walked away, but others stayed to watch, and pretty soon we all had our dicks out and started wanking."

Johnny seemed surprised that I had never masturbated with another guy before. He said that he had jerked off with all the freshmen football players and several of the sophomores. He said they had often had shooting contests, "But after what I just saw," he added, "I'd bet you'd win hands down." I'm sure I blushed, but at the same time, I felt really proud.

By that time, we were both rubbing our swelling cocks in our jeans again. I'm sure he was just as ready to jerk off again as I was, but I thought we really should get back to the house before my parents started to get suspicious.

Just as it was a rule that I had to do my chores when I got home from school, it was also a rule in our house that I had to do my homework before supper. ('Supper' is what farm folks call the evening meal, what city folks call 'dinner.')

Despite that rule, I convinced my parents to let Johnny and me go out and play some two-man football before the sun went down. Dad balked, but Mom convinced him that it would be all right. "Supper's gonna be a little later tonight anyway," she told him, "and he can do his homework after we eat."

I don't know, but I suspect she just made that up to give me a little more time to get acquainted with Johnny.

It being October, most of the crops had been harvested, so the field was barren, which gave Johnny and me plenty of room to run. At first, we just tossed the ball back and forth like Mike had done with me when I was little, but I could tell that Johnny wanted more, so I said, "Go long." He looked at me like, "You're a nerd, dude. You're really gonna throw the ball that far?" But he had seen me shirtless, so he knew that I had some muscles, and off he went.

I could tell right off the bat that Johnny was a very skilled athlete. Just like Mike, he had speed and agility like someone older.

As Johnny ran across the field, I kept motioning for him to run farther and farther away. He glared at me dubiously but kept going. Finally, I threw him the bomb, and he caught it like it was destined for him. "Holy shit, man. Lucky shot," he said while walking the ball back to me. "Bet you can't do that again."

But, of course, I did do it again. And again. And again. After half a dozen perfect passes and an equal number of perfect catches, Johnny just froze and stared at me. "OK, but can you catch?"

"Try me," I boasted. I ran about 20 yards, and Johnny hit me with an easy pass. Tossing the ball back to him, I said just one word, "Farther." Johnny threw a 40-yard pass, which I caught effortlessly. "Farther," I demanded. Almost defiantly, Johnny threw a bomb clear down the length of the field. I had to leap high into the air to catch it, but catch it I did.

"Hrmp," Johnny snorted. "If you could just play defense, you might actually be worth something."

"See that post?" I asked, pointing to one side of the field, "and that one?" (on the opposite side).

Johnny nodded in the affirmative as if to say, "What of it?"

"That's the goal line. I'll throw you a short pass, and you try to get past me."

Johnny snorted again but took off after the ball. He ran it back in a zigzag pattern, but I still caught him and brought him down. I must confess that his sweaty, naked torso felt really good against my body. We ran several more plays, and I tackled him every time, each time lingering atop his body a bit longer.

"That was fucking amazing, dude. How did you learn to play football like that?"

"From my brother, Mike," I told him.

"Hold on," he flinched. "Mike? Mike Murphy? No way, dude. You're not fuckin' telling me that Michael Murphy is your damn brother! Mike Murphy...the All-American Mike Murphy at UT?"

"Afraid so," I said, feigning modesty but bursting with pride.

"Holy shit! That guy is a football legend. Coach says he's sure to be drafted by the pros in the first round this spring, and my dad agrees."

"Yeah, he's hoping to get drafted by the Cowboys, but who knows?"

We played a bit longer, switching roles. I would throw to him, and he would hit me. Neither of us ever missed a ball.

"Damn, Rick. You could be just as good as your brother. You must have football in your genes. How come you're not on our team? We could really use you."

I feigned a lack of interest, claiming that I wanted to focus more on academics. I was too embarrassed to tell him that our family just couldn't afford to hire someone to pick up my chores if I stayed after school for football practice. The weather had not been good to us farmers the past couple of years, so as much as I wanted to follow in my brother's illustrious footsteps, I had to accept the fact that it just wasn't in the cards.

3 Homework and Dirty Talk

Over supper, Johnny charmed my folks with praise for their sons—both of their sons. I was somewhat embarrassed but also flattered. He also complimented Mom's cooking and Dad's industriousness in keeping the farm going. When we finished eating, Johnny said to Mom, "Why don't you go take a load off your feet, Mrs. Murphy? Rick and I can take care of the dishes." Mom, of course, was very impressed, but Dad reminded me that I still had homework to do, so when I headed back upstairs, Johnny said to Mom, "OK, then I guess it's just you and me, Mrs. Murphy."

When Johnny finally came up to my room to join me, I asked, "It took you an hour to do the dishes?"

"Nah. I've been chatting with your dad about stuff."

"Stuff?"

"You know...football, the weather, the new farm bill that's just been introduced in Congress." I laughed it off like he was wasting his time trying to impress me. I didn't learn until the next day that he actually did know everything there was to know about that farm bill, including which congressmen and senators were likely to support it and which ones weren't.

"Whatchya workin' on?" he asked, leaning over my shoulder. I could feel his body heat beating down on my neck.

"English Lit," I mumbled. Johnny and I had different English teachers, and even though the curriculum was pretty standardized, each teacher was free to use whatever materials he or she wanted. "Mrs. Bagley gave us a list of quotes from various works, and we have to find out who wrote them and which works they're in."

"Cool," he said, "Like what?"

"Well, this one is from *Hamlet*. Shakespeare." And I read out, "Those friends thou hast and their adoption tried, grapple them to thy soul with hoops of steel."

"Ah, yes," said Johnny. "Polonius' advice to his son Laertes as he and Hamlet set sail for France. Most people are familiar with the line, 'Neither a borrower nor a lender be' from that soliloquy, but I like the line you just read."

Who the fuck do you think you're fooling? Mr. Kaplan must have given your class the same assignment earlier.

"What else ya got?" he asked, stepping away from my desk as if to size up the room.

"Well, I'm a little unsure about this one: 'Do not do unto others as you would that they should do unto you. Their tastes may not be the same.' Sounds like Oscar Wilde, but I'm not sure."

"George Bernard Shaw," said Johnny matter-of-factly. And before I could question him, he added, "Most people think that Wilde and Shaw were British because they did most of their writing there, but actually they were both born and educated in Ireland. Of course, you knew that, being Irish and all."

"Who the hell are you?" I asked incredulously.

"Just a dumb jock," he offered, like it was no big deal. "You done now?"

Speechless, I just nodded and put away my books.

"Good. I believe you had some pictures to show me."

Yes, my walls were covered with pictures of Mike, including some of Mike and me together. Johnny and I talked more about football and, of course, what all 14-year-old boys are obsessed with: sex.

"We'd better get ready for bed," I said. "You're probably not used to getting up as early as I am, but I've got chores to do in the morning before we catch the school bus." We stripped down to our briefs, but we didn't go to bed right away. Instead, we continued our conversation about the favorite topic of boys everywhere.

I was dying to know more about his experiences jerking off with other guys on the football team, but I didn't want him to think that I was queer, so I was relieved when he volunteered the information.

"Circle jerks?" I asked.

"Yeah, sometimes we stand or sit around in a circle and jerk off. The object of the game is to see who can cum first. In one variation, we don't beat ourselves off; each guy pumps the man next to him. The guy who finishes last has to clean up the mess."

It was all I could do to keep my jaw from hitting the floor. *Wow! That's a lot of cum.*

"Dude, if you expect me to sleep in that bed with you, you're gonna have to do something about that submarine," he insisted, pointing at the tent in my briefs.

"Submarine?"

"Yeah, it's big and hard and full of semen, isn't it?"

I had to laugh in spite of myself.

"And," he continued, "I'll be damned if I'm gonna let you be poking me with that thing all night."

"Well, looks to me like you're launching a pretty big sub yourself," I said, pointing at the bulge in his briefs.

As he pulled down his underwear and sat on the bed, I pulled down mine and sat in my desk chair facing him. We started out stroking ourselves slowly and gradually picked up the pace. Shortly, he gave me a questioning look. No words were spoken, but I knew what he was asking me. I simply nodded, pulled my chair closer to him, reached out, and took his cock in my hand. At the same time, he took over pumping my man meat. As soon as I felt his skin on mine, an electric shock zapped me.

"Oh fuck!"

"Feels good, doesn't it?"

"Fuck yeah," I gushed.

Maybe it was just the novelty of having another man's hand on my dick for the first time, but having him jerk me off felt better than jerking myself off. And I don't know, but it looked like he might have felt the same way.

"Oh shit!" he exclaimed. "Damn motherfucker!"

His dirty talk turned me on even more, so I reciprocated.

"Fuck, man. Your hand on my cock feels fuckin' fantastic. My dick never felt so gooood."

"It feels...." From the way his body twitched, I could tell that another electric shock had interrupted his speech. "Are you sure you've never done this before? You're a helluva lot better at it than Hightower." (Boys on the football team often called each other by their last names, as their coaches usually did.)

I smirked at the thought of being able to please him more than one of his teammates had. Seeing precum forming on the tip of his dick, I reached over with my free hand and wiped off the nectar with my finger and brought it to my mouth. His eyes squinted as if to disapprove, but his throbbing cock told me otherwise. It began to pulsate, so I knew he was getting close, as was I. I slowed my pumping almost to a halt.

"What the fuck are you doing, man? Don't stop now. You're fuckin' killing me, dude. Beat the shit out of that motherfucker!" I relished in the thought of torturing my new friend—like a gentleman, of course—but I acquiesced to his wishes and picked up the pace. The throbbing increased. The closer he got, the tighter he squeezed my dick with one hand and practically choked the bed sheet to death with the other. All I could think of was that I was glad he was squeezing my dick and not my balls.

He scrunched up his face just as he exploded all over himself...and me! I would swear that he shot out even more semen than he had that afternoon. I worried that he was going to scream as he had then, causing my parents to barge in to see what was the matter, so I grabbed a pillow and covered his mouth. Sure enough, he screamed into the pillow. His spasms continued for what seemed like forever until he fell back on the bed gasping for breath, releasing my cock in the process. When he finally came back down to Earth, he grasped for words to describe the intense feeling he had just experienced, and then it hit him.

"Oh my god, champ. I'm so sorry. I was so wrapped up in my own orgasm that I completely lost track of yours. We've gotta get you off too."

As he grasped my still-hard dick again, two thoughts consumed me. One was that it was so considerate of him to want to please me as I had pleased him. *I think I was wrong about you. You're really a nice guy.*

The second thought that hit me was that he had called me 'champ.' Nobody but Mike had ever called me that before, and I'm sure that I hadn't told him about that. I don't know where it came from, but it felt incredibly good.

Refocusing on my tingling cock, I suddenly became aware that he was now pulling on my dick with both hands. He must have seen my eyes widen, so he explained, "Jeez, champ"—there it was again, and my cock pulsated in response—"I can't believe how big this motherfucker is. It's a fucking monster." His flattery almost brought me to a climax, but he suddenly let go. I glared at him in shock, and before I could say anything, he sneered, "How the hell do you like it, motherfucker?"

Stunned and without realizing that I had loads of his cum on one of my hands, I grabbed his shoulders and commanded, "I'm gonna fuckin' burn your ass, you sonofabitch, if you don't jerk off that fuckin' monster right now." I could see him struggling to suppress his mischievous glee as he wrapped both hands around my cock again and resumed pumping and pulling. "Oh, gawd. It feels so goddam good."

"Cum for me, champ. Shoot that fuckin' load. Blow the goddam roof off this fuckin' house. Give it to—"

And I did. The first load shot way over his head and landed on the wall behind him. The second one flew even higher. The third one hit him in the face and almost put one eye out. The fourth and fifth volleys coated his chest and abs. It all happened so fast that he barely had time to react. "What the fuck, dude?" he exclaimed as he reflexively released his grip on my still-pulsating member. Not quite spent, I fell back in my chair, gripping my own cock now, and the next three loads covered my pecs and abs. Number nine soaked my pubes, and the last two spilled over the head of my cock and dribbled onto my hand.

When I finally stopped hyperventilating and opened my eyes, I could hardly believe the beautiful carnage that we had just created. My gawd, there was cum everywhere. Johnny spoke before I could, "Jeeezus, man! You came more than the whole fuckin' football team. If I hadn't seen you cum this afternoon, I would have sworn that you had been saving up for months. Who knew that two balls could hold that much juice?"

I laughed, but I had to suppress it because I was still struggling to catch my breath. When my capacity for speech finally returned, I gloated, "You look like shit, man."

"Oh yeah? Well, you look like a fucking snowman." I had to laugh in spite of myself. I swirled around and sat on the bed next to Johnny. The two of us fell back on the bed, our arms touching. We turned our heads, our eyes connecting, smiling at each other.

"Oh shit, buddy, let me get that jizz before it oozes down into your eye." *'Buddy?' Where did that word come from? I don't know, but it just seems right.* Johnny and I had started the day as strangers—aloof strangers at that—but we had become acquaintances, and now were we actually becoming friends?

I reached over and gently (dare I say 'lovingly'?) wiped my cum from Johnny's eyebrow.

"Umm, Rick, I hope I didn't offend you with my foul language. I guess I just got carried away."

"Are you fuckin' crazy?" I asked. "I thought it was spec-fucking-tacular. It was so hot, it really turned me on and got my juices flowing. I wish I had recorded it so I could play it back whenever I wanted. I could listen to you talk like that all day."

Johnny smiled back at me with a mixture of bewilderment and delight.

"Let's clean up," I said. My parents' bedroom was on the first floor, so I wasn't too concerned when we traipsed to the bathroom with nothing on but our cum and our devilish grins. I suggested that Johnny shower first while I took a piss and brushed my teeth.

After a few minutes, Johnny pulled back the curtain and asked, "I dunno. Do you think I got it all? I inspected his body as thoroughly as I dared.

"I think so," I said. "Hey, how about you step aside, let me wash up, and you can check to see if I got it all too." That was a mistake. I immediately started to pop another boner, and so did he. We agreed to jerk off again in the shower.

Johnny peed and brushed his teeth while I turned down the bed covers. When he came back into my bedroom, I was already lying down on my back under the covers on one side. He crawled in naked, as I was.

"You'd better roll over and face the other way, champ. I'll be damned if I'm gonna have you poking me with that bazooka all night."

"I could say the same to you, buddy, but I probably would never even feel that little peanut."

"Oh, dude, you're asking for a whoopin'."

"Yeah, you and what army?"

We continued swapping friendly insults until we eventually drifted off to sleep.

I don't know what he dreamed about that night, but I know that we both woke up with morning wood. Of course, we wasted no time jerking off again, but even so, I went through the entire school day holding books in front of my crotch.

We got back our algebra tests. I scored a pretty respectable 97, but when I asked Johnny how he had done, he just replied, "OK," and we left it at that.

4 Football Night

It was a Friday—football night—practically a state holiday in Texas. Up north, football is just a game, but in Texas, it is a religion—right up there with Protestantism, Conservatism, and Capitalism.

After school, Johnny stayed behind in the gym while I took the bus home and rushed through my chores. I hadn't been to a football game since Mike graduated, but I begged my folks to let me go, and they finally relented. Truth be told, I think they were secretly thrilled that I was finally coming out of my shell. And they really liked Johnny.

Of course, I was still too young to get a driver's license, so Johnny arranged for Hightower's parents to pick me up. Yeah, *that* Hightower. *Oh, the irony.*

Freshmen were members of the junior varsity team and generally didn't get to play with the varsity team, but they were required to suit up anyway, and when the team's wide receiver got injured in the first quarter, Johnny was drafted to replace him. It was a good thing, too. At the end of the first quarter, we were trailing 10 to nothing, but by half-time, we trailed by only three points, and we ended up winning the game by 21, thanks to Johnny's three touchdowns. Johnny was named the game's MVP, unprecedented for a freshman, but very well deserved.

On the field, Johnny was a perfect blending of science and art as well as strength. He was a thing of beauty. I could just imagine Leonardo da Vinci and Leroy Neiman fighting over the commission to memorialize him on canvas—Leonardo with his understanding of anatomy as the substructure of portraiture and Neiman with his ability to capture the dynamics and passion of sports.

Unlike most people, I had seen Johnny naked, so I knew how beautiful his body was, but that's not what I'm talking about. I'm talking about his athleticism. Like my brother Mike, he ran like a jaguar and leaped like a gazelle with the fluidity and grace of a ballet dancer.

But he played the game with his mind as well as his body. With every move, you could just see him computing every variable: the trajectory of the ball in motion, propulsion, and resistance. And like a champion chess player, he always knew where every man was on the field at all times. Even when he couldn't see them, he could apply the laws of physics to calculate their locations and how fast they could move in any direction, so he always knew where he and the ball needed to be.

I knew that night that this man had a stellar career ahead of him. Maybe he would be a professional athlete, maybe a Nobel physicist, or possibly a pioneering astronaut, but one way or another, Johnny Andersen was destined for the stars.

The Hightowers drove us back to my house, praising Johnny the whole time. It may seem odd since I had nothing to do with Johnny's success, but I actually felt proud, much like I used to feel with Mike.

When we got back to my house it was late, but Mom and Dad were still up, and I babbled on and on to them about what a great game it was and how great Johnny was. I think I actually embarrassed him, but I couldn't help it. It was all my parents could do to keep from bursting with joy—joy for Johnny, yes, but mostly joy for my newfound zest for life.

Of course, Johnny and I exchanged amicable insults before masturbating and going to bed. I had showered before going to the game, and Johnny had showered at the gym after the game, so we skipped the showers and just washed up with wet wash cloths.

In the morning, we jacked off again and washed up. When Johnny went to the bathroom, I started tidying my room, and when I picked up one of his shirts from the floor, a folded sheet of paper fell out of the pocket. I picked it up, thinking nothing of it until I recognized it as his algebra test paper. I wouldn't have paid it any attention, but the grade was clearly visible. He had scored a perfect 100. *What the...?* As I unfolded the paper, I saw that he had not only answered every question correctly, but he had provided proofs for every solution. Clearly, Johnny was no dumb jock. The sonofabitch was a friggin' genius—at least as far as math was concerned.

School was easy for me, but I still had to study to maintain straight A's—unlike Johnny, who, as he once told me, had a "pornogra...er... photographic memory." He could read or hear something once, and it was forever etched into his brain.

He was more than a walking encyclopedia, though. He had a unique way of thinking. He could analyze a problem or situation down to its finest detail, but he could also connect seemingly unrelated elements or events and synthesize them into a unified whole. Most people lean more toward the ability to analyze or to synthesize; rare are the people who can do both well, and nobody did it as well as Johnny.

I re-folded the test paper and put it back into his shirt pocket. Obviously, he didn't want to make a show of his talent, so I never mentioned it.

Though it was a Saturday, I still had chores to do—work never ends on a farm—but with Johnny's help I also had more free time, which Johnny and I spent playing football, chatting, and just generally having a good time. We were actually grateful when time came to check up on the sheep because it gave us the opportunity to jerk off at our leisure. Naturally, I tortured Johnny with my stop-and-start antics, and he thrilled me with the nastiest, most vulgar language he could dredge up from his perverted mental thesaurus.

When we got back to the house, Mom was in the garden, and Dad had run to the farm supply store, so when the phone rang, I picked it up. "It's your mom, buddy."

"Yeah, he calls me 'buddy'," I heard him tell her. "Yeah, I guess you could say that we hit it off, and Mr. and Mrs. Murphy have been super. I still think I'm old enough that I could have taken care of myself at home, but I'm glad I got to come here. They're really nice people." After a brief pause, he continued, "Yeah, the game was great. We won by 21 points." He never told her that he had scored those three touchdowns. "Oh, OK, well you and Dad do what you have to do. Don't worry about me. I'll be just fine here...if they'll keep me."

"She wants to talk to you," Johnny said, handing the phone back to me. I listened attentively as Mrs. Andersen explained that they would have to stay in Louisiana a bit longer to wrap up her aunt's affairs. She wanted me to ask my folks if they would mind keeping Johnny for a couple more days.

"Oh, I don't have to ask them," I assured her. They love having him here. I think they would adopt him if they could." She laughed heartily.

"He didn't tell you about last night's game, did he?" I asked. I informed her that Johnny had practically won the game single-handedly and was named MVP. She seemed mildly surprised, but I guess she really knew her son.

"Sometimes he's a bit more modest than he needs to be," she explained. *Yeah, like not telling anybody that he's a friggin' Einstein.*

When Dad came home and walked through the front door with Mom, I told them about the phone call and explained that Johnny would be staying with us for a couple more days.

"Well, of course, you're welcome to stay here, Johnny," Mom assured him. "We're delighted to have you."

After supper, Johnny again volunteered himself and me to wash the dishes, and this time Mom accepted graciously. "Your folks are really nice," he confided to me as I washed the dishes and he dried. I had to confess that I was a very fortunate kid. "God only knows what went wrong with you," he teased.

I splashed dish water in his face, and he retaliated with mock boxing jabs until Dad's voice boomed from the den, "You boys better behave or you'll be sleeping in the pig sty tonight." We choked back our giggles and finished cleaning the kitchen.

Before going up to my room, we sat in the den and watched TV with my folks for about an hour. I was dying to get upstairs, but I also wanted to show my parents that I really did appreciate them. And I didn't want them to get suspicious about what we were doing up there.

That night was a repeat of what we had done our first night together. We talked, exchanged friendly barbs, jerked each other off, showered, beat off again, and drifted off to sleep telling each other how shitty the other man was. It was a match made in heaven.

The next three days were more of the same except that our barbs got sharper, and Johnny's language got raunchier and more perverse, much to my delight.

5 Weekend at Johnny's

On Tuesday, Mr. Andersen called to let Johnny know that they would be getting home very late and suggested that he spend the night with us, and they would pick him up after school the next afternoon. I spent all day Wednesday in a funk. I knew that I would still see Johnny at school, but I wondered if we would ever get to spend any more "private time" together.

That afternoon, as I was about to get on the school bus to go home, I heard Johnny yell, "Rick! Rick!" I turned to see Johnny running toward me with the broadest smile spread across his face. "My folks are here, and they want to drive you home."

"Thanks, but—"

"Oh, stuff it, asshole. They want to thank your folks for letting me stay with you these past few days, so you're coming with us whether you like it or not." The ride was very pleasant. I had never ridden in a Lexus before, and Mr. and Mrs. Andersen were so nice. They kept saying how much they appreciated our looking out for Johnny in their absence and how much he had enjoyed his time with us and what a good influence I had been on him. *Me, a good influence on him? Really? What the hell?*

When we got to our house, the Andersens repeated their thanks to my parents, and Mrs. Andersen gave my mom a ceramic vase she had picked up in Louisiana. It was a perfect gift. Mom loves gardening, and the vase was pretty but not so expensive as to make her feel indebted or embarrassed.

"Please let us return your generosity," Mrs. Andersen said to my folks. "We would love to have Rick stay with us for a few days." I couldn't believe my ears. I was thrilled, but I knew there was no way my folks would let me out of my chores that long, and I was right. My dad thanked the Andersens for the offer but declined.

"How about a compromise?" said Mr. Andersen. "What if I pick up Rick after he has finished his chores Friday afternoon and take him with us to the game?" (It was an away game, but the host team was not far.) "He can stay with us Friday night and through the weekend, but I'll bring the boys over every morning and every afternoon to take care of their chores."

"Oh, that's very generous of you to offer," said Mom, "but—"

"We accept," my dad interjected.

I was stunned. I thought my mom might accept the offer, but I never thought my dad would be the one to do it. I jumped up and hugged him right then and there, and I must admit that I was surprised when Johnny hugged my parents too.

After school on Friday, Johnny and I walked the short distance to his house. When I saw it, I thought my eyes would pop out of my head. It was the Taylor

Mansion. Of course, everybody in town knew the Taylor Mansion—it was a local landmark—but I had no idea who lived there.

Wide stairs led up to the front porch, held up by Greco-Roman columns, a motif carried through in the foyer and living room. Crystal chandeliers hung over the living room and dining room, which were furnished nicely, but not extravagantly. In short, the house was a lot like Johnny, a class act, but not ostentatious.

"Hi, mom," said Johnny, greeting Mrs. Andersen in the kitchen with a peck on the cheek. "I'm starved," he announced. "What've we got to eat?" he asked as he opened the refrigerator door and surveyed the contents.

"There are some cookies on the table, but just one. You don't want to spoil your dinner."

She spotted me when she turned to brush Johnny away from the fridge. "Rick! So nice to have you with us." She dropped the kitchen tools she had been working with, wiped her hands on her apron, and rushed over to give me a great big hug and a kiss on the cheek. "I hope you like lasagna." I assured her that I did.

"Your dad will be home from work in an hour or two," she said to Johnny. "And I need to run to the supermarket. You boys will be all right until I get back, won't you?"

"Of course, Mom."

"And no playing football in the house," she lectured as she walked to the garage.

Johnny rolled his eyes and directed me, "This way, champ." He led me through the large family room and through the sliding glass doors to the patio and the biggest swimming pool that I had ever seen. "Wanna take a dip?" Johnny asked.

"I didn't bring a suit," I said.

"Well, there isn't anybody here but the two of us, and you ain't got nuthin' I ain't seen before." And with that, he stripped down to his birthday suit and dived in. I thought the water would be too cold, but the pool was heated, so I stripped and dived in too.

We swam a few laps and got into a water fight and swam some more. After about half an hour of that, Johnny hopped out of the pool and lay naked on one of the chaise lounges, so I followed and lay in another lounge beside him. We didn't do much but hypothesize about the meaning of life and other mundane topics. All the while, though, Johnny played idly with his dick and balls. He wasn't hard, but he sure as hell was getting a rise out of me.

Much to my surprise, he reached over and started stroking my dick. He had never initiated contact before, and now he had one hand on my family jewels and one on his own. I don't know if it was the feel of his own cock in his own hand or the feel of his hand on my cock, but in no time at all he was sporting a huge, rock-hard missile.

When I saw how inflated he was, I reached across and started priming his cock as he continued to cup his balls. He had much less control than I did and started pulsating before I was even ready. I could feel that he was getting close, so I sat up on the edge of my chair to get a better grip.

All of a sudden, he jumped up and screamed, "Garage door! Mom's home!" But it was too late; he shot a huge load right into my face.

In a panic to get away before his mom could spot us, he snatched up our clothes, grabbed my free hand, and dragged me up the back stairs. After he pulled me into his room and closed the door, he took several deep breaths before he turned and, for the first time, discovered what he had done. After the initial shock, he collapsed on the floor, laughing hysterically. He was laughing so hard that he couldn't speak, only point at my face. In a brief moment of semi-composure, he said, "Dude..." but he was too torn up to complete the sentence.

"What?" I asked in an incredulous tone, and when I opened my mouth to speak, a load of cum dribbled down onto my chin. Johnny laughed so hard that he curled up into a little ball, rolling on the floor. When he finally gained enough composure to speak, he said, "Sorry, buddy, but you look like somebody just dumped a truckload of mayonnaise on your face."

"Well," I replied, "Sommmebody just did."

"Are you boys all right up there?" came Mrs. Andersen's voice.

Still laughing, Johnny cracked open the door and yelled back, "We're fine." And then he whispered aside to me, "At least, *one* of us is."

"We're just changing out of our swimsuits," he yelled back to his mother. "We'll be down in a minute." Then, laughing all the way, he led me to the bathroom to wash up.

When I came out of the bathroom, I found Johnny standing in front of his dresser, still naked as a jaybird. I had never really noticed before what a fine ass he had. When he spotted me in the mirror, he turned and tossed me a pair of gym shorts and a tank top. He picked a football jersey and another pair of gym shorts for himself. He put on the gym shorts minus underwear, so I followed his example.

When we got halfway down the stairs, Johnny turned to see if I was all right, and when he did, he gasped, "Oh, shit, dude. You missed a spot." He wiped a finger across my forehead to erase a spot of cum that I had not washed away and reflexively licked that finger clean. Without a beat, he ushered me on to the kitchen.

When we re-entered the kitchen, Mr. Andersen greeted me with a hearty handshake and his other hand on my bare upper arm. "Good lord," he exclaimed, squeezing my bicep, "He's got more muscle than you, Johnny." I figured he was just trying to be hospitable, but his touch caused my dick to twitch nevertheless.

When Mrs. Andersen turned away from the sink to face us, she gasped, "My word! You look like a wet cat. Jonathan Llewellyn Andersen, you march yourself right back up those stairs and comb that shaggy mop of yours."

As we retreated, Mr. Andersen walked between us with his hands on our shoulders and whispered to us with a smirk, "And while you're at it, you might want to put on some underwear."

As soon as we got back to Johnny's room, he turned to me and asked, "Underwear? What the hell did you do, man?" My dick replied with another twitch. "What the fuck, Rick?" Johnny sighed with his hands on his hips.

"Gimme a break, Luuuuu Ellen!" I snapped. "I didn't have the advantage of having just emptied my nut sack all over somebody's face."

"Sorry about that," he said. And with a little squeeze of my semi-erect dick, he added, "I'll pay you back later."

He reached back into his dresser drawer and pulled out two jockstraps, handing me one and keeping one for himself. “Maybe this will restrain you...and if it doesn’t, I guess we’ll have to get you a chastity belt.”

As Johnny went into the bathroom to comb his hair, I rubbed the jockstrap through my fingers, brushed it against my face, sniffed it, and put it between my lips. After I put it on, I felt like pinching myself. I couldn’t believe I was wearing one of The Great Johnny Andersen’s jockstraps. I wondered how much cum and man sweat had been washed out of that little piece of fabric.

When we got back to the kitchen, Mrs. Andersen asked, “What were you boys laughing so hard about anyway?”

Mrs. Andersen looked at Johnny. Johnny looked at me. I looked at Johnny. Johnny looked at Mr. Andersen. Mr. Andersen looked at Johnny. Johnny looked at me, and finally, I blurted out, “Pigs.” Mrs. Andersen raised her signature eyebrow, Mr. Andersen squinted, and I thought Johnny was going to have a seizure.

“Pigs?” asked Mrs. Andersen, her eyebrow still arched.

“Uh, yes ma’am,” I tried to explain. “I was telling Johnny about some of my humorous experiences with pigs on the farm.”

“I know what you mean,” chimed in Mr. Andersen. “We had pigs on our farm in Salado, and, yeah, we had some pretty funny experiences with them too.”

Johnny was about to burst, so he grabbed my arm and said to his parents, straining to get the words out, “Porky and I will go set the table.” Mrs. Andersen looked at Mr. Andersen. Mr. Andersen looked at Mrs. Andersen.

Once in the dining room, Johnny backed me into a corner and whispered to me, "Pigs? Pigs? I can't believe you just lied to my parents about PIGS!"

"Well, what was I supposed to tell them, Luuu Ellen? That you were laughing hysterically because you had just plastered my face with your baby batter?"

"Hey, it's a family name, dildo."

"Nah, I think it was your name before the surgery."

At dinner, Johnny and I both took extra-large helpings and then went back for seconds. "You boys had better leave room for dessert," Mr. Andersen teased.

"Oh, we will, Dad. We will."

After a big bowl of Blue Bell rocky road ice cream and a couple of Mrs. Andersen's homemade chocolate chip cookies, Johnny and I cleared the table and put the dirty dishes in the dishwasher. "That was delicious, Mrs. Andersen," I said. "Really delicious." She thanked me and kissed me on the cheek again.

I was dying to get back upstairs, and I knew Johnny was too. The jockstrap I was wearing was successful in keeping me from pitching a tent in the borrowed gym shorts, but it couldn't keep my balls from aching. Regardless, Johnny's parents had been away for nearly a week, so I respected his need to spend a little time with them.

In the family room, Mr. and Mrs. Andersen summarized their trip to Shreveport, bringing Johnny greetings from relatives he barely knew and skipping over the morbid details of their aunt's death.

Then, changing the subject, Mr. Andersen asked his son, "So, what's this I hear about you playing a little football Friday night?"

"Yeah, Coach let me in the game."

"Let you in the game?" I snapped. "You *were* the game, buddy!" Scooting forward to the edge of my seat, I turned to Mr. Andersen and gave him a play-by-play description of his son's triumph on the field. I practically acted out Johnny's maneuvers. The Andersens listened politely, but looking back, I'm sure they were laughing inside at my fervor, especially since I stole all of Johnny's thunder.

"You shoulda seen him, sir. He was fan-fu...uh... he was fantastic!" Johnny rolled his eyes at me, Mrs. Andersen raised an eyebrow, and Mr. Andersen struggled mightily to suppress a chuckle.

"Well, it sounds like you had a great game," Mr. Andersen complimented his son. "I'm sorry we missed it."

"Oh, I'm sure you'll get another chance," I popped up. "Coach Davis is sure to start Johnny in every game for the rest of the season."

"Oh, shut up, dude!" Johnny chided me. "Let's go back to my room," he commanded, pulling my arm, "before you turn my parents into zombies."

Mr. and Mrs. Andersen finally released their suppressed laughter and thanked me for sharing the experience with them. As Johnny literally dragged me up the stairs, I turned my head and thanked Mrs. Andersen again for the delicious dinner, but she was too consumed with holding her side and wiping tears of laughter from her cheeks to reply. She just waved her hand at me as if to say, "Get out of here before you kill me, dear." (Thus, I saw where Johnny inherited his laugh.)

On entering his room, Johnny released my arm, threw himself onto his bed, embraced a pillow, and cracked up. "You are so fuckin' looney, dude. You are a riot."

"Whaaaat?" I asked. "You *were* great Friday night."

"OK, and you were great under the oak tree at your place, but you don't hear me bending your folks' ears about it."

As I surveyed the room, a picture on the dresser caught my attention. "Who's this?" I asked, pointing at the cute little boy with the curly blond hair.

"Who do you think, douche bag?"

"Well, if I knew, I wouldn't be asking, butt plug." (If nothing else, I had Johnny to thank for expanding my vocabulary.)

"It's me, you idiot."

"Really? Damn! You used to be sooo cute. What the hell happened?"

"You're what happened, dickhead," throwing a pillow at me. "You've completely ruined me."

I've ruined you? Is there a hidden message in that confession that neither of us wants to admit?

I caught the foam-stuffed pillow and beat him with it as he rolled over in a fetal position and cackled interminably. I jumped on top of him and started punching him lightly with my fists. He rolled back over, shielded himself with the pillow, and we wrestled for control of it. After several minutes with one of us on top and then the other, Johnny reached around my waist and grabbed my crotch.

"Say 'uncle,'" he demanded.

"Eat me!" I replied.

"Well, I won't do that," he scoffed, "but I guess I do owe you one." And with that he slid his hand under my shorts and jockstrap and began to tug on my dick.

"Mmmm," I moaned. "That feels really good, but you know what would make it even better?"

"What?"

"This," said I, getting up, stripping off the clothes he had loaned me, and climbing naked back onto the bed. Johnny didn't bother to get up; he just hurriedly pulled off his clothes lying down and tossed them aside. As we lay side by side on the bed, as we had done previously by the pool, Johnny massaged my nut sack gently and petted my cock slowly. Since I was already semi-erect, I reached full saturation in no time at all. As he stroked me, Johnny talked dirty to me, but not in the aggressive way he had done before. No, I felt the warmth of his breath as he whispered the delicious filth softly into my ear.

With the first spasm of my engorged tool, Johnny repositioned himself between my spread legs and pumped harder with both hands. I was so tense that I clinched my eyes shut when I started to explode. "Oh fuck! Oh shit! Jeeezus Fuckin' Christ!" I screamed *sotto voce* as my canon shot one volley after another. My body jerked for at least two minutes before I could muster the strength to re-open my eyes, and when I finally did, I was shocked at the sight before me. Johnny's face was soaked with my cum. Unlike me earlier, he had plenty of warning. He purposely took my jizz on that adorable dimpled face.

"Oh shit, man! What the fuck did you do that for? Oh, buddy, you know you didn't have to do that."

He didn't speak. He couldn't. His lips were pursed tightly to prevent any of the cream from dripping into his mouth. I so much wanted to reach out and pull his naked body on top of mine, lick his goo-covered face, and bury my tongue deep in his mouth, but I knew that was just a fantasy that I could experience only in my dreams...as I would frequently.

When Johnny returned from washing his face, he came back and lay beside me again on the bed. "You really didn't have to do that, man. I never expected—"

"Fair is fair. Now shut the fuck up and go to sleep." Before I did, though, I faced him and wiped a finger across his forehead. "You missed a spot," I lied. He smiled before turning faux serious again.

"This is a queen-size bed, shitface. You stay on your side, and I'll stay on mine. I don't want your damn pole poking me in my ribs all night."

"Oh, I won't be aiming for your ribs," I retorted with a devilish grin. He elbowed me, and we both rolled over, facing in opposite directions. In the morning, though, I awoke to the feel of Sleeping Beauty's chest pressed against my back, his arm draped over my torso, and his morning wood poking me in the...well, let's just say it wasn't in my ribs.

6 November

"Good news," I announced to the Andersens one Saturday at their house. "Mike's coming home for Thanksgiving."

"Really, can I meet him?"

"Heck, no!" I teased Johnny. "I'm keeping him as far away from you as possible." Johnny pouted while his parents chuckled.

"Actually," I corrected myself, "Mom and Dad would like for all of you to join us for Thanksgiving dinner."

Johnny was so excited that I thought he would start turning cartwheels right there in the family room.

"Please thank your parents for the invitation, Rick," said Mr. Andersen, "but we're planning to have Thanksgiving dinner—"

"Tell your parents that we accept," interrupted Mrs. Andersen.

"But I thought you wanted to—"

"Why cook when I don't have to?" Mrs. Andersen explained. "Besides, all the ladies in the garden club say that Faith Murphy is the best cook in West Texas.

And you can always take me out for a fancy feast the day after."

Johnny looked like a little kid who had just gotten a pony for Christmas.

Mrs. Andersen cooked anyway. Mom made the main dishes, but Mrs. Andersen brought a casserole and a couple of pies. Johnny fawned all over Mike, who took it graciously. I'm sure he was used to overexuberant fans, though I thought I'd have to throw a bucket of ice water over Johnny. After we watched a football game on TV, Mike said, "Well, team, why don't we go outside and toss the football around a bit?" I thought Johnny was going to tear out the hinges as he bolted through the doorway.

After a few warm-up drills, Mike announced, "Scrimmage. Shirts versus skins. I call shirts." Johnny and I wasted no time ripping off our shirts. Even though it was late November, it was a pretty, sunny day, and we knew that we would both be sweating soon anyway. We would have played the rest of the afternoon and well into the night had Mr. Andersen not announced that they had to take Johnny home.

Mike had beaten Johnny and me by one touchdown, and I'm sure he was going easy on us.

Walking back to the house to shower and change clothes, I asked Mike, "So what do you think of Johnny?"

"He's good," Mike drolled.

"Good? He's fucking fantastic!"

Mike raised an eyebrow at my language. The fact is that we had not grown up using that kind of language in our house.

"If that bastard is corrupting you," Mike mocked, "I'll beat the shit out of that goddam little motherfucker." Of course, I couldn't help but laugh at the farcical contrast.

All the way back to the house, I must have sounded to Mike the way I had sounded to Mr. and Mrs. Andersen when I told them about Johnny's first game of the season. Mike listened politely and smiled at the change that he had witness come over me since he had gone away to college.

When we got upstairs, I went to my old room to dump my shirt, and Mike went to his old room, now my room, but his for that weekend.

"You decent?" I called through the cracked door of his/my/his room.

"No, but I'm dressed," came Mike's reply. It was a running joke we had worn out years before.

As I entered the room, Mike was sorting his clothes on the bed, and I walked around and hopped up on the foot of the bed.

"You know, champ, this is your room now," he said. "You really didn't have to give it up for me."

"I know, but you're taller, so it makes sense for you to have the bigger bed."

"Well, at the rate you're growing, pretty soon you're going to be as tall as I am, if not taller."

He was right, but he had always been my idol, so I couldn't imagine myself being as tall or as fit as he was.

As we chatted about school—his and mine—and, of course, about football, Mike carried his clothes from the bed to the dresser where he began to undress. When he pulled off his pants, I gasped involuntarily. Mike turned to see me gaping at his red underwear, briefs with a hefty pouch to make his assets look bigger, as if he needed any help in that regard. He chuckled at my reaction. "Pretty snazzy, huh? And the girls really love them."

"The briefs or what's in them?" I asked.

It was a bold question coming from me. Given the difference in our ages, Mike and I had never really talked to each other like that before.

"Oh, my! Somebody really has corrupted you," he giggled. "And speaking of girls, are you seeing anybody now?"

"Nah," I replied.

"How come?"

"You know what it's like when you live on a farm. You just don't have a lot of free time."

"As I recall, I managed to date a bit when I was your age."

"When you were my age, you were probably shagging every girl in school," which elicited another quizzical look from my big brother. "I'm sorry," I hastened to add. "That was out of line."

"If you want to talk about my sex life...or yours...I'm wide open, but that's not what gets under my craw."

"What do you mean?"

"You just don't get it, do you?"

"What?" I asked, perplexed.

Mike just stared at me like he was about to explode.

"What?" I repeated.

"Come over here, bro!" he commanded, with his hands firmly planted on his hips as if he were getting ready to attack.

I just sat there with a confused—and frightened—look on my face.

"Get your ass over her right now," he demanded, indicating the space right in front of him.

I strolled over cautiously as if I were walking into the lion's den. He grabbed me by the shoulders and positioned me between himself and the mirror atop the dresser. Pointing at our dual images, he asked, "What do you see?"

"I see you and me," I stammered.

"And how tall do you look compared to me?"

"You're taller," I said.

"By how much?"

"Several inches," I ventured.

"More like two," he snapped.

"Now, make a muscle," he commanded, flexing his arms to demonstrate.

I did as I was told.

"Look at those shoulders. You inherited those broad shoulders from me," he quipped. We both laughed, but I could see what he meant. Dad had broad shoulders too.

"How big would you say those biceps are?"

"I dunno. Twelve, thirteen inches maybe."

"I didn't ask you how big Johnny's biceps are," he snapped. "I asked you how big yours are."

The suggestion that my biceps could be bigger than Johnny's left me speechless.

"At least 16, I'd guess. Maybe more," he continued. "Now, how many 15-year-old guys do you know with 16-inch biceps? Not many. Not damn many."

Moving around to face me, he punched me a couple of times in the chest. "Those pecs are rock solid, champ. They're not as fully developed as mine, but you'll get there sooner than you think."

He ran his hands down the sides of my torso and across my belly. "Look at those abs. You're gonna have a six pack in no time."

Then he grabbed me by the chin. "Chiseled jawline. Your friend Johnny has a cute baby face that I'm sure the girls just love at this stage, but this jaw...this is a man's jaw. This is your ticket to heaven, champ."

Next he dropped to the floor and rubbed his cupped hands up and down my legs. "Fucking quads, man. Johnny hasn't got quads like these, and you're just getting started."

With his face almost in my crotch, my dick started to twitch in my sweatpants.

Getting up off his knees, he grasped my shoulders again and drilled his eyes into mine. "Rick, I know you think your friend Johnny is some kind of superhero. Sure, he's a hot jock, smart, good looking, and he seems like a nice kid. I like him. But trust me. He ain't got nothin' on you. You are all those things and more."

"But—"

"But nothing. And don't interrupt me when I'm ripping you a new one, OK?"

I nodded.

"Rick, I also know that you have always looked up to me, and I'm flattered. No, I'm honored. And humbled. But Rick, you are not me, and you're not Johnny, and you don't need to be. Bro, you're a fucking Captain America. You just don't see it yet, but I can tell you who will see it if you'll just let them." Seeing the puzzlement on my face, he explained. "I'll bet you that every girl at that goddam high school is dying to get into your pants, and from what I can tell," as he glanced at my crotch, "they'll be damn thrilled when they do."

Once he broke his grip, he said, "I'm gonna take a shower now, and while I'm doing that, you're gonna stand right here and stare into that mirror until you see what I see. You're going to stare at it until you see Patrick Captain Fuckin' America Murphy." And with that, he dropped his sexy red briefs and headed for the bathroom.

Trying to overlook my beet-red face, I surveyed my body in the mirror from head to toe and took stock of what I saw. Mike was right. I had been too hard on myself. I was really starting to come into my own.

Having caught a glimpse of Mike's dick when he pulled off his briefs, I pulled down my sweats and compared mine to my recollection of his, and I'll be damned if I wasn't convinced that mine was almost as big.

I reached down and picked up the red briefs he had left on the floor and sniffed them, as I had done with Johnny's jockstrap. Mike's underwear had a much stronger musky aroma than the jockstrap, but, then again, the jockstrap had been fresh. *Should I or shouldn't I? Oh, what the hell!* As I began to put them on, I marveled at the way they looked on me. I modelled them in the mirror and strutted around the room, occasionally fluffing my package. I flexed my muscles and boldly announced, "Patrick Captain Fuckin' America Murphy to the rescue!"

That night, I jacked off in front of the mirror, visualizing myself in those red briefs and imagining girls swooning all over me. When I came, I made quite a mess on the mirror, but if I do say so myself, it was a sight to behold.

After my morning masturbation routine, I ran downstairs for breakfast and was delighted to find that Mike had not left yet. He stayed for dinner, and between doing my chores and watching more football on TV, we tossed the ball around some more, and even though I knew he would beat me, I played with a confidence that I had never felt before.

When I went to my room to go to bed that night, I discovered something on my floor: Mike's sexy red briefs. Had he simply forgotten them, or had he intentionally left them for me? I couldn't decide whether to wash them or keep the manly, musky smell. I eventually decided to wash them but not before a week's worth of jacking off with them. To this day, that red brief has an honored place alongside Mike's note about the "old oak tree" and, of course, that legendary blue bandana.

7 The NFL Draft – Late April

On the last Saturday of April, the entire Murphy and Andersen clans, including Mike, gathered in front of the Andersen's large-screen TV to watch the first day of the NFL Draft. As expected, Mike was drafted in the first round—not by the Dallas Cowboys, but by the San Francisco 49ers. It was a bittersweet celebration, but more sweet than bitter. Even before all the hugs and pats on the back had been exchanged, the phone rang. "It's for Mike," announced Johnny.

"That was my agent," Mike reported after completing the call. "He wants me in New York tomorrow morning to begin contract negotiations. He has booked me on a red-eye flight out of Austin."

"You have an agent now?" asked Dad.

"New York?" asked Mom.

"Yes ma'am. All the team owners are there for the draft, and so is my agent. He said he has some other matters he wants to discuss with me too, but he didn't say what."

"I think you just didn't want to have to sleep in the single bed tonight," I teased.

"Anything to get away from you, bro."

On Monday morning the news broke even before Mike had a chance to call us: he had just signed a four-year contract for $16 million a year. The press was calling him the Sixteen-Million-Dollar Man.

Big deal. I'm Patrick Captain Fuckin' America Murphy!

From New York, Mike had to fly back to Austin for the last two weeks of his college career. Then, one day after school, I arrived home to find a very sexy sports car parked in front of our house. When I ran into the house, I found Dad scolding Mike for spending his money frivolously and even before he had received his first paycheck.

Mike explained that he had not spent any of his money on the car. "Those 'other matters' my agent wanted to discuss with me," he explained, "were commercial endorsements." Spreading his arms like a male peacock flaunting its feathers on the make, Mike declared, "You are looking at the new spokesman for Lexus...as well as several other big companies."

Mike went on to explain that the contract requires that he not be seen in public driving anything but a Lexus, which they will provide. "That's a very snazzy car," said Dad. "They couldn't have given you something less flashy?"

Lexus, said Mike, was getting ready to introduce a new performance car that they described as 'strong and fast; bold, but dependable; revolutionary, but classy; and, of course, sexy,' "so that's why they chose me," he boasted, with his nose facetiously turned up in the air like a flippant drama queen. Mom and Dad had to chuckle despite themselves.

"What are the 'other big companies' you mentioned?" I quizzed.

"Well, I'm glad you asked that," he said, handing me an envelope he had pulled out of the pocket of his new Brooks Brothers sports coat.

"What's this?" I asked.

"Why don't you open it and find out?"

From the envelope, I pulled out two cards, one with the Levi's logo and the other from Apple, both headquartered in the San Francisco Bay Area. "What am I supposed to do with these?" I asked.

Mike called them "account cards." The Levi's card, he explained, had a cash value of $5,000, which I could spend on any Levi's products, and the Apple card had a $10,000 value.

"My Lord," said Mom. "You're going to spoil that boy rotten."

"I think he can handle it," Mike said.

"Can I go show Johnny now?" I asked.

"I have a better idea," Mike suggested. "Why don't we all go? Dad can drive the Lexus over there, and Mom can drive us back." On the way to the Andersen's, dad commented on how well the car handled, and Mom gushed over the luxurious interior.

Of course, $15,000 in account cards was peanuts to Johnny, but he was very gracious because he knew how much it meant to me. And he was thrilled to see Mike again.

Back at the house, Mom set about getting supper on the table while I sat in the living room making lists of things I planned to buy. Dad and Mike stood on the front porch catching up.

"That was really nice what you did for your brother," said Dad.

"Well, I just told the marketing execs that if they wanted me to be their spokesman," said Mike, "the cards had to be part of the deal. Anyway, I think he's worth it."

I didn't know if they realized that I could hear them, but I could.

"I don't know what you said or did to Rick when you were here last Thanksgiving," Dad said to Mike, "but whatever it was has really changed him. He's really matured. He was always a good kid...like you were...but he's becoming a man now."

"I'm glad you brought that up," said Mike, "because I wanted to talk to you about that... about Rick. I think you should let him go out for football this fall."

I was shocked, but I knew that would never happen. Football would take too much time away from my chores.

"He's a great kid, Dad, and he's smart as a whip, but he also has a natural talent for football, and he needs to experience what it's like to be part of a team."

And here comes the door slamming in my face.

"I've always wanted to give him that," said Dad, "but who's going to do his chores if he's spending his time on football?"

"We'll hire somebody," said Mike. "Actually, I've already put out some feelers."

"Oh, really? And since when did this become your farm?" Dad scoffed.

"Dad, you and Mom have busted your tails for us, and there's no way we'll ever be able to repay you. The things that are coming to me now are there because you and Mom made them possible."

"You don't owe us anyth—"

"Dad, if you won't let me do this for you, let me do it for Rick...and Mom."

Dad just stared at Mike for a few moments before walking back into the house. "Rick," he addressed me, "would you be interested in trying out for the football team?"

The rest of the spring and summer passed like a Texas twister. Mike spent as much time with us as he could between quick trips to New York and San Francisco. One day in early June, Mike sent me out to his car with instructions to bring in the stuff from the trunk.

"Have you and Mom ever had a vacation?" Mike asked Dad. "Son, you know how it is running a farm."

"Just as I thought," replied Mike, "and you probably never even had a honeymoon, did you?" Without waiting for the answer, which he knew to be negative, he handed Mom an envelope with two first-class tickets to Hawaii—just as I was coming through the front door with the luggage set he had sent me to fetch.

"But where would we stay?" asked Mom. "Marriott Hotels—one week in Honolulu and one on Maui. I just signed an endorsement contract with them. They're paying for the flights as well as all of your accommodations and meals. You'd better go start packing," he said. "The limo is coming to pick you up first thing in the morning."

"But I don't have anything to wear," protested Mom. "Pack light," said Mike. "There's a shopping mall in the basement of the Honolulu Marriott, and anything you buy there can go on your hotel bill."

"But why the rush?" asked Dad. Mike explained that he and I would both be going off to training camp soon and that Mom and Dad needed to take their trip while we were still around.

"Oh, so you're going to look after the farm while we're gone?"

"Heck, no!" scoffed Mike. "That's Rick's job. I'll be here to supervise—which means that I get to sleep late—but Rick will be the one actually running the place."

"Me?" I asked, with my eyes popping out of my head.

"Why not? You know this farm better than I do and almost as well as Dad." Then, turning to Dad, he added, "You said yourself that he's practically a man now. Here's his chance to prove it to you."

The next night, Mom called from Hawaii to let us know that they had arrived safely. "It's the honeymoon suite," she gushed.

"Oh, really?" Mike pretended to be surprised.

Mom went on and on about how nice everyone had been—from the limo drivers in Austin and Honolulu to the bellboys at the Marriott—and how the hotel manager had greeted them on their arrival and handed them an envelope containing $2,500 "to cover any expenses outside of the hotel."

What Mike didn't tell Mom was that as soon as I had finished my morning chores, he had taken me to Austin in his snazzy Lexus sports car to use my cards from Levi's and Apple. I bought jeans, of course, but also some shirts and a couple of jackets.

At the Apple store, I picked out a desktop for the farm, a laptop for myself, software, a printer, and other accessories. When I went to pay for everything, the manager said that my purchases had exceeded the $10,000 limit on the card. I started to put some of the things aside, but Mike advised the manager to call the customer service number on the back of the card. A short time later, the manager handed the card back to me and told me that everything had been taken care of.

"Thanks," I said, "but I guess I won't be needing this card anymore."

"Oh, Mr. Murphy" (he called me by my last name), "the gentleman on the phone authorized your purchases. Your card still has its full balance." I couldn't believe my ears. I couldn't wait to get home with that computer so I could start jerking off to porn videos.

Back at the farm that evening, Mike and I reviewed résumés of candidates for the farmhand positions, and we conducted six interviews the next morning. Of course, Mike was with me through the entire process, but he had me take the lead. "You're the boss," he said. "You make the decisions." I hired two men, Eddie and Carlos, and they reported for work the next morning.

Like me, both men had grown up on local farms. Unlike me, Eddie actually enjoyed getting his hands in the dirt. Carlos was eager, but he had ambitions to become an agricultural businessman. He had already completed several courses at the local community college.

Both men were fluent in Spanish as well as English, as were all of the members of my family. When you grow up in South Texas, you either thank your lucky stars for the opportunity to learn another language and appreciate another culture, or you bury your head in the ethnocentric sand and let the world pass you by.

Carlos was Mexican-American, but he was hardly an immigrant. His family had been working the land we were on for generations, long before Southern plantation owners goaded Congress into launching the Mexican-American war in order to bring Texas into the Union as a slave state.

During the two weeks that Mom and Dad were gone, Mike and I reviewed Dad's books for the farm, and Mike showed me how to computerize all of the records. After all, he had just graduated from the University of Texas with a degree in business.

When Mom and Dad returned from their "honeymoon," I introduced them to Carlos and Eddie, our new farmhands, and showed them the surprise I had for them.

Behind the barn, we had erected a combined bunkhouse, guesthouse, and office. At the center of the building were a small den and a kitchenette with seating at the counter. On one side of the building was a bedroom with two bunk beds (and room for more), a large bathroom, and an office where we had set up the desktop computer and a printer. On the other side of the building was a large bedroom suite with a king-size bed.

"And this will be my room when I'm here," said Mike.

"Oh, so you've decided that too, have you?" asked Dad.

"Well," replied Mike. "The boss (pointing at me) did say that I should sleep in the barn."

"How did you manage to do all this in just two weeks?" Mom asked. Mike explained that through his contacts at ESPN he had talked to some folks at HGTV, and they had agreed to erect the building in exchange for the rights to film the project for a future broadcast.

The next morning, Dad, Mike, and I followed Eddie and Carlos as they did the morning chores. Dad expressed his surprise and pleasure at how efficiently they worked. "Rick's a good trainer," Mike told Dad.

After breakfast, Mike said, "Let's go to the office," where we showed Mom and Dad how to use the computer to keep track of the financial records as well as websites that could help with planting and harvesting schedules, weather forecasts, and farming trends. Mom and Dad picked it all up very quickly, which is a good thing because Mike announced that he and I would be leaving in three days and would be gone for a week.

"Oh, where are you taking our young farm manager?" Dad asked.

"Yeah, where are we going?" I asked, surprised as anyone.

"Hawaii," replied Mike.

"Hawaii?" Mom asked.

"Are you going to check up on what we did when we were there?" asked Dad.

Mike chuckled and explained that on his last trip to New York, he had signed a contract with Denier.

"Denier? Who's that?" asked Mom.

"It's a Barcelona-based company that makes swimsuits and underwear for men under the trade name ES." Mike did not mention that the company also had product lines called Addicted and AD Fetish. I guess he didn't want our folks to freak out. Quickly refocusing the conversation, Mike added, "They want me to do a photo shoot in Hawaii for their new advertising campaign."

“Does this mean that we’re going to be seeing you strutting around on national TV wearing nothing but your underwear?” asked Dad.

Mike explained that the photos would appear mostly in magazines and websites. “Compared to Marriott, Lexus, and Apple,” Mike said, “it’s a relatively small company, but I thought it might be fun, and my agent thinks it will be good for my image.”

“Oh, you’ve got an image now?” Dad asked. “And does your brother have one too?”

“No...well...not yet,” replied Mike. “But he’s been working pretty hard, and I thought he deserved a little vacation before he goes off to football camp.”

“I can’t wait to tell Johnny,” I huffed. “He’s going to be very jealous.”

“Not really,” said Mike. “He’s going with us. I cleared it with his folks yesterday.”

8 AL-OHHH-HA!

At the Honolulu Marriott, Johnny and I shared a room with two queen-size beds. The morning after we arrived, we dressed in our swimsuits to hit the beach, but we had to stop at Mike's suite first. He had asked us to stop by to meet the photographer who was coming to get acquainted and talk about what to expect in the shoot. When the knock on the door to Mike's suite came, Mike was in the bathroom, so Johnny answered the door.

"Oh, yes, definitely," said the photographer with an Italian accent, sizing him up. "You shall be exquisite *modella* for *la campagna*."

"Oh, I'm not Mr. Murphy," Johnny corrected him. "He's inside."

And when the photographer entered the suite, he approached me enthusiastically with his hand outstretched, "Such pleasure to meet you, Mr. Murphy. I am so looking forward to working with you."

"Yes, that is Mr. Murphy," said Mike exiting the bathroom, "but he's not the Mr. Murphy you'll be working with. I am."

"*Perdonami*," exclaimed Armando—he went by only the one name—"but such an abundance of male *bellezza*. Such a pity to have only one of you to work with." Johnny and I had to giggle.

Mike shook hands with Armando and motioned for him to sit on the sofa, where Armando also placed the large suitcase he had carried in with him. Johnny and I told him how happy we were to meet him and said we were headed for the beach.

"Arresto!" Armando practically yelled at us. "Stop! Stop! Stop! You cannot go to beach dressed in such *stracci*...how you say, 'rags?'" he insisted. "Come, come."

We walked back over to the sofa where he practically ordered us to remove our swimsuits. Johnny and I looked to Mike, who just shrugged as if to say, "Don't look at me; it's your junk."

Johnny dropped his baggy suit, but I kept mine on for the moment. *"Magnifico!"* proclaimed Armando. "Turn."

"Huh?" Johnny asked.

"Show me your *culo*, your ass. I cannot select right costume for you without assessing entire body." Johnny turned 180 degrees as instructed. *"Perfetto!* You have exquisite ass," he pronounced, launching into a rapid-fire soliloquy in Italian, from which we were only able to catch one word: 'Michelangelo.' And we caught that only because he emphasized it so vigorously. Johnny didn't know whether to blush, burst out laughing, or run like hell.

With Johnny standing before us naked as a Rodin sculpture, Armando opened his suitcase and rifled through the mass of swimsuits he had brought, occasionally selecting one, holding it up to Johnny's crotch and ass, and throwing it on the floor until he finally came to the "right" one. He ultimately decided on a baby blue bikini with navy blue stripes in a chevron pattern that drew the eye to his crotch.

"Put on this one," he commanded, and when Johnny did, Armando spent what seemed to me to be an inordinate amount of time checking the fit. Ultimately, he decreed, *"Perfetto!"*

When Johnny pointed out that the suit was cut so low that it exposed some of his pubes, Armando smiled from cheek to cheek and assured him, "It is modern fashion. Girls will fight over you now."

"You," Armando ushered me forward. "Show me what you have," but I was already starting to pop a boner. I was hoping that no one had noticed, but Mike had, and Johnny and Armando probably had too. I coughed and made an excuse that I needed a glass of water, so I went into the bathroom, concentrated on a movie I had seen in which one of the characters was repeatedly kicked in the balls, and didn't come out until my boner had receded—most of the way anyway.

When I returned to the sitting room and dropped my swimsuit for Armando, he gasped, *"Gesu Christo!"* making the sign of the cross. "You have *il pene mostruoso*."

After crossing himself again, he instructed, *"Girarsi,"* indicating with the rotation of a finger that I should turn around, and so I did. Though Armando had laid hands on Johnny quite liberally, he did so only after Johnny had donned the swimsuit. With me, he rubbed his hands all over my naked ass, "accidentally" brushed against my balls, and even combed out my public hairs with his fingers. I felt like a horse being put up for auction, and I'm pretty sure I caught the words *'cavallo'* (horse) and *'stallone'* (stud) in his ramblings.

Turning once again to the open suitcase, Armando rummaged through about five times as many swimsuits as he had for Johnny and finally shouted, "Eureka!" handing me a fiery red bikini with a deep-cut white pouch that clearly showed the outline of my shaft, helmet, and ridge—a feature known in the fashion world as VPN (visible penis line). A metal ring held together the very narrow waist band on the side of each hip, and a third, larger ring substituted for a belt buckle, revealing far more of my pubes than I thought might be legal. The seat was just wide enough to cover my butt crack but narrow enough to expose the dimples in my butt cheeks. I looked to Mike for his judgement, but all he did was cover his mouth to conceal a massive, devilish grin.

When we started to exit Mike's suite in our new ultra-revealing swimsuits, I reached for our old suits on the floor, but Armando beat me to them, threw them in the waste basket, and pantomimed spitting on them. As we walked out the door, Mike chuckled, "You boys have fun."

Johnny was chomping at the bit to get to the beach, but I convinced him that we had to go back to our room and jerk off first unless he wanted me to embarrass the hell out of him as we walked through the hotel lobby.

We spent most of that time on the beach eyeing beautiful girls and young women in their thongs and string bikinis, and we got many stares—from guys as well as gals—and even a few whistles in return. Of course, we spent a lot of time adjusting our junk or rolling over on our stomachs, and we had to run back to our hotel room once to jerk off again.

Just as we were getting ready to go back to the hotel a second time, we were approached by two gorgeous blondes who introduced themselves as Britta and Inga. We were skeptical when they told us they were Swedish college students on summer vacation. They didn't look that old to us, but since they seemed eager to discover what law of physics was keeping our skimpy swimsuits together, we weren't about to argue about calendars.

To make a long story short, we ended up back in our hotel room with those two "older women" teaching us the facts of life...well... some of the facts anyway.

Britta got Johnny naked first, and when Inga got my swimsuit off, she swooned, "Oooh, this one is huge."

Britta responded, "If you can't handle it, leave it for me, and I will take care of it as soon as I finish with this one." When she went down on me the first time, I thought I was going to die from ecstasy. *So that's what it feels like to have a mouth instead of a hand on your cock.*

When I regained enough sanity to open my eyes, I looked over to discover that Johnny was experiencing the same joy that I was. To be perfectly honest, I didn't know if I was turned on more by the sight of the naked young woman, Johnny 's face as he fluctuated between grinning and grimacing through the agony and ecstasy, or his dick getting moisturized by her wet tongue.

After several minutes, our Swedish vixens muttered something in their native language and switched places, Inga on Johnny and Britta on me. They took their time deep kissing us, licking our bodies from head to toe, gently nibbling on our nipples, and swallowing our cocks. Even though my erect dick was almost seven inches at the time, I was amazed at how much of it they could swallow, and it seemed that Johnny was impressed with that too.

Every time either Johnny or I would get close to shooting, they would let up and switch places again. After nearly an hour of that sweet torture, they finally let us explode. And when we did, they licked up the ambrosia, kissed each other, and then kissed us.

My first blow job and my first cum kiss. I was in friggin' heaven. I wasn't sure how Johnny felt about his cum kiss, but he must have thought it was worth the price of the blow job because I didn't hear him complain.

Between the blow jobs and the jet lag, Johnny and I were exhausted. The four of us ended up in one bed with Johnny and me in the middle and one of the blonde bombshells on either side of us. Inga and Britta encouraged us to take a nap so that we would be rested enough to do it again, but when we woke, they were gone, and Johnny and I found ourselves hugging each other. The ladies left a note thanking us for a good time and promising to see us again, but they never did. Johnny and I decided to shower and go back to the beach, but when we looked for our babe-magnet swimsuits, they were gone too. We concluded that the blondes must have taken them for souvenirs.

When we went back to Mike's suite to meet him for dinner, Armando was still there. They had spent the whole day sorting through and trying on various swimsuits. When we asked Armando if we could have our old swimsuits back, he said that the maid had already emptied the trash.

"What happened to the ones he gave you this morning?" Mike asked.

Sheepishly, I answered, "Well, we...kinda lost them."

"Aha!" shouted the photographer. "Armando told you that girls would love you!" He pointed to a pile of swimsuits on the floor.

"Those are the ones I tried on and Armando rejected," said Mike.

"They are all *eccelente,"* he said, "but not right for this shoot."

When Johnny and I began to sort through them, Armando insisted, "Take all. I am done with those." And so we did.

The next day, Armando photographed Mike in countless poses by the hotel pool and different beaches. Everywhere they went, Mike drew a throng of admirers, not because he was a famous football player, but because he was a gorgeous hunk wearing practically nothing in public. Johnny and I dubbed Mike's new fans "the Murphy thong throng."

The third day was spent trying on numerous pairs of underwear, and the fourth day, Armando photographed Mike wearing that underwear in his suite and even in some public locations. Many of the poses were very provocative: getting in and out of bed, getting dressed or undressed, pulling down his briefs halfway, exposing practically all of his pubes and even a hint of the base of his shaft. Johnny and I watched some of the session and then went back to our room to jerk off before heading back to the beach, where we had hoped (unsuccessfully) to find our Swedish bombshells or other equally uninhibited women.

On the fifth day, we decided to skip the beach when we learned that Armando was bringing in six gorgeous models, two women and four men, to supplement the shots in endless permutations. Of course, Johnny was eager to check out the female models, and I was too, but I didn't let on that I was just as curious to meet the male models and see how they looked in the sexy threads.

In one scene, Mike sat on the bed alone, completely naked, legs crossed to conceal his privates. The featured underwear simply lay on the bed next to him. In a variation, Mike held the underwear up to his nose to sniff it. In another pose, Mike sat on the bed putting on a sock with his legs spread in such a way as to draw the eye to his bulging underwear.

Then, Armando slowly began adding models in various combinations: one model standing or sitting behind him wearing the ES and Addicted underwear or posing completely naked with his junk concealed only by Mike's shoulder, a woman or man lying under the covers (partially) behind him, a woman and a man, two women, two men, Mike lying under the covers with various combinations of models in different poses, dressed or undressed.

In another scene, Mike stood completely naked looking into a dresser drawer full of underwear, as if trying to decide which pair to wear for his hot date. His image was reflected in the mirror and his cock and balls were concealed only by the drawer shot at just the right angle. Then, as before, Armando shot the same scene with different combinations of models in an assortment of poses.

Once, Armando had two of the male models go into the bathroom, and when they came back out a few minutes later, their underwear was filled out a bit more than before. When it hit me what they had done, my own underwear began to fill out more. One of the hunks seemed to take note and winked at me. Later, he slipped me a piece of paper with his room number on it.

In one of the outdoor scenes, two of the male models, dressed as cops, led Mike, handcuffed and wearing only his very revealing underwear, to a police cruiser. In another, he stood in front of a burning apartment building next to a fire engine and surrounded by four male models dressed as firemen. Of course, the building was not really on fire (though many of the onlookers were), but Armando said that effect would be added in the final production. Of course, it goes without saying that all of the outdoor shoots were traffic stoppers.

Armando repeatedly tried to convince Johnny and me to pose in some of the shots, and Johnny would have killed to be photographed lying in bed between the two female models, but Mike put his foot down on that. "They're 15!" he yelled at Armando. "Leave them alone. You can call them in three years." Mike did allow us to act as extras in some of the outdoor shots, but we were fully clothed and surrounded by other extras who were also completely dressed.

Johnny fell all over himself trying to coax the two female models to his hotel room, but I have no doubt that they spent the night in Mike's room, so Johnny and I contented ourselves with swapping fantasies of sex with them...and sex with the two of them plus the two Swedes. Then, of course, we jacked off.

When we got home from Hawaii, Johnny and I each discovered that we had an extra suitcase. We had not noticed them before because Mike had bought each of us a new set of luggage, which had been handled mostly by bellmen and skycaps. When we opened the extra suitcases at home, we found them filled with the swimsuits and underwear from the photo sessions—the ones he and Mike had used and the ones they had discarded. I couldn't wait to wear some of them to football camp.

9 Football Season

When Mike, Johnny, and I got back from Hawaii, Dad told us how pleased he had been with Eddie and Carlos, the two farmhands we had hired. It was a relief, because I had only two more weeks at home before I was scheduled to go to my first football camp.

Football camp literally was a camp, which is to say that it was held at a former campground in the woods near Fort Hood in Killeen, Texas. The practice field divided the camp into two sections. One had buildings that resembled a motel, and the other had cabins resembling a military base. You can guess which one they put us in. We were assigned by classes in four cabins (more like bunkhouses), each containing four bunk beds.

The training was rigorous in the Texas summer heat and humidity. By the end of the first day, we were all exhausted, but it was a good exhaustion. I had put in long, hard days at the farm, so I could take it better than some of the guys, even some of the seniors who had been playing football for three years or more, but I had never before felt the sense of accomplishment that I did at football camp. In time, I would come to realize that my work on the farm deserved just as much appreciation as my work at football camp, but at the moment, I was in sweat heaven.

The "motel" section on the other side of the practice field had private or semi-private showers, but our side of the camp had one big community shower, much like our locker room back at school.

I was always razzed as a kid. The other boys would call me Smirky Murphy, Murph the Smurf, and worse. It was all verbal, never physical. As long as my brother Mike was around, they wouldn't dare touch me, and even after Mike went away to college, his legacy was enough to keep me safe from physical bullying.

Back then, I just took the name-calling and internalized it. I didn't know how to punch back verbally without escalating things. Johnny changed that in me. Name-calling became not an insult, but a way of male bonding.

At school, before I met Johnny, I was too self-conscious to change in front of the guys, let alone shower with them. I would go off to the most remote corner of the room and change with my back to anybody nearby. But my experiences with Johnny (and, of course, the two Swedes) built up my self-assurance. When my teammates hit the showers at the end of the first day of training camp, I had no qualms about joining them.

As I was undressing, Hershel Morgan hollered from the showers, "Hey, Murphy, are you still fucking those pretty little sheep?"

"Well," I shot back, "It's better than those ugly cows you've been humping."

Morgan seemed stunned at first, but Johnny laughed hysterically, and the other guys followed suit, pointing fingers at Morgan, and punching him in the arm with their fists. "I guess he told you, Morgan," said one guy. "Way to go, Murphy," said another. And then even Morgan had to laugh.

Then Czynski asked, "Murphy, is it difficult to keep those sheep satisfied?"

"No harder than keeping your mama satisfied," I quipped. I thought Czynski was going to charge right at me and beat the shit out of me for that one, but he stopped short, glared at me, and cracked up, as did all the other guys.

At that point, I pulled down my gym shorts and revealed my huge cock to them for the first time. I tried nobly to keep my eyes off their dicks as I entered the showers, but they didn't have any qualms about staring at mine, which, even flaccid, was bigger than any of theirs—much bigger, in fact. Nobody said anything, but they all gawked. Johnny was the only one who didn't seem shocked because, of course, he had seen it many times before. I think he got a kick, though, out of watching everyone else's reaction.

Hightower finally broke the awkward silence as I stepped into the shower with the jocks. Pointing straight at my dick, he asked, "Murphy, aren't you a little big for those poor little sheep?"

"Yeah," I bemoaned, "I guess I'm gonna hafta start hunting for some bigger ass." And with that, I aimed my big cock directly at him and shook it.

The reactions came out in rapid succession:

"Oh, my gawd, Hightower, you better run."

"Yeah, Hightower, he's liable to kill you with that big thing."

"It's hunting season, Hightower, and you're about to become somebody's trophy."

And all the guys grabbed their dicks and started aiming them at Hightower.

Hightower and I laughed along with everyone else, but I soon realized that my little stunt might not have been such a great idea. My cock started to rise, and I thought I would die, but then I noticed that Johnny was starting to pop a boner too, and then Morgan, and even Hightower. Finally, Hightower raised his hand in a kind of salute and shouted, "Circle jerk!"

"Circle jerk!" repeated Johnny.

And then everyone joined in a chant, "Circle jerk! Circle jerk. Circle jerk!"

I wasn't the first one to shoot, but I wasn't the last one either. I did shoot the farthest, though, and that won me some additional admiration from the guys. It was a shame to see all that delicious nectar go down the drain, but a couple of shots from somewhere did hit my feet and legs. More importantly, in that moment, I felt something that I had never really felt before. It could be described as orgasmic, but not sexual, if that makes any sense. For the first time in my life, aside from my family, I really felt like I belonged.

Every evening at football camp, some of the players would sit around a fire pit (even after dark it was still too hot to have an actual fire) talking about football and girls, girls and football, football and girls. On our last night, Hightower challenged each man to tell of his best sexual conquest. Most of us were sophomores with just a couple of freshmen and juniors, so we all understood, though did not admit, that most, if not all, of our stories were just made up, but they were still provocative enough to produce hard-ons all around.

When it came my turn, I told a variation of the escapade Johnny and I had experienced in Hawaii with the two Swedish girls. Even though Johnny and I had doubted that they were actually college students, we maintained the ruse just because it made the story sound even more salacious. Of course, I omitted any details that might be construed as queer, and when Johnny picked up the story, he claimed that we had actually fucked the girls. I don't know if any of the guys actually believed our story or not, but they ate it all up just the same. In fact, it was more titillation than some of them could stand, so out came the dicks.

I had grown quite a bit since the lecture from Mike last Thanksgiving and was already one of the tallest men on the football team and had bulked up some too. When school started that fall, I thought that I was getting a little more attention from the girls than before, but I wasn't sure. Then came the first game of the season.

I had expected Coach Davis to put me in as quarterback, but he chose instead to make me the halfback. His reasoning was that we already had a pretty good quarterback but no one to fill the halfback spot. He also explained that I would make a good halfback because I had the speed, agility, and versatility plus the ability to think on my feet.

With Johnny as wide receiver and me at halfback, our team won the season opener 42-0. Johnny caught every pass thrown to him and scored three touchdowns. I recovered one fumble and ran for two more touchdowns. Our quarterback, a senior, was named

MVP, but Coach Davis singled out Johnny and me as runners up. The next Monday, it seemed like every girl in school knew my name and couldn't wait to sit next to me in class or in the cafeteria.

"Hey, dial back the pheromones, asshole," Johnny teased. "If you keep this up, there won't be any pussy left for me."

"Suck it up, has-been," I retorted.

Our second game was an away game, which we also won quite handily, and this time, I was named the MVP. I felt that Johnny and I should have shared the honor, but I had to admit that the recognition was nice to have, and my parents were thrilled when they heard the news.

The front seats on the bus were usually accorded to the cheerleaders, so when I boarded for the return trip, I sat at the center of the bus, but when Johnny got on, he grabbed my arm and commanded, "With me." He took me to the back row and shoved me to one side while he sat on the other. I questioned the move since the back rows were usually reserved for upper classmen, who claimed it as their "make-out territory."

"Usually," he confirmed, "but tonight you're the MVP—" and before he could finish the sentence, two of the cheerleaders came between us and sat down. "Champ," he continued, indicating the one sitting next to him, "this is Cindy, and this (indicating the one sitting next to me) is Debbie."

The girls briefly flattered us on our performance—on the field, that is—but Johnny wasted no more time with the small talk, and I followed his lead. Back in Hawaii, the "college women" had been the aggressors, but this time, Johnny and I manned up and took the lead. The girls seemed to appreciate it because they responded accordingly.

For the first half hour, it was mostly kissing, including French kissing, and light fondling. Johnny did manage to get one hand inside of Cindy's top while I only got far enough to squeeze Debbie's breast through her uniform. I was actually surprised when Debbie began rubbing my crotch since I had not seen Cindy doing that to Johnny. At that point, all I could think of was how friggin' impossible it was to undo my damn football pants.

When we got back to school and hit the showers, Johnny proclaimed, "Debbie likes you. A lot!" And gazing at my schlong, he added, "I think she's gonna like you a lot more pretty soon."

The next day Mike, who had evidently heard the news of my MVP award from someone, called to congratulate me. That really thrilled me and built up my confidence even more. Without going into any details, I also told him about my encounter with the cheerleaders, and he congratulated me on that achievement as well.

For the rest of the season, home games alternated with away games, and on the way back from away games, we were joined at the back of the bus by different cheerleaders until we had gone through all of them, even the seniors. And then we started over again switching partners. On the weekends when we had home games, we hung out with other girls who were not on the cheerleading squad, but who, as Mike had put it, were "thrilled to get into our pants."

From the beginning of the season, we watched Mike play football on TV, which meant that we also watched his ads for Levi's and Lexus. One of the

Levi's ads showed Mike putting on or taking off a pair of jeans. His Addicted briefs were clearly evident. But there was one ad in which he appeared to be going commando.

The Lexus campaign was built around the words Mike had used to describe the car—and himself. They interspersed clips of him playing football with scenes of him in various settings. One ad began with the camera focused in slow motion on the muscles in Mike's bare upper arm as he was throwing a football. That was quickly followed by a clip of Mike's cherry red sports car (or one just like it) accelerating from zero to 60 in less than 5 seconds. Then, the word "Power" flashed on the screen. In the second scene, Mike was shown running down the field, evading tacklers, and the word "Agility" popped up. Then we saw the Lexus racing down a highway, passing everything in sight, and the caption read simply, "Speed." The final scene combined a clip of Mike crossing the goal line with a picture of the Lexus getting the checkered flag on a racetrack.

The second Lexus ad practically broke the internet the next day. It showed Mike driving a black version of the same car up to a luxury hotel. He got out of the car wearing a tuxedo that fit him to a T and was approached by a gorgeous woman in a black evening gown. The caption read, "Classy." Then the camera showed the woman slowly circling the car, tracing the lines with her finger until she reached Mike, and then rubbing her hands seductively down the lapels of his tux. The solo word at the end of the scene was "Style." The final scene showed Mike walking out of the beautiful woman's hotel room. She was now scantily clad in a sexy negligee, and Mike was dressed in his tuxedo with his tie undone, his shirt unbuttoned halfway, and his coat thrown over his shoulder. When he got back into the Lexus, the camera showed Mike smirking at himself in the mirror before speeding off. The caption read, "Performance."

A third commercial used the words "pass," "receive," and "score." I'll just let your imagination run away with that one.

His print ads for Denier also began appearing in magazines such as *Men's Health, GQ, and Playboy,* with the caption "They feel as good when you put them on, as when you take them off."

The very provocative underwear ads also appeared in women's magazines such as *Vogue, Allure, and Playgirl,* with the suggestion that the underwear would make a rewarding Christmas present for that "special" occasion. The caption on some of them read, "Buy them for him, buy them for yourself."

I asked Mike over the phone if his teammates were razzing him about the ads, and he said that some of the guys had clipped the ads out of magazines and taped them onto their lockers. "They're just jealous," he laughed, "because I'm getting all the girls."

I mentioned the razzing to Johnny in the locker room one day and by the end of that week, every player on our team had posted one of Mike's print ads inside his locker. Of course, most of them put up ads featuring Mike with the beautiful female models, and some posted ads with only Mike's picture. Others created a collage, posting a large picture of Mike surrounded by smaller pictures from various magazines.

I don't know if they did it because they all revered Mike almost as much as I did or if they did it to razz me. "That's OK," I told them. "The inside of my barn is wallpapered with pinups of your girlfriends and sisters."

10 Sweet Sixteen

Johnny and I were both born in October, just days apart. From our first away game, our birthdays were only a couple of months away, but we could barely wait. Dating had been difficult without a car, but come October, we would be 16 and able to drive. And sure enough, we both got our driver's licenses on our birthdays.

The Andersens suggested that we have a joint birthday party at their house the following weekend. Mom made two birthday cakes, and Mrs. Andersen decorated them. Johnny's was white and blue (our school colors) and adorned with confectionary football gear. Mine was white and green and decorated with leprechauns and four-leaf clovers—plus a 49ers helmet in honor of Mike, who couldn't be there because he had a game in New Orleans that weekend.

Dad and Mr. Andersen took turns grilling hamburgers and hot dogs while the kids swam in and danced by the pool. Johnny opened his presents, which consisted mostly of football paraphernalia and memorabilia, but he saved a few that had been tucked away. A couple of the kids had bought me similar presents, but most of them hadn't known me very long, and maybe they figured it was really Johnny's party since it was held at his place. I really didn't mind. I was just thrilled to be part of the action.

After the other kids had all left, Mrs. Andersen suggested that we open the remaining presents. The Andersens gave me a couple of shirts and slacks, and my folks gave Johnny the same. Everyone laughed at how "great minds think alike."

We were surprised to discover that we had each received a package from Mike. Each contained a folding 8x10 picture frame with three panels. On the left panel, we had identical press photos of Mike in his 49ers uniform. Of course, they were autographed. The middle frame held a picture of Mike, Johnny, and me leaning against the hood of his cherry red sports car, a picture that Mom had taken and we had all forgotten about. Johnny's third frame and mine were different. His was a picture taken by a newspaper sports photographer when Johnny scored his first touchdown of the season. Mine was a picture of me receiving my first MVP award. I don't know who was more thrilled, Johnny or me.

"One more," said Mr. Andersen, handing Johnny a rather large box. When Johnny started unwrapping it, he discovered that there was another box tucked inside, and when he opened that one, there was another one, and another one, and another one, nested like a matryoshka, a Russian nesting doll. When he finally got to the end, he opened a small box to discover a key.

"What's this?" Johnny asked.

"Well," explained Mr. Andersen, "your mother has been pestering me" (Mrs. Andersen slapped him on the arm) "for a new car, so you get the leftovers." Johnny was getting the family's Lexus. I think I was thrilled as much as he was because now we would be able to go on real dates and not have to rely on anyone else to give us a ride.

"Oh," said Mrs. Andersen, "it seems like we missed one." I fully expected her to hand it to Johnny, but instead, she handed it to me.

"What's this?" I asked.

"Well, open it," said Dad, "and find out."

"Don't get overly excited," said Johnny. "It's probably just one box inside of another one."

When I opened it, I was speechless. It was an illustrated guide to the *Book of Kells*, Ireland's most prized national treasure. The *Book of Kells*, I explained to everyone when I regained my faculty of speech, is a richly illustrated eighth- or ninth-century manuscript of the four Gospels housed at Trinity College, Dublin.

"How did you know?" I asked Mrs. Andersen.

"Don't look at me," she replied. "Johnny picked it out."

When I gaped at Johnny, he replied, "Ever since I've known you, you've done nothing but brag about how you're going to be the greatest Irish-American writer since Eugene O'Neill." Everyone laughed at the faux sarcasm except me. I was still in shock. Johnny may have gotten the most expensive birthday present, but I got the richest one.

Though I had ridden to the party with my parents, Johnny insisted on driving me home in his newly acquired Lexus. On the way, he told me that he would call Cindy and Debbie, the cheerleaders, and ask them for a double date the next weekend.

When we got back to the farm, my dad said that there was a package waiting for me on the porch when they got home. "I put it on your bed," he said. Johnny and I ran upstairs to see what it was.

"It's from Italy," I exclaimed.

"Well, don't just stand there, *signore*," he mocked. "Open it!"

Inside the box was a paper bag and two larger items. I opened the bag and pulled out two swimsuits identical to the ones that the Swedish girls had taken as souvenirs. Johnny and I laughed and said in unison, "Armando!"

I reached back into the box and pulled out two identical photo albums. They contained prints from Mike's photo shoot, including the ones in which Johnny and I had served as extras, but they also contained pictures that did not appear in the ads.

Professional photographers take dozens of shots just to get one great one. Armando's camera was constantly clicking away, so he got some shots of the models as they repositioned themselves, which may explain why he had gotten some pictures of Mike totally nude. There was the scene of Mike sitting on the bed with his legs crossed, but Armando had also captured Mike before and after he crossed his legs. Armando had also photographed Mike standing naked in front of a dresser with an open drawer blocking his genitals, but his camera had also captured images of Mike when the drawer was closed and Mike's junk was fully exposed.

The albums also contained photos of the other models that were not included in the advertising campaign, and in many of them, the models—male and female—were completely nude, and in a few shots, some of the male models were partially erect.

Some people, I am sure, would have considered those pictures pornographic, but I saw them as works of art, pictures that belonged in a museum. I had thought of Armando as just an eccentric, if not perverted, picture taker, but I now realized that he was a master artist.

I handed one of the albums to Johnny and hugged the other one to my chest. I was speechless, and I think Johnny was too until he noticed something else in the box. "What's that?" he asked.

I pulled out two envelopes containing notes to each of us. The handwritten notes said pretty much the same thing, but it was gracious of Armando to have personalized them, I thought. In the notes, Armando thanked us both for "modeling for him." Heck, all we did was stand in a crowd.

"You were the most beautiful models there—two of the most beautiful models I have ever seen, in fact. It is such a pity that Mr. Murphy would not let me photograph you more. I hope that someday you will give me the honor of capturing that beauty for all of eternity."

For the second time in just a few minutes, Johnny and I were speechless.

That night, as I nestled in my bed, I spread out several of the sexiest photos of Mike against the footboard and leaned back against the headboard and beat off. I did not fantasize about having sex with Mike. Oh hell, God no! But I did imagine him watching me. I just wanted to show him what I could do. And when I blew my load, I would swear that I saw him smiling back at me from those photographs.

The day after our joint birthday celebration, Sunday, we watched Mike and the 49ers play the New Orleans Saints on TV, and then Johnny and I went "cruising," which is to say that we just drove, going nowhere in particular. Johnny even let me drive the Lexus a bit.

On Monday, Johnny told me that he had plans after school and that I would have to take the bus home, which was no big deal since it was what I had always done. When I walked up the dirt road to our farmhouse, I was surprised to see a strange vehicle, a late-model Ford Explorer in our driveway. When I reached the porch, I was shocked to see Mike coming out of the house. "Happy Birthday, champ," he greeted me.

"What? How?" I stammered.

He explained that he had taken a slight detour flying back from New Orleans to San Francisco. "Sorry I missed your 'sweet 16' party," he said. "I hear it was quite an affair."

"It most definitely was," I assured him, and I thanked him for the present of the framed pictures. "I think Johnny will prize his even more than the Lexus," I laughed.

"And speaking of Lexus cars," I added, "how's yours? Don't tell me you've crashed it already. You haven't lost that endorsement contract, have you? Did you rent that Explorer at the airport?"

"No," he laughed. "I believe that car belongs to 'the greatest Irish-American writer since Eugene O'Neill.'"

I started to laugh, and then it hit me. "You don't mean...you can't mean—"

"Happy birthday, champ," he said, holding up the key.

"What is all the commotion?" asked Dad, stepping out of the house onto the porch—as if he and Mom didn't already know.

"My Lord," protested Mom. "You're going to spoil that boy rotten."

"Don't worry, Mom. It's last year's model," he joked.

When we all went to get a closer look, everyone took a turn pointing out certain features of the SUV. "This is actually better than Johnny's Lexus," said Mike, nudging me in the ribs with his elbow. "The rear seat folds down," he clucked.

"Michael Sean Murphy!" Mom scolded.

"Can I go show Johnny?" I asked.

"Well, it is a school night," said Mom.

"Let him go," said Mike. "If he makes anything less than an A on his next report card, "I'll personally come back here and take back that SUV."

Johnny walked back to the Explorer with me and said for me to look into the glove compartment when I got to Johnny's house. When I did, I found two packages of condoms. I kept the extra-large set for myself and gave the other one to Johnny.

A couple of days later, just as we were finishing our supper, we heard a car coming up the driveway. Mom looked out the kitchen window to see a pearly white Lexus sedan coming to a halt. "Oh, it's Emily (Mrs. Andersen)," said Mom. "Bill (Mr. Andersen) did say that he was going to buy her a new car to replace the one they gave Johnny."

When we all went outside to greet Mrs. Andersen, though, it wasn't she, but a young man nattily dressed in a stylish blue business suit. "I have a delivery for a Mrs. Murphy," he said, meeting us at the foot of the porch steps. When Mom identified herself, the man handed her a clipboard and said, "Sign here please."

When the man said nothing more, Mom asked, "Is the package in the car?"

"The package," said the man, pulling a set of keys out of his coat pocket, "*IS* the car."

As the three of us were oohing and aahing over the luxurious Lexus, a silver Ford pickup pulled up behind the car. When a woman clad in Dockers and a Levi's shirt stepped out, we assumed that she was there to drive the man in the blue suit back to town. "Mr. Daniel Murphy?" she asked, not sure if that was me or Dad. "That's me," said Dad, and the woman handed him an envelope. Inside were a key and a card that read, "Sorry, Dad. Lexus doesn't make pickups."

Now armed with cars of our own, Johnny and I began dating girls much more frequently. In the early days, we often double dated, sometimes with his car, sometimes with mine, and Mike was right: the fold-down rear seat was very useful.

The Saturday after Johnny and I became 16, we double dated with Cindy and Debbie, the two cheer-leaders we had made out with on the bus, and that was the night we lost our virginity—twice, if there can be such a thing—which is to say that Johnny fucked Cindy while I fucked Debbie, and then we switched partners and did it again. Of course, Johnny and I used the condoms that Mike had so fortuitously given us.

No longer virgins, Johnny and I dated often, sometimes together, sometimes separately, though the double dates became less and less frequent. Word around campus—and every high school campus within 50 miles apparently—was that we were boffing a different girl (or girls) every night, but that was just hyperbole. Johnny did date a lot, and I had as many opportunities as I could handle, but even with two new workers, I still had responsibilities on the farm, and I still had to study so that Mike wouldn't take back my new Explorer.

11 French Exposure

Mike was not able to come home for Thanksgiving or Christmas, but he sent Mom and Dad tickets to spend the December holidays in Australia, where it is summer at that time of the year, which meant that I was left in charge of the farm those two weeks. Of course, we had Eddie and Carlos to do the work, but I had to oversee things. The Andersens invited me to spend Christmas Day with them, and Johnny and I were able to hang out together some, but he also had other family obligations...when he was not "deflowering every virgin in West Texas."

Once the NFL season was over, Mike spent more time at the farm, but he was always coming and going. He would be home for a few days and off to New York or San Francisco on business or some other exciting place to film TV commercials or make public appearances. His ads the first season had made him a national celebrity, and he was appearing frequently on TV talk shows. He had picked up endorsement contracts with eight or 10 more companies: cereals, shaving products, athletic shoes, airlines, and even women's lingerie. By Memorial

Day, he was making more money from endorsements than he was from playing football.

With summer approaching, I asked Mike if he would be doing another photo shoot in Hawaii, hoping that he would take Johnny and me along again, but he said no, he would not be going to Hawaii, and when he saw the disappointment on my face, he added, "The French Riviera this year." Then when he saw my excitement, he continued, "I was thinking of just taking Johnny this year." For just a second or two, I was shocked, but I quickly realized that he was just teasing me. "How's your French?" he asked.

Since Mike was a little more prepared for this photo shoot and not quite as rushed as the year before, he scheduled two weeks, one for the shoot and one to play tourist. The three of us spent seven days exploring Paris and the French countryside.

The photo shoot had a different theme that year with a different photographer, a Frenchman. Claude was younger, much more handsome, and not quite as intense as Armando, and he took a very personal approach to his work. He insisted on spending a whole day with Mike getting to know him before starting to shoot. He wanted to understand "who you are as a person, a man" and not just his body, and since Johnny and I were a part of who Mike was, Claude insisted on having us participate.

Claude met us at our hotel in Nice for breakfast and stayed with us until bedtime. He led us on a walking tour of Old Nice, took us to the Palais de Festivals, where the Cannes Film Festival is held every year, and suggested other tourist sites we might want to take in.

But he spent most of the time asking us about our lives. He wanted to know about football, not the game so much as our commitment to it. He quickly latched onto the fact that all three of us are fairly intelligent, so he asked about what kind of books we like to read, our favorite artists and philosophers, and our personal heroes. He asked Johnny and me what we wanted to study in college, and he asked Mike what he would be doing if he were not playing football. He asked about Mom and Dad and what it had been like for Mike and me growing up on a farm. He asked about our thoughts on religion, politics, and current events. And after we had eaten dinner and returned to Mike's suite, he asked about our sex lives.

"That's kind of personal," Mike said.

"Yes, of course," he replied. "It is your personality, not just your body, that I must photograph. Sex is a fundamental element of life, is it not? Sex is what we are selling in this advertising campaign. In order to capture your sexuality, I need to understand it."

Mike thought for a minute and came to the conclusion that Claude's premise made some sense. When Mike began to talk about his sexuality, Johnny and I got up to leave, but Mike said, "Guys, if this is going to make you uncomfortable, I understand, but I trust you, and if you want to stay, I don't mind."

I was touched by the confidence Mike was entrusting to us and the sense that Johnny and I were mature enough to be part of the discussion. I think Mike had also surmised that we were both no longer virgins.

Claude asked Mike about his early experiences with masturbation and whether he had ever masturbated with other boys. Mike acknowledged that he had masturbated with other boys, and when Claude asked if he had ever jerked another boy off or had another boy jerk him off, he said that he had, but "only a few times." Mike talked about those experiences and said that he had stopped masturbating regularly with other boys when he started dating girls, but that he had masturbated with other guys three or four more times until he graduated from high school.

When asked how often he masturbated today, Mike said it varied depending on circumstances and opportunities, but on average, probably once or twice a day.

"So, you have never sucked another man's cock?" Claude asked.

"No, Mike replied. "I don't think there's anything wrong with that," he added. "It's just not my thing."

"When did you lose your virginity?" Claude asked.

"Well, I was hoping to do it tonight," Mike joked, and then he added that it had happened when he was 14. I was a little surprised by that since I was 16 when I lost mine, but I guess I shouldn't have been surprised considering how good-looking and self-assured he was...even back then.

Mike described his first experience in some detail, with Claude's encouragement, and then chronicled his "conquests" through high school and college. He said he was most sexually active when he was in college because as a star football player, he attracted many women who wanted to sleep with him. He also admitted that he had participated in group sex, i.e. orgies, and had experienced sex with as many as three or four women at a time. Asked if he was still as promiscuous today, he said no. He explained that he enjoyed sex very much but that he now likes to get to know the women he dates "as people, not just as sex objects." I don't know if he was being totally honest about that or if he was just trying to send a message to Johnny and me.

When Claude turned to Johnny and me and asked us about our early experiences, Mike said, "That's it. You can ask me whatever you want, but these guys are off limits. I'll see you in the morning," and with that, Mike ushered Claude to the door. Johnny and I got up to leave also, but Mike stopped us. He put one hand on my shoulder and one on Johnny's and looked us straight in the eye.

"Guys," he said. "I hope I have not embarrassed you tonight. It's just that I feel that we Americans treat sex too much as if it's something dirty, and it's not. Claude was right; it's a natural part of life, and it's a beautiful thing when it's handled properly." He took a deep breath and continued, "It's late and I'm tired, and I have to get up and go to work in the morning, but I want you to hear this: if you have any questions or want to talk about anything we discussed tonight, let's do it. I want you to feel that you can talk to me about anything."

Back in our room, Johnny and I just looked at each other with our minds glazed over. Mike had shared so much with us. He had bared his soul, a significant part of it anyway, and we just didn't know what to make of it. We each had a thousand questions and didn't know where to start. I had gotten erections quite a few times as Mike talked, and I'm sure that Johnny had too. Hell, I imagine that Claude did too, and maybe even Mike had himself. But at that moment, Johnny and I were too overwhelmed to get horny. We just said good night to each other and went to bed.

That night I must have dreamed of Mike masturbating, including the first time I saw him masturbating under the old oak tree and the thought of him participating in an orgy—because I woke up with a raging hard-on. And I noticed that Johnny did too. So, of course, we had to jerk off before we went down to breakfast.

Claude wasn't kidding when he said that he wanted to capture Mike's personality and not just his body in the photo session. He photographed Mike being whimsical in a pillow fight, being cerebral reading a book in bed, and being romantic waltzing with one of the beautiful models.

He also took lots of close-ups of Mike—not of his crotch, but of his face. These were later used in storyboard ads and became an international sensation because of the emotion they conveyed. Many readers said that they felt as if Mike were looking directly into their souls. Mike received thousands of fan mail letters from women (and men) requesting autographed photos and quite a few that included marriage proposals. These close-ups were also Mike's favorites... and Mom and Dad's.

In one of the most memorable photo sets, the most beautiful of the female models stood in front of an ornate gold dresser and mirror that looked like they had come from the Palace of Versailles. She wore a gorgeous black evening gown with slits up the side, revealing titillating parts of her legs. Mike stood behind her, his face also visible in the mirror. He was dressed only in very sexy briefs that accentuated his bulge from the profile. With one hand, he was pulling back her long black hair, and with the other he was reaching over her shoulder to help her dab a hint of perfume on her neck.

Though the photo shoot was for Denier, when they declined to use that particular photo because "it wasn't a good fit for that campaign," Claude showed it to Yves Saint Laurent, who negotiated for the rights on a one-time arrangement. The photo appeared in YSL ads in every woman's magazine right at the beginning of the Christmas season—in a couple of instances, even on the cover. It won numerous advertising awards and became very popular in every corner of the globe. When YSL sales soared, along with magazine sales, the company offered Claude and Mike both long-term contracts.

Like Armando the year before, Claude begged Mike to let him photograph Johnny and me until Mike acquiesced to letting us be extras in a scene as long as we were fully clothed. Then, he allowed us to appear in the background in a shot by the pool provided that our swimsuits were not too skimpy and the scene was not too risqué. "Yes, I understand that you're selling sex," he told Claude, "but it's my sex you're selling, not theirs." We ended up being among the people sitting around the pool in lounge chairs, which took me back to that day when Johnny spooged all over my face beside his swimming pool.

Claude also shot a set of photos in the hotel's fitness center, and Mike let us be in those shots with the stipulation that we wore gym shorts and not sexy underwear or swimsuits. In some scenes we wore tank tops, and in others we were shirtless, as were Mike and the other models. Claude took lots of shots of Mike bench pressing with one of the models spotting him. In some shots, the spotter was female, in some male. In a variation, Mike was spotting the model, who was looking straight up at his crotch.

In other shots, Mike did squats, bicep curls, leg extensions, and other exercises. Some of these pictures were taken after he had worked up a sweat, the moisture making the fabric around his pubic region and his butt crack semi-transparent.

In the locker room, Claude photographed Mike dressing and undressing, and Mike let us be extras in some of those shots with the stipulation that our faces were not to be shown.

Claude even had Mike showering, naked of course, with his genitals concealed by an object or a person in the foreground. In one case it was a female model sitting on a bench looking directly at Mike and dangling a pair of underwear in her hand as if to say, "What would you give me for this?" From one angle, it was her head that blocked the view of Mike's genitals, from another it was the dangling underwear.

In another context, two male models stood in the foreground facing each other wearing only sexy designer jockstraps, their pouches bulging toward each other. Their bodies framed a view of Mike standing between them in the background with only the steam from the hot shower providing an opaque cover for his family jewels.

When Johnny and I were not observing or participating in the photo sessions, we spent most of our time seeing the sights of the French Riviera and cruising the beaches. Given the fact that most of the girls wore string bikinis or thongs and some were topless, it was not surprising that many of the guys on the beach sported boners. Because it was so commonplace, most went without particular notice, but Johnny and I were drawing quite a few looks anyway, so when we got stiffies, they definitely did not go unnoticed. I thought quite a few of the girls—

and even some of the guys—were game to mount us right there on the beach. Needless to say, we managed to escort several back to our hotel room or theirs.

And, of course, Johnny and I bedded all three of the female models Claude had hired, and I beat off with one of the male models as well. That model wanted to do much more, but I drew the line. As an enticement, he even offered to include one of the female models in a threesome. It was a very tempting offer. I declined to have sex with him, but Johnny and I did allow him to beat off while watching us fuck the three girls on our last night there. He talked dirty the whole time, which was a real turn on for me.

After our guests said *au revoir* and returned to their own rooms, Johnny and I reflected on the week's events. Naturally, we talked about our sexcapades, the photo sessions, and that first night when Mike shared so much with us. We began by reviewing many of the experiences that Mike related, but then our conversation became more contemplative. We started asking ourselves what all of that really meant to us. We talked about our sexuality not only in the present context, but also what it might mean for our futures.

We recalled how Mike had answered when Claude asked him if he had ever considered having sex with a man or if he would consider it, so Johnny and I put the same question to each other. Johnny confessed that the thought of sex with another man had crossed his mind and, like Mike, it did not evoke any negative feelings in him, but it just wasn't something that appealed to him.

I told Johnny that the thought had also crossed my mind more than once. I informed him that the male model who had just left our room had propositioned me, and I had turned him down. I confessed to Johnny that I did not find the guy unattractive or the thought of having sex with him unappealing. I just wasn't ready to undertake that experiment. I told him that I was still exploring my sexuality and did not really know who or what I was in that regard.

These were thoughts and feelings that I had never shared with anyone else before—I'm not sure I had even admitted them to myself—and I was enormously relieved that Johnny listened like a true friend: listening, not judging. Ultimately, we agreed that we should be open to new experiences, deciding for ourselves about our sexuality and not letting others determine our sexuality for us.

12 Troy

When we got back home to Texas from France, we had only a couple of weeks to prepare for football camp. Just two days before we were to leave for camp, Johnny, Mike, and I each received a package from Claude. They contained albums of the photo shoot much like the ones that Armando had sent the year before except that these also had pictures of Johnny and me lounging by the hotel pool and working out in the fitness center. Among these were not only the "official" photos, but also close-ups shot from different angles. They were really no different from the type of photos that anyone might take on a family vacation except that they were so professionally done that they seemed more like works of art than mere snapshots, so we had no qualms about showing them to our parents. Even Mike, who had placed strict limits on how Claude was permitted to photograph us, was impressed.

Johnny seemed almost like a different person at football camp. He was still basically the same ole Johnny, but he approached the game with a new, deeper sense of commitment. Paradoxically, he had a greater sense that it was just a game. What really seemed to matter to him more than the score were the people: the players, the coaches, the student body, the families. Ironically, as a result, he played even better than before, and he was rewarded by his teammates, who voted him co-captain along with our quarterback, Matt Williams, a senior.

In accordance with tradition, we gathered around the imaginary campfire the last night of camp for storytelling and bragging of our conquests, which were largely as imaginary as the flames in the pit. Of course, what everyone was eager to hear about, especially after the tales we had told the year before, were our experiences in France. I led our accounts, embellishing some details and omitting others. Johnny followed with his own elaborations, but, of course, there was actually more truth in the story this year than before, and he relayed that truth with what I can only call "respect" and "maturity." When it came time for the ritual circle jerk, Johnny participated, but it seemed that he did so more out of a sense of camaraderie and responsibility than mere juvenile revelry.

The second week of school, after we had already won our first game 38-7, Coach Davis introduced a new member of the team, Troy Mazure, a transfer student from Chicago. Like Johnny and me, he was a junior. "Troy has some experience playing back there," said Coach, "so I'm sure he will be an asset to this team. I want you men to welcome him to the team, to the school, and to the community."

After all the members of the team shook his hand and welcomed him, we hit the field for practice, but Coach pulled aside Matt and Johnny and reminded them that it was their duty as team captains to ensure

Troy's successful transition into the team and to the school.

Johnny and I had always had lockers next to each other, but Johnny suggested that I move down one so we could put Troy between us. At first, I thought Johnny was just ribbing me, but then I realized that he was serious. Johnny wasn't just being a good host, though. He was assuming his role as the leader of the team. He was manning up. I had always admired Johnny, but now I could see that he was really earning that admiration.

With Johnny on one side of Troy and me on the other, I felt like one of two bookends. While Johnny had that cute baby face, Troy was more ruggedly handsome, like a young Paul Walker or Antonio Banderas, Jr., with a five o'clock shadow that presented itself at full force before noon. Johnny had medium-length brownish blond hair, while Troy had longer, dark brown hair that hung over his thick black eyebrows and shaded his brown eyes that were so dark, they looked almost black.

I had shot up a lot over the spring and summer, so Johnny, Troy, and I were about the same height, around six feet, and we all had that V-shaped mesomorphic body—broad shoulders and chests, narrow waists, and rock-hard six-pack abs—but Johnny's body was perfectly proportioned while Troy's was just a tad on the husky side. Johnny's body didn't have a hair on it (except where it really counted), while Troy was covered with thick fur on his chest, belly, arms, and legs.

Both had beautiful cut cocks, slightly above average, but not nearly as big as mine. The penis of the average American male when erect ranges from 4.7 inches to 6.3, with the average being 5.1 inches.

Having seen Johnny's erect penis, I estimated it to be around the top of the range, and though I had not seen Troy's penis erect (yet), based on its flaccid size, I guessed that it would be about the same as Johnny's. Mine was about 7 inches and still growing. I used to tease them that even if they tied their dicks together end to end, theirs would still not be as big as mine. Of course, that is an exaggeration. Slightly.

Johnny exuded amiability and self-assurance while Troy conveyed a touch of innocence along with a hint of the feral in his pheromones. Both were sexy as hell, but in very different ways.

"What's with all the pin-ups of Mike Murphy?" Troy asked Johnny. Some of the guys still had pictures from Mike's magazine ads the year before on their lockers, some had removed them, and some had replaced them or added to them with photos from our more recent shoot in France. A few had even put up ads with Johnny and me in the background, and a couple had drawn mustaches or devil's horns on our faces.

"Ask Rick," said Johnny with a smirk.

"Oh, the guys are just razzing me," I said.

"You? What's this got to do with you?" he asked. Johnny grinned more broadly, and I thought he was going to burst out laughing.

"Let me re-introduce myself," I said. "My name's Rick Murphy."

"Yeah, I got that, but.... Oh, wait. Murphy. You're not...I mean he's not? Oh, shit!" And with that, Johnny did burst out laughing.

"It's OK," I said, slapping Troy on the back to reassure him. "Happens all the time. And yes, Mike Murphy is my brother."

"Oh, my god! That must be...I mean what's that like? I mean...."

"It's great," I said. "I couldn't ask for a better—"

"And he's a super great guy," Johnny jumped in. "You'll love him."

"You mean I might get to meet him?"

"Sure," I replied. "He doesn't get home much during the season, but when he does, we'll have you over. He loves meeting my friends."

Troy didn't respond immediately, but I had the sense that he hadn't expected to hear the word 'friends.' He smiled, and I slapped him on the back again.

Upon reflection, it dawned on me that the word 'friends' was new to me too. Oh, I knew people, and we were friendly with each other, but it was not until I joined the football team that I really felt like I had friends.

That Friday, we had an away game, which meant cheerleaders at the back of the bus. I got the sense that Johnny contemplated inviting Troy to sit with us but decided that such a move might be premature, so instead, he gave up his back seat to Matt Williams and sat with Troy in the row right behind the cheerleaders up front. I followed suit, giving up my seat to whomever Matt wanted to assign to it and sat across from Johnny and Troy.

The next day, Saturday, Mom asked me to help her load some things into her car after breakfast. "What's up?" asked Dad. "You leaving us?" he teased.

"Oh, you know I would never leave you, dear. You'd be totally helpless without me."

And people wonder where I get my vicious sense of humor.

"No. You recall that Edna Fowler's mother lives over in Bryan and is homebound." Dad nodded, knowing that Edna Fowler was a member of Mom's garden club. "Well," she continued, "Edna asked if anyone would like to help her put together a bouquet to send to her mother. Apparently, the health department has hired an itinerant nurse who's going that way today, and we all agreed to put together several arrangements for her to distribute to the patients on her route." Neither Dad nor I was surprised. It was the kind of thing that Mom and her friends did all the time. It just seemed like a perfectly normal gesture to them.

I helped mom load three boxes of bouquets and potted plants into her Lexus, and about 30 minutes after Mom left, she called and asked Dad to meet her at the nurse's house. "Her car won't start, and I thought maybe you could take a look at it."

Since Carlos had everything under control at the farm (Eddie had the day off), I decided to ride with Dad. Dad is not exactly a mechanic...and I'm certainly not...but Dad has had some experience doing routine maintenance on tractors and such, and I thought he might need an extra hand.

"This is Sarah," said Mom when we got to the house. Dad and I shook hands with the attractive but distraught lady.

"So, what's the problem?" Dad asked.

"I don't know. It just won't start."

"Well, let's take a look. Pop the lid for me, Rick."

And just as I was about to get into the car, a voice called out, "Hey, jerk! Don't steal our car!"

Mom, Dad, and Sarah looked shocked, but when I turned around, I saw that it was Troy. "Troy! Hey, man, you live here?"

"Yeah," he said. "Just moved in."

I gave him a hearty handshake with a jerk and quipped, motioning to Sarah, "Well, this can't be your mother. She's way too pretty."

Troy punched me on the arm, and our parents breathed a sigh of relief. "I can see that your son has kissed the Blarney Stone," said Sarah, Mrs. Mazure.

"Sometimes I think he's swallowed it," Dad replied.

Turning to Troy and me, Mom said, "I take it that you two know each other"

"Yeah," I replied. "Troy's our new back-up quarterback. But I'm sure we'll have a winning season anyway."

"Oh, stop that," Mom scolded me with a chuckle. "You're going to make these folks feel unwelcome."

"Not at all," replied Mrs. Mazure. "I believe that this is the young man who Troy told me has been so nice to him since he enrolled at school here."

"No, Mom. That was the other guy, Johnny. This is the one that I told you I felt sorry for because he didn't know the difference between a football and a shuttlecock."

And before I could hit back, Troy reached out his hand to greet Mom and Dad and said, "You've got a really great son, Mr. and Mrs. Murphy...and I guess this one's not too bad either." Mom and Dad laughed, and Mrs. Mazure looked perplexed.

"Their other son," Troy explained to his mother, is Mike Murphy."

"Mike Murphy?" asked Mom.

"You'll have to forgive my mother," said Troy, winking at my parents. "She doesn't really follow pro football. He's with the San Francisco 49ers," he turned to his mother and explained, "and one of the best quarterbacks who has ever played the game." Then he turned to my parents and, with a second wink, said, "I guess one out of two isn't so bad."

Mrs. Mazure gave her son another "Troy Mazure!"

"Ahem," Dad grunted, "let's see what we can do with this car. Troy, would you like to do the honors and pop the hood for me? OK, now start the ignition." Dead silence. Not even a sputter. "Was it like this when you tried to start it this morning?" Dad asked Mrs. Mazure.

"No," she said. "It sputtered a few times but wouldn't start, and finally it just stopped altogether."

"Has this sputtering happened before?"

"Yes, off and on for a couple of weeks, but I've just been so busy what with the move and the new job and all—"

"Of course," Mom reassured her with a gentle hand on her shoulder.

"Have you ever changed the fuel injectors?" Dad asked to a blank stare.

"I'm sorry," she lamented. "My husband always took care of things like that."

"Mom and Dad are divorced," Troy explained.

"It could just be the spark plugs or the wires, which wouldn't be too bad, but if it's the fuel injectors, that could get quite expensive, and with a car this old, you'd probably be better off just replacing the car."

Seeing the concern on Mrs. Mazure's face, Dad said, "Let me pull the spark plugs and see what we can do. When Mrs. Mazure asked how long that would take, Dad explained that he had to go back to the farm and get some tools, come back and pull the plugs, go to the store for new ones, come back and install them, and see if that solved the problem. "Probably about two hours," said Dad.

"Oh, dear," said Mrs. Mazure, apparently on the verge of tears. "There are patients counting on me, and I hate to disappoint them, especially on my first week on the job."

"We've got this," affirmed Mom. "I'll take you on your runs, Sarah, while the boys see what they can do with this car."

"Oh, I couldn't ask you to do that," Sarah objected.

"You didn't ask," said Mom. "I offered."

"But I have to go all the way to Bryan," which was more than an hour away.

"I know," said Mom. "Edna Fowler's mother lives there, and I haven't seen her in ages. Besides," she added, "it will be so refreshing to talk to someone about something other than football." Mrs. Mazure relented; nobody argues with my Mom.

"Troy, go with Mr. Murphy to get the spark plugs. I'll get you some money." She looked at Dad for his approval, and Dad, always a man of few words, just nodded his permission.

While Mrs. Mazure and Troy went back inside to get their things, Mom said to me, "When you get back to the house, I want you to make a phone call."

When Mom and Mrs. Mazure got back that afternoon, Dad, Troy, and I were waiting with the bad news. Replacing the spark plugs did not work; it was probably the fuel injectors.

"Do you have more runs to make tomorrow?" Mom asked Mrs. Mazure, and she replied that she was off for the next two days.

"Good," said Mom. "Rick and I will be back here early Tuesday morning. Rick can drive Troy to school, and I'll take you wherever you need to go. Meanwhile, we'll keep working on ideas, and either of you can call us if you need anything before Tuesday." Mrs. Mazure tried to object, but once Mom has issued her declaration, it's pointless to argue with her. We all exchanged phone numbers, and on Monday morning, Troy walked to school. His house was not far from the campus.

On Tuesday morning, Mom and I left the house early to go back to the Mazure's house. Since we didn't know what we would find when we got there, we took separate vehicles. When we rang the doorbell, Mrs. Mazure seemed almost surprised to see us. "I'm sorry," said Mom. "Do you have company?" gesturing to the unexpected Lexus SUV parked in her driveway.

"Oh, Faith. I'm so sorry. I should have called you, but everything's just been—"

"That's quite all right, so—

"Come in, Faith. Come in, Rick. Troy will be down in a minute." She invited us to sit down and continued, "You simply will not believe what happened. Yesterday afternoon, when Troy was still at school, a woman came to the door and introduced herself as Heidi Bergman, the Director of Market Research at Lexus, the car company...oh, but of course, you know that."

Obviously, Mrs. Mazure was so overcome with excitement that she could barely collect her thoughts.

"So, anyway, she asked if I was Sarah Mazure, and I assured her that I was. Then she asked if I was an itinerant nurse and if my job required me to drive more than 300 miles a week. So, I asked, 'Yes, what's this about?' She said that I had been identified as 'part of a demographic' they were looking for 'to assist in a research project.' I was curious, naturally, so she explained that they were entering the beta phase of a new product and were looking for people to participate. Of course, I know what a beta test is, but I asked her exactly what kind of beta test this was. She said that they would soon be introducing a new SUV hybrid and wanted people who drive a lot to test the car and give them feedback.

"I told her that I couldn't afford a Lexus," and she just smiled and said, "Oh, you don't have to pay for anything.' She went on to explain that the company would loan the car to me for one year. Every three months, I am to fill out a brief feedback questionnaire and possibly participate in a telephone interview.

"'Ms. Bergman,' I said, 'Right now I couldn't even afford the insurance on a car like that.'

'Oh, we cover the insurance, routine maintenance, everything. There is absolutely no cost to you whatsoever.'

"Well, Faith, as you can imagine, I couldn't believe my ears. My car breaks down and two days later, someone is loaning me a Lexus free of charge."

Mom started to tell her how wonderful that was and how happy we all were for her when she launched into her monologue again.

"And then Heidi...Ms. Bergman...oh, she was so nice...she said that their research had indicated that I had a son of driving age and she wanted to know if he was home. I told her that Troy was at football practice and would be home in about an hour. So, she suggested that we fill out the necessary paperwork, which she had in her bag, and that she could go over all the controls and features of the car—the one she had driven up in—with Troy and me together when he got home."

"So, that's the car in the driveway?" Mom asked.

"How do you like our new car?" asked Troy, coming down the stairs with his backpack over his shoulder. "Isn't it great?"

Mom and I both agreed that it was great.

Mrs. Mazure offered to show us all the fancy stuff in the car, but Mom reminded her that Troy and I had to get to school and that she had to get on the road to her patients. "Let's do it when you have more time," Mom said.

All day long at school, Troy cornered everybody he knew, mostly the guys on the football team, and gave them every detail about the new car. You would have thought he was on ecstasy or something.

Mom called Mrs. Mazure that night to see how the car had performed on her patient run, and I called Troy. He told me that his mom had allowed him to drive it to the campus and back but that he could only drive it with her in the car because he only had a driver's permit. I offered to take him down to DMV whenever he was ready.

A few days later, Troy put up a picture of Mike in his locker. It was from an ad using one of the provocative photos taken in the hotel fitness center.

13 Birthday and Holiday Surprises

In October, Johnny and I celebrated our seventeenth birthdays together as we had celebrated our sixteenth. We invited Troy and his mom to join us. I got almost as many presents as Johnny did that year, but he was most excited about the present he got from Mike, an autographed football "from the game where I scored the winning touchdown against the Cowboys." It was a bit of intentional irony since Johnny had always been a big Cowboy fan before he met us.

We had our traditional Thanksgiving dinner at our house with the Andersens and the Mazures, and we even invited Carlos and Eddie to join us.

The week before school was to let out for Christmas break, Mrs. Mazure asked us if we were going to the school's annual Christmas concert. We hadn't planned on it—after all, it didn't involve football—but when she told us that Troy would be singing in the choir, Mom said, "Well, of course, we'll go. We can't miss that."

Troy had a deep, very sexy speaking voice—I thought he'd be great on radio—but it had never occurred to me that he might be a good singer. When we sat down in the auditorium that night, Mom, looking at the program, said, "Oh, look. Troy has a solo." Sure enough, it was the last song listed on the program.

The concert was not bad for a small-town high school. The program included a mixture of hymns and secular Christmas carols. When it came time for the final number, Troy stepped down from the risers and took center stage. The stage lights were dimmed, and a spotlight focused on him. He began to sing "Adeste Fideles," in Latin, of course, *a cappella,* and my jaw nearly hit the floor. He had the most beautiful baritone voice I had ever heard.

On the second verse, the concert band and the rest of the choir joined in, but his voice rang out over them all. After the second verse, they switched to the English version, "O, Come All Ye Faithful." He held the last note for what seemed like forever, and when he finished, the audience gave him a spontaneous standing ovation. When it seemed like the applause would never stop, we began to hear shouts of "bravo" and "encore." Obviously, those comments were directed specifically at Troy and not to the choir in general.

Troy started to walk back to his place among the choir, but the choir director stopped him, whispered something in his ear, and redirected him front and center. The director may have prepared an encore for the choir, but if she had, she shelved it and gave the floor to Troy. He took a couple of deep breaths and then launched into the most stirring *a cappella* rendition of "O Holy Night."

Anyone who is familiar with the song knows that the notes go up on the chorus, but Troy exceeded that. With an arpeggio, he went up two whole octaves, which suggested to us that Troy might have had opera training. Of course, I had no idea what an arpeggio was until Mrs. Andersen explained it to us later. (It seems that she had taken piano lessons as a child.)

As I listened in awe as Troy sang the second and third verses, I thought I was in the presence of an angel, and he was singing only to me.

Even before he finished, at least half of the audience was moved to tears. My own eyes were watery. I was too stunned to cry, but I noticed that even Johnny wiped an eye. After the climax, there was dead silence in the auditorium. The audience was too stunned to react. Then, all of a sudden the audience erupted in thunderous applause that had to have lasted for a good five minutes. There were even more shouts for an encore, but the director took the stage and thanked everyone for coming.

When the members of the choir came out front to greet the people from the audience, Troy was mobbed by his throng of new fans, and when word circulated that the choir director had hired a videographer to record the concert, everybody insisted on having a copy. I purchased two and sent one to Mike.

When the crowd dispersed, I tried to tell Troy how much he had impressed me, but I couldn't rally the words to come out of my mouth. Johnny rescued me with these words: "Dude, you've been holding out on us." That performance was the talk of the town for weeks and weeks.

We celebrated Christmas at the Andersen's, who decided not to go away to visit relatives that year. Mike's presents to Mom and Dad came in two envelopes. One was an all-expense-paid vacation cruising up Alaska's Inside Passage, followed by a train excursion through the Canadian Rockies, ending up at Niagra Falls. The trip was booked for next summer. The other envelope contained a letter from the bank informing them that their mortgages on the farm were all paid up. When times had gotten bad a few years back, Dad had to take out a second mortgage, but now he was debt free.

Troy, Johnny, and I each got an autographed picture of Mike in his 49ers uniform and several gift certificates. Troy also got a hand-written note from Mike saying how much he had enjoyed the tape of the Christmas concert that I had sent him. Troy was thrilled.

After dinner, we had all settled in the family room when the doorbell rang. "Who could that possibly be?" asked Mr. Andersen.

"I'll get it," said Johnny. And the next thing we heard was, "Oh, my god, what are you do—" But the unexpected guest swept past him before he could finish the sentence and burst into the family room.

"Oh, my god!" I echoed Johnny's reaction.

Everyone else in the room looked to Johnny and me for an explanation, but before we could offer up one, the man went straight to Mom, kissed the back of her hand, and said, "Mrs. Murphy, I would recognize you anywhere. Now I know where your sons got their beautiful looks." And before she could thank him, he extended his hand to Dad and said, "Mr. Murphy, such an honor to meet the father of two such outstanding young men. They are so beautiful in their bodies, in their minds, and in their hearts," and no sooner had he said it when he whirled around and greeted the Andersens in similar fashion, praising them as Johnny's parents.

“And who is this extraordinary man?” he asked, grabbing Troy’s chin and sizing him up. “Last night I stayed in hotel in town and everyone was talking about ‘the young man with the golden voice.’ You must sing Iago in *Otelo,*” he insisted.

“I love Verdi,” said Troy.

“And you must be his sister,” he said to Troy’s mother, who actually blushed.

“Mom, Dad, everyone,” I finally managed to interject. “I would like you to meet Armando.”

“He’s the photographer who shot the photos of Mike in Hawaii last year,” chimed in Johnny.

With this sudden clarification, everyone re-greeted the Italian photographer and complimented him on his work. “It is not work,” he said, “when you have such beautiful models for your art.”

“What are you doing here?” I asked Armando.

“Patrick!” Mom scolded. “Your manners.”

“I’m sorry,” I corrected. “I meant, what brings you to Texas?”

“Hot shot actress in Hollywood ask me to photograph her for portrait. Ugh! Movie stars!” he practically cursed. “But trip give me chance to come here to ask your parents,” he said to a roomful of puzzled faces. “I asked to photograph your sons in Hawaii,” he said to Johnny’s parents and mine, “but Mr. Murphy…er…Mr. Mike—such a nice man—he tell me, ‘No. They are too young.’ And then I see photographs taken by Claude, that hack”—and he mocked spitting on the floor as he had done with our “rags” of swimsuits in Hawaii—“and I think, Armando must photograph these men and show the world what real art is.”

And after every sentence, he mumbled something in Italian.

Johnny and I were ready to crawl under the sofa, our parents didn't know whether to gloat or laugh, Mrs. Mazure must have been thinking "who are these crazy people I've gotten myself mixed up with?" and Troy looked like he couldn't wait to get back to school so he could use the incident to embarrass the hell out of us.

"Forgive me for intrusion in your holiday," he said, "but I come to bring you present, the gift of my art."

"What is he talking about?" Dad asked me, confused and perhaps a bit perturbed.

"I think he's saying he wants to photograph us."

"Si," he confirmed. "No *nudo*. Only *rispetto*. Like businessman. *Bellissimo*."

"So, you're saying that you want to photograph Johnny and Rick in business suits?" asked Mrs. Mazure.

"*Si, bella signora*. But no, not only signore Johnny and signore Rick, but also I must photograph this *bella signore*," he said, gesturing toward Troy. "I give you photographs free. You can use for your high school...how do you say...yearbook. You can use for apply for job...or university. Everyone will love you."

Our parents all smiled at each other, not knowing quite what to do with this situation.

"How do you plan to do this work...this art?" asked Mr. Andersen. "I mean, when? Where?"

"*Qui*," Armando answered. "Here. *Adesso*. Now."

We were all stunned. "*Un momento*," he practically commanded. "Signore Johnny, *venire*. Signore Rick, come," so Johnny and I followed him out the front door to a cargo van parked out front with Troy following behind, more out of curiosity than anything else. Armando opened the back doors and ordered, "Bring, bring." Inside the van was a clothes rack carrying at least a dozen men's suits. "Inside," he said, "Inside. Now. Go."

Johnny and I took the rack of suits out of the van and began to roll it to the front door. Seeing Troy standing there, Armando commanded, "*Venire, venire*. Come, come." And he directed Troy to carry some of the large metal cases into the house.

In the foyer, he filtered through the suit bags, selecting a suit, shirt and tie for Johnny and pushing him upstairs to change. Then, he did the same for Troy, and then me. As we were heading up the stairs, we heard Armando ask Mr. Andersen, "Where shall I set up?"

He was a whirlwind. It all happened so fast that our parents were at a loss to pause it, let alone stop it.

When we came back downstairs in the suits Armando had selected for each of us, our parents literally gasped.

"Oh, my word," said Mrs. Mazure.

"Johnny!" said Mrs. Andersen.

And I thought Mom was going to cry.

"*Bello*!" proclaimed Armando. "Three subjects for Michelangelo, no?"

"Nice threads," remarked Dad.

"They should be," replied Mr. Andersen. "Those," he said, recognizing the style and obvious quality, "are Dolce and Gabbana suits." Seeing that the name meant nothing to Dad, he added, "Six to eight thousand apiece." Mrs. Mazure gasped, while Mom and Mrs. Andersen looked at each other with astonishment.

Armando ushered the three of us into the living room where he had set up his equipment. "Johnny, stand. There." Troy and I watched as Armando took dozens and dozens of shots with various poses in different locations within the room. When he was done, he led Johnny back to the clothes rack, picked out another suit, and sent him upstairs to change again. Next, it was Troy's turn and then mine.

When the three of us came back downstairs in the formal tuxedos Armando had selected, I thought our moms were going to faint. Mrs. Andersen waved her hand in front of her face as if to fight off the vapors. "Don't you boys ever go out in public dressed like that," said Mr. Andersen. "We don't have an army to fight off the girls."

Armando repeated the sequence of sessions, first with Johnny, then Troy, and finally me.

After we changed back into our "street clothes," we came back downstairs, put the suits back on the rack, and helped Armando load his equipment back into the rented van. We came back in to find our parents surrounding him in the foyer and thanking him profusely. He insisted that he should be thanking them, and when we started to take the suit rack back to his van, he rejected our assistance.

"Too much work carry back to Italy," he said. "You keep." We all tried to decline his generosity, but he was gone before we knew it.

When we sat back down in the family room, Mom began to cry. "What's wrong?" I asked her. "My baby is not a little boy anymore. He's a man now." The other mothers nodded in agreement and wiped tears from their eyes as well.

Perhaps to lighten the mood, Troy spoke up, "Man, Armando really hates that Claude guy, doesn't he?"

"Why do you say that?" I asked.

"The whole time he was here," replied Troy, "he kept cursing him."

"How do you know?" asked Johnny. "Oh, wait. You're kidding, right? You don't actually speak...? Oh, my god! You've been holding out on us again."

When everyone looked to Troy for an explanation, he said, "I've been studying Italian for six years now. If you're going to sing opera, you really must learn the language. I mean, you can memorize the words. That's easy enough, but if you want to capture the full meaning of what the composer is trying to convey, you have to understand the cultural context and all the linguistic nuances."

"Well, look at you, Professor Pavarotti," teased Johnny.

About 10 days later, Mrs. Andersen called and asked us to come over. She had something for us, she said. When we got to their house, Troy and his mom were already there in the family room. Mrs. Andersen handed Mom and Mrs. Mazure each a package. They unwrapped them to find sets of photographs of their sons. "We've already opened ours," said Mr. Andersen.

The Andersens looked on as Mom and Dad and Mrs. Mazure thumbed through the photos speechlessly. When Mom had gone through the set, she went through them again and finally sank back into the sofa. "When he boasted about being an artist," said Mom, "he wasn't kidding. These are the most gorgeous photographs I have ever seen in my life."

Mrs. Mazure and Mrs. Andersen agreed. Mr. Andersen and Dad just smiled and nodded their agreement. "Careful, Faith," said Dad. "You don't want all this praise to go to the boys' heads. They're hard enough to handle as it is." Of course, everyone knew that he was joking. His words notwithstanding, he was practically beaming with pride.

"There's something else," said Mr. Andersen, handing Troy's mom and mine each an envelope. Mom read her note silently and then passed it to Dad, who read it and turned to me.

"He wants our permission to photograph you in his studio in Rome. He says that he understands that you are under age 'by American standards' and must have your parents' permission. He promises that the photos will be 'tasteful, not vulgar,' and he has offered to pay our expenses as well to observe the photo session to ensure that everything is proper and acceptable."

"Wow! Italy," exclaimed Troy. "You lucky stiffs."

"Troy," said Mrs. Mazure, "This note says us too." Troy's eyes nearly popped out of his head.

"There's more," she said. "He has shown your photographs to executives at Dolce and Gabbana in Milan, and they are interested in discussing a modeling contract, depending on the additional portfolio he would compile in Rome. And he insists that he can line up other sponsors as well."

Our parents just looked at each other in astonishment.

"Can we, Mom?" asked Troy. "It's Italy, Mom. Italy!"

She looked to the Andersens, who looked to my parents. Finally, Dad spoke. "It sounds like a real opportunity," he conceded, "but I would like to see what Mike thinks. He knows this Armando, and he's had lots of experience with this kind of thing. Let's see what he says."

Our parents all agreed that getting Mike's input would be a good idea. Dad called when we got home and left a message. Mike called back the next day, and Dad filled him in. Mike asked to speak to me. "Do you really want to do this, champ?" I assured him that I did and so did Johnny and Troy. I told him that going to Italy was a life-long dream to Troy.

I gave the phone back to Dad, and Mike told him that he thought it would be all right as long as our parents were there to make sure that Armando did not "get carried away."

He asked if Armando had given us any timeframe, and Dad said he had not. Mike said to give him a week or so to check on something. He said that he wanted to talk to some people and that it might take some time. He didn't say who these people were or what he wanted to ask them, and Dad didn't question him on that. For the next several days, we were on pins and needles waiting for Mike to call back.

Then, one day, Dad called a meeting of the "Italian Tuxedos Club" at our house. After The Andersens and Mazures had all arrived, Dad said we just needed to wait a few more minutes for another guest. Dad always did love a mystery, especially when he was the only one with the clues. About 10 minutes later, the door opened, and in walked Mike.

Everyone was so excited to see him, we practically tackled him, but I don't think anybody was more excited than Troy. It was his first time to meet Mike. He thanked him for the autographed photo, and Mike replied that with the football season now over, he would be around—in and out actually—for a few months and that he expected to hear Troy sing for him. "Save me a couple of tickets for your spring concert," he said. Troy was practically giddy.

Mike motioned for everyone to sit down and began his exposition. "As you all know, I told Dad that I thought it would be OK for you to accept Armando's offer, but I wanted to check on some things first. I called my agent in New York, and he made some calls to our contacts in Barcelona, Denier's headquarters. I wanted to find out if we could schedule my next photo shoot in Rome with Armando so we could all go together, but it turns out that they want to do the shoot in Greece with an Olympics theme, and they've already lined up a Greek photographer.

Seeing the look of looming dejection on our faces, Mike hastened to add, "Don't kill me now, guys. I've got a plan I'd like to run by you." He continued, "As soon as I find out the dates for that shoot, we can contact Armando to see if we can schedule your shoot (pointing to us guys) the week before or the week after. You (indicating our parents) can chaperone, but I'll be around to answer any questions or to intervene if necessary. And," he added, "if there are any contract negotiations, I can probably help with that too."

Everyone agreed that this was a reasonable plan—hell, it was a fantastic plan—and we were all excited about the prospect of getting to visit both Greece and Italy.

"Now," said Mike, "which one of you guys wants to go get my luggage out of the car and take it to the guest house?" The three of us practically tripped over each other rushing out to the car.

The day after Mike came home, Troy and Johnny virtually leaped out of their skins when Mike suggested a scrimmage. "You and Johnny have really matured," said Mike after the scrimmage, "on the field and off. I'm really proud of you."

I did a kind of "aw shucks" gesture and asked what he thought of Troy.

"On the field or off?" he asked.

"Both," I replied.

"He's got a helluva voice," Mike said, "and from all I've heard, he's a really nice kid. You three guys make a good team. As a quarterback," he continued, "he's good. He has the potential to be very good, maybe even excellent, but the question is, does he want it as much as he wants his music? You and Johnny are exceptional, you can handle more than one thing and do them all well. Not many people can do that."

"Would you help him?" I asked Mike, "Coach him?" Mike understood better than anybody that Johnny's success as a wide receiver and mine as a halfback depended on having a good quarterback.

Mike just smiled and said, "I'll do what I can."

14 Underwear Party

As promised, Mike was in and out—home for a few days, gone for a few days, and so on and so on. Once, he even went to Washington with a group of executives from Lexus and other car companies to testify about automobile safety. Lexus had sent engineers and lawyers as well as vice presidents. Mike's role was just to add some "star power," and it evidently worked because the hearing was covered live by CNN, ESPN, MSNBC, and C-SPAN and reported on all the evening newscasts. We watched it on the new big-screen TV that Mike had given us and, of course, recorded it.

Mike surprised everyone, including the team from Lexus, with his knowledge of the subject. He demonstrated a reasonable knowledge of the engineering issues, but he seemed to understand the legal issues at least well as the lawyers and much better than the Congressmen. I knew that Mike had taken a course in business law at UT, but his expertise went way beyond that. He had done his homework, and it showed.

Leaving the Capitol, Mike was mobbed by reporters, and he had to fly to New York for a few days to accept all the requests from Ellen DeGeneres, Andy Cohen, Stephen Colbert, and other talk show hosts. He was no longer a celebrity; he was a sensation and was dubbed "America's Most Eligible Bachelor."

The day that Mike got back home, he got a call from his agent informing him that Lexus had tripled his consulting contract and would be sending him a very large bonus. When Mike thanked his agent for his hard work on his behalf, the agent said, "I should probably claim that I sweated bullets to get that money, but the truth is that it was not a hard sell at all." Still, Mike told the agent to keep half of the bonus for himself and give the other half to his favorite charity. It was not until years later that we learned that he had kept none of the money but had, instead, donated all of it to shelters for LGBT kids in four Deep South states. When asked why he had chosen those particular charities, he replied simply, "That's where the most acute need was."

When he was home, Mike always made time to work with Troy. Neither he nor I ever explicitly told Troy of our conspiracy. We just made it seem like spontaneous football, but it was obvious to me and probably to Johnny that Mike was actually coaching Troy, and by the time we got to the next football camp, the results were clearly evident. Coach Davis was pleased to say the least.

Like many of the guys on the football team, Troy had put up a picture of Mike inside his locker door when he first came to our school, but I noticed that he had replaced it with a different one. I asked him why he didn't use the one that Mike had sent him for Christmas. "Oh, I don't want to ruin that one," he said. "That one is now framed and hanging on the wall in my bedroom."

Over the next several days, Troy added smaller pictures in a collage around the big one in the center. Most of the guys had posted pictures that highlighted the female models, but I noticed that Troy had posted some with the male models. Even though I had been present for some of the photo shoots, I had not seen those particular ads in print, so I asked him where he had gotten them, and the next day he slipped me a piece of paper listing several URLs.

When I got home, I learned that these were websites catering to gay men, and some of them were downright pornographic, but there in a side panel were Addicted ads featuring Mike in his seductive underwear with links to other sites with even more provocative pictures. Suddenly, I understood why the photographers had taken photographs that were far too sultry to appear in mainstream magazines. Those photos were not for the mainstream magazines; they were for these websites. At first, I was shocked, but then I realized that if Ben Cohen had no objections to being featured in gay magazines, why not Mike? After that realization, it suddenly dawned on me: What was Troy doing on those sites anyway?

Martin Luther King's Birthday Weekend found everyone away except Troy and me. His mom had to spend the weekend at a palliative care seminar in Fort Worth. The Andersens, including Johnny, decided to get away to Cancun for the weekend. Mike flew back to New York to fit together the final arrangements for our upcoming trip to Greece and Italy, and he took Mom and Dad with him to take in a couple of Broadway plays. Because of Mike's celebrity status, they were invited backstage to meet the performers.

Troy had been asking me about our photo shoots in anticipation of his and ours. He had not been to either of our football camps when Johnny and I told our stories, so he had only heard second-hand accounts from other players. After some prodding, I finally admitted that there was more to the stories.

"Why don't you come by my place on Sunday?" I suggested. "I'll show you some pictures that didn't make the ads."

When Troy arrived Sunday afternoon, I led him to my room. I began by showing him prints that had made it into some ads and then the ones that didn't.

"Oh, I've seen that one in an ad," he said. It was a picture of Mike with a couple of the male models.

"Online?" I asked, and he confirmed my suspicion.

"If you think that's something," I said, "wait until you get a load of this one," and I flipped to the back of the album and showed him a print of the same scene but with the models fully exposed. I thought his eyes were going to pop out of his head. What's more, I thought something was about to pop out of his pants as well. And mine too.

"It's warm in here," I said. "Would you like something to drink?" He nodded yes, and I went down to the kitchen and brought back two Pepsis.

"So, where did you get all that sexy underwear I see you wearing in the locker room?" he asked. He already knew that Armando had given Johnny and me a pair of swimsuits to wear to the beach, but he didn't know that Armando and Claude had given us the entire batches.

"I've got them all in a suitcase," I said. "Wanna see?"

Troy jumped at the chance. In fact, the intensity of his enthusiasm surprised me a little, but I thought it was flattering. And cute.

I began the "swimsuit and underwear tour" by showing him the one that I had worn to the beach in Hawaii the first day...or rather...the replacement that Armando had sent me.

"Were you actually able to fit into that thing?" he asked. "I mean, you are awfully big down there."

I chuckled, and I don't know what possessed me, but I said, "Here, I'll show you." I didn't think anything of stripping in front of Troy since he had seen me naked in the locker room and in the showers. Then, I put on the infamous red-and-white swimsuit that Armando had selected for me and modeled it for Troy.

I had to laugh when Troy whistled. I took it as friendly teasing from a teammate.

Still in that swimsuit, I invited Troy to rifle through the array of swimsuits and underwear in the suitcase. One by one, we pulled out items and talked about which of our teammates and classmates would look good—or not—in each one. Then, we giggled like a couple of tweenage girls as we talked about which of our teachers would look good or not.

"I've never seen you wear this one at school," he gasped, holding up a brief with a transparent pouch.

"Are you kidding?" I gasped back. "The guys would never let me hear the end of it. Besides," I winked, "That one's for 'special' occasions."

Troy winked back.

"Oh, you would never be able to get into this one," said Troy, holding up an ultra-skimpy bikini.

"No," I conceded, "but maybe you would." When he threw me a funny look, I explained, "Not to say that you're small; you're just not as big as I am."

"Nobody's as big as you, champ." *Champ? Where did that come from? You must have heard Mike or Johnny call me that sometime.*

I laughed and then said, "Why don't you try it on and see?"

"You're sure?" he asked.

Just as he had seen me naked before, I had seen him naked in the locker room, so I really didn't think anything of it.

Troy stripped and put on the skimpy bikini. He actually looked pretty good in it. "Not bad," I said, "as long as you don't pop a boner." We both laughed, but I thought I did see his cock twitch. "Or maybe you'd look even better in it *with* a boner," I dared to say.

When he took it off, I suggested that while he was still naked, he try on some of the other items. A couple of times, I helped him adjust the fabric as Armando had done for me. "Oooh," he said. "You'd better stop that if you don't want me to poke a hole in this thing."

When we had gone through about half of the items, Troy, once again completely naked, asked me to tell him more about how we had met the Swedish college students on the beach. I did, and this time, I omitted none of the juicy details.

"Holy shit!" he exclaimed. "They actually kissed you after sucking you off?"

Fearing that I was about to cross a line, I ventured, "So, have you ever sucked cock?"

"A few," he confirmed.

"Bet you've never sucked one this big," I said, pulling down my swimsuit.

Troy practically dove for my cock and swallowed as much of it as he could. He was much more talented than any of the Texas girls who had sucked my dick. I'd put him on a par with the Swedish women.

Troy had my cock rock hard and extended to its full seven inches in no time. All my inhibitions, all of my pent-up frustrations flew out the window. I had to have him. I shoved him back on the bed and crawled on top of him. I pinned him to the bed and sank my tongue into his mouth. I was determined to lick his tonsils. It was so unlike me. I had never kissed a boy, and it wasn't my nature to be so aggressive. I slid up his body to his shoulders, grabbed the back of his head, thrust my cock into his mouth, and began fucking his face.

My term as the vandal was short-lived, though. Troy flipped me over and took the role of alpha male. He stretched my body out and lay on top of me. The scratching of his fur against my skin drove me wild. Our hard dicks rubbed against each other as he kissed me, alternating between deep, aggressive kisses and soft, loving ones. I would never have imagined that a boy could kiss like that.

He pulled back and just stared at my face as if he were studying a painting. Then he leaned slowly toward me, but instead of kissing my lips, he gently kissed my forehead and then my eyelids. He kissed his way across my right temple and over to my ear, which he took deliberately into his mouth and massaged with his tongue. He gently nibbled on my ear lobe and then worked his way back across my face to the left ear.

He kissed my cheeks, jaw, and chin, and then he retraced his steps, licking my face instead of kissing it. He licked his way down my neck and all across my chest to my arm pits. When he got to my nipples, he licked first and then sucked. I had never entertained the thought that my nipples could be so sensitive or so sensual.

He licked his way down to my navel and swirled his tongue around there before moving down to my pubic region. He didn't just lick my pubic hairs, he sucked on them as if they provided some sort of life-affirming nectar. He rubbed his stubbled cheeks over my dick but did not lick or suck it. Instead, he by-passed that organ and moved on to my balls, which he licked and then sucked, taking each one into his mouth separately.

Surely he will return to my aching cock now, I thought, but he didn't. He continued on his course and licked my perineum, again sucking on the hairs there. Finally—*oh please, God, please*—he made his way back to the base of my cock, where he paused to look up at me and smile. His eyes said, "I've got you now. You're mine, Achilles."

Seeing the sweet agony in my face, he licked my cock slowly from the base to the tip, his eyes still sending intoxicating darts into my soul. *Oh, God, please, please, please, make him do it. Now dammit!* He licked a spiral path from the base of my cock to the tip and teased the piss slit before slowly slipping his lips over my helmet. Then, without warning, he plunged his mouth down over my cock, digging as far as he could before gagging and having to relent.

"You're too fucking big, stud," he choked.

"Sorry," I squealed.

He smiled, "But you're so fucking hot, I've got to have you."

He lunged at my cock again and took in as much as he could manage. When he had to concede that he could not take it all, he wrapped one hand around the bottom half of my shaft and concentrated his oral ministrations on the top half. He pumped and sucked in unison.

The girls who had sucked me off merely rubbed my penis with their lips, but Troy actually sucked it, applying pressure with his tongue. His technique was amazing for someone who claimed to have limited experience.

My cock grew so tight that I thought the skin would flake off. Electric shocks flashed from my dick through my entire body. I felt as if I were caught in a lightning storm.

My cock began to throb, driving me to clench my teeth and claw at the bedspread until at last I exploded into his mouth with the force of a torpedo. To the extent that I was sentient at all, I imagined that I must have killed Troy. Surely, I had blasted a hole through the back of his skull.

Then I came again and again and again and.... And with each thrust, I shook so violently that I thought I would propel myself off the bed and onto the floor...or wherever one goes after such an explosive experience.

I felt as if every cell of my body had been turned inside out, sucked into a Texas cyclone, and blasted into the clouds. I thought the aftershocks would never stop, but when they began to wane and I regained enough strength to open my eyes again, I saw the face of an angel. Troy gently pulled my chin down to open my mouth. Then he opened his and kissed me.

I scanned his beautiful body with my eyes to discover that he was still hard as a rock. I tried to get up, but I was too exhausted. “Easy, stud, easy,” he said.

I pointed to his stiff shaft and tried to speak, but the words would not come. "It's all right," he comforted me. "There's plenty of time. We can take care of that later."

Totally drained, I did not even realize that I had dozed off. I have no idea how much time passed before I woke up to find Troy's head nestled against my shoulder and his hand cupping my balls. After several attempts, I finally managed to stand up and Troy began to stir, and that's when it hit, that call emanating from downstairs.

"Rick! Rick! Are you here?"

"Oh shit! It's Johnny!"

15 Missed a Spot

I panicked and tried to think what to do when I heard Johnny's footsteps climbing the stairs. Johnny had spent so much time at our house that he was practically considered family, so it was not uncommon for him just to walk right in. I quickly grabbed a pair of underwear and pulled them on, but Troy was not so quick. He had managed to pull up a pair halfway when the door opened.

"Oh, hey, Troy," Johnny said nonchalantly, strolling right past me and plopping himself on the bed as if he had seen absolutely nothing out of the ordinary. "Come to see Rick's underwear collection? Yeah, I've had a few 'undies parties' myself with the stuff we've collected from Mike's photoshoots."

"You?" It's the only word I could manage to get out.

"Yeah, Hightower asked to see them, and then Morgan, and then Czynski. Hell, I might as well have invited the whole team and gotten it over with."

Troy and I laughed, and before we could say anything else, Johnny pointed at the briefs Troy had barely managed to get on. "Those look good on you, Troy." It was the ultra-skimpy bikini. "You should have seen Rick trying to get that horse cock of his into them. He tucked and squirmed like a contortionist. I thought he was going to castrate himself before he finally gave up."

Troy and I couldn't help but laugh, which gave us a chance to catch our breath and relax a bit. Troy even plopped down on the bed across from Johnny.

"Did you get the same collection?" asked Troy, surprising me that he had regained his composure. I was not so quick.

"I'm thirsty. Anybody want a glass of water?" I asked, trying to change the subject...and the atmosphere.

They both nodded in the affirmative, and I left the room. Actually, I was dying to pee, and I used the water as an excuse to go to the bathroom. After I emptied my bladder and splashed water on my face, I went down to the kitchen and returned to my room with three bottles of water.

During my absence, Johnny and Troy had gotten into a conversation as natural as the sun rising in the east and setting in the west. They were going through the rest of the underwear, commenting on them and joking around. They had begun talking about which faculty member would look good in which pair, just as Troy and I had done earlier. *Earlier? What time is it? What day is it? What year is it?*

"What are you doing here anyway?" I asked Johnny. Then, suddenly realizing how that must have sounded, I added, "I mean, I thought you and your folks weren't coming back until tomorrow."

"There was some kind of emergency at Dad's company," he said, "so we had to come back early, and I thought I'd swing by and see if you wanted to grab a burger."

"Well—"

"How about you, Troy? You hungry?" Johnny continued.

If Troy was half as hungry as I was, he was starving.

I ordered a triple burger with large fries and a large vanilla shake. "He's a growing boy," Johnny said to Troy, pointing his finger at my crotch.

When we got back to the farm, I was exhausted despite the nap earlier. *How long did I sleep anyway?*

I really just wanted to go to bed—preferably with Troy—but Johnny kept Troy engaged. It was becoming clear to me that Johnny had taken control of the day, but I really didn't know what to make of that.

When Johnny announced that he should leave, Troy mentioned that his mom had also gone away for the weekend.

"Well, if you have no commitments," said Johnny, "why don't you just stay here?" I couldn't believe Johnny was reading my mind. "They've got a guest house behind the barn."

"Why don't you think about it," I said, "while I walk Johnny out?"

After we walked down the stairs and out to the front porch, Johnny turned to me, wiped a finger across my forehead, licked it, and said, "Missed a spot."

My jaw practically hit the ground, and when Johnny got to his car, he turned, looked me in the eye, winked, and gave me a thumbs-up.

"You sonofabitch," I said to no one there. *You knew all along.*

When I got back to my room, Troy had already stripped again in preparation for bed. "Collect your things," I commanded. "I'm taking you to the guest house."

Troy looked at me with a combination of bewilderment and dejection. "It's good," I reassured him. "The guest house has a king-size bed."

Lying naked together in the guest house, Troy and I kissed and fondled each other, but I was just too exhausted to go any further. "It's OK," he said. "We've got all the time in the world."

The next morning, I awoke early, as I always did. Troy was still asleep, and I was almost overcome by the sight of him. He looked so peaceful and so beautiful. I wanted so much to grab him up in my arms and squeeze him, but I also wanted him to rest.

I decided to go into the kitchenette to see if there was any orange juice in the fridge when I started to hear rumblings in the room that we called the bunkhouse. Of course, I thought, Carlos and Eddie are getting up to do the morning chores, the ones that I used to do. But the sounds I heard were not those of two men getting dressed. They were moans and grunts. Hmmm. Carlos and Eddie were cultivating more than crops, it seemed. I slipped back into the guest room so as not to disturb them.

"Morning, handsome," Troy said when he awoke much later.

"Ah, you're awake," I said.

"Awake and rarin' to go," he said. "Come here, gorgeous."

I removed the underwear I had put on and crawled naked back into bed next to Troy.

As I held Troy in my arms, I confessed to him that I had never lain with a guy before—not like this anyway. I told him that this was also my first time kissing a boy and my first time getting a blow job from one.

And I told him that I had never sucked off a guy. "Something tells me," he said, "that you've got a lot of firsts yet to come."

He rolled over to face me and gave me the most sensual kiss. He started to re-enact the kissing and licking pattern that he had demonstrated the night before, but I stopped him, looked him in the eyes, and whispered, "No. Now it's my turn." I flipped him over on his back and began kissing and licking him from head to toe. When I got to his beautiful cock, I just rubbed it softly against my cheek and moved on. Eventually, I came back to that holy place and kissed the tip of his penis. It was a new experience for me to put my mouth on another man's penis, but it felt so good and so right.

I sucked and swallowed as much of Troy's penis as I could, trying to emulate the techniques he had employed on me. I took short breaks periodically to rise up and kiss his lips and then go back down on him. When he began to squirm and moan louder and his dick began to pulsate, I knew he was close. When he finally exploded in my mouth, I was a bit shocked at first, but shocked in a good way. A very good way. It felt like another milestone in my sexual development, not just because I did it, but because I did it with a guy I really liked. I couldn't imagine anything else being so delicious.

Troy and I lay in bed together for the longest time just holding each other. I had never really cuddled with any of the girls I had hooked up with. We just fucked and moved on. Or fucked, rested a few minutes, and fucked again.

"That was incredible," Troy finally declared.

"Yeah?" I asked. "Was it really or are you just trying to be polite?"

"Oh, baby, I would never deliberately try to be nice to you," he teased. "No, seriously, I did not know that a blow job could feel that good. I mean, I haven't had a lot, but that one was probably the best."

"I don't know whether being called a great cocksucker is a compliment or not," I said, "but I'll take it." Following another stretch of silence when we just enjoyed being with each other, I asked, "Have you ever...I mean...have you—"

"...fucked a guy?" he completed my question. "No," he replied. "In that regard, I'm still a virgin."

"Have you thought about it? Is it something you think you might like to do?"

"Sure. I've thought about it," Troy said. "As to whether I would like it, I guess I won't really know until I've tried it."

"But you would try it, huh?"

"Yeah, I think so...with the right guy...at the right time."

Of course, I wanted to ask who, when, but I decided to let it go for now.

Troy and I showered, ate breakfast, and sucked each other off again. That was my first experience with a 69. I was experiencing lots of firsts.

Since our parents would soon be returning from their trips, we decided to take separate cars into town for lunch so we could go our separate ways afterwards. Troy suggested that we invite Johnny to join us for lunch, and I said, "Sure. Why not?"

Having Johnny join us for lunch felt a bit strange. I wouldn't say that it was uncomfortable. It was more like we all shared a secret that nobody was ready to talk openly about yet.

When everyone got back from their weekend getaways, Mike called another meeting of the Italian Tuxedos Club. He began by explaining that while they were in New York, he and our parents had met with his agent to finalize plans for our trip to Greece and Italy. They had worked out the schedule with the Denier folks about the shoot in Greece and with Armando for the one in Rome, and they had also negotiated who would pay for different parts of the trip.

"But don't worry about that," he said. "Everything's been taken care of. You won't have to pay for a thing." Our family and the Andersens were not surprised since their sons had been through this kind of experience already, but Mrs. Mazure and Troy were bowled over.

"So, here's the plan," Mike continued. He explained that he and the three boys—"yes," he said, eyeing Troy, "*three* boys—will go first to Greece for a week. It will be a good opportunity for Troy to observe my shoot so he can get a sense of what to expect with Armando's shoot in Rome. For that leg of the trip," he added, "the parents are welcome to come along or not. The choice is yours." Everyone looked at each other as if trying to figure out who would be crazy enough to pass up the opportunity.

"From Greece, we'll fly to Rome for your shoot," he said, pointing to Troy, Johnny, and me. Everyone needs to be in Rome because you have to supervise the shoot.

"Now, Phase Three," Mike announced, much to our confusion." *There's a Phase Three?*

"From Rome, I'm taking my family to Ireland for a week to explore our roots. The rest of you can join us, go your own way, or come home." After a bit of murmuring among ourselves, Mike almost shouted sternly, "Except you!" he said, pointing to Troy. Troy looked like he had just been shot.

"You, my good friend, will remain in Italy for another month." Troy and his mother were both star-struck. "I have arranged for you to take an intensive advanced course in Italian."

"'Advanced' means you get to learn all the dirty words," Johnny elbowed Troy.

"Jonathan Andersen!" Mrs. Andersen scolded. *At least she didn't call him Jonathan Luuu Ellen Andersen that time.*

"That course will take place not only in Rome, but also in Florence, Venice, Milan, or wherever you decide to go. In Milan, you will have a tour of La Scala, the famous opera house, and meet with faculty from the Academy for the Performing Arts. I didn't know if you would want to take lessons from them or just have discussions, so you can let me know, and I'll pass the word along."

"Mrs. Mazure," Mike continued, "You can stay with Troy or I can arrange for someone to oversee him. And, like I said, everything's covered."

We were all flabbergasted. Troy, Johnny, and I ran up to my room to plot all the crazy things we were going to do as our parents remained downstairs to talk about what they needed to do to keep us from going bonkers. From then until June, it was hard to focus on anything else, but focus we must.

Troy and I played again the following weekend and agreed that we would continue our budding relationship, but not exclusively. We agreed that we liked each other and wanted to see how things developed, but we also agreed that we both needed to get more experience with other people to see if our feelings for each other were real.

I continued to hang with girls, often ending up in bed, but sometimes not. I had more double dates with Johnny, but those were becoming fewer and farther between. I even took Hightower's sister to the junior prom. Hightower took me aside before the dance and told me that if I did anything to hurt his sister, he would rip my balls off, and I knew that he was only half kidding. I dated girls not just to "pass" for straight, but also because I really enjoyed being with them. I still didn't know if I was gay, straight, bisexual, or something else. It was just too early to decide, and I saw no reason to try to rush the process—or if there even needed to be a process.

I also met up with guys I found online or were introduced to by Troy. A couple of times, Troy took me to "bate parties" in Temple or Killeen. Typically, these parties consisted of a group of guys sitting around in a room jerking off (i.e. "bating"), either individually or in concert with each other. Troy told me...and even showed me...other rooms where guys were doing more: sucking each other off or fucking. I didn't know quite what to make of it all...but my dick did.

16 Solos and Duets

The spring choral concert was scheduled for a Friday night the middle of April, one week before Good Friday, which was late that year. Mike told Troy to get him two tickets. "I wouldn't miss it for the world," he said, causing Troy to just beam.

The day of the concert, Mike informed us that he needed to go to the airport to pick up someone. He assured us that he would be back in time for the concert. Another mystery.

Mike arrived at the school auditorium just as we did. "Mom, Dad. I'd like you to meet Maria Bianchi." We were all stunned, not that Mike had brought a date or that he had brought a pretty one, but that she was drop-dead gorgeous, the most beautiful woman I had ever seen in my life. She had raven hair, dark eyes, a beautiful complexion, and a perfect figure in her "little black dress." She reminded me of Catherine Zeta-Jones in *Zorro*, but even more beautiful, if you can imagine such a thing. The men, even my dad, almost melted to the ground, and the women looked at her with awe.

Mike introduced Maria all around—except to Troy, of course, who was backstage with the rest of the chorus.

"You just flew in today?" asked Dad.

"Yes."

"And where are you from?" asked Mom.

"New York City."

"And what do you do there?"

"I'm a teacher."

"Oh, what do you teach?"

But before she could answer, the ushers urged everyone to take their seats.

Ms. Garcia, the choir director, had reserved seats for us in the front row. Maria sat in the aisle seat next to Mike. I sat next to Mike with Mom and Dad on the other side of me and the Andersens and Mrs. Mazure on down the row. When we were seated, Dad leaned over and whispered to Mom, "Looks like somebody's been making all those trips to New York for something more than business."

"Oh, look," said Mrs. Andersen, holding up her program. "Troy has two solos, one right before intermission and one at the end."

The girls in the choir, dressed in knee-length black dresses or skirts, entered from stage right and took their places. The boys, dressed in suits and ties, entered from stage left. Of course, Troy wore his seven-thousand-dollar Dolce and Gabbana suit.

The program consisted of an eclectic mix of popular songs and non-traditional pieces designed to highlight the various strengths within the chorus. There were several that I had never heard of and a couple that I could not even pronounce.

The first part of the program was pretty good. I didn't fall asleep. But, of course, everyone was waiting for Troy's solo.

"This next song," announced Ms. Garcia, "features Troy Mazure, who will give us a little introduction."

Troy stepped downstage center. "'Strange Feelings,' by Robert Milton Ingram," he said, "is a song about the cognitive dissonance, the inner conflicts, that a person feels when he or she falls in love, perhaps for the first time. Like 'I Don't Know How to Love Him' from *Jesus Christ, Superstar,* this song can be a woman singing about her man, a man singing about his woman, or either singing about their love for Jesus. Listen to these lyrics." And he recited one verse:

Why do the clouds smell like jasmine and fruit on the vine?
Why does the rain taste like honey and strawberry wine?
Why does the wind whisper poems and sonnets of love?
Why do their words float like angels from heaven above?
What are these strange and mysterious feelings in me?

Troy took one step back, took two deep breaths, and let the music take over.

When he finished the final chorus...

Why is everything strange?
Am I going insane?

Am I losing my mind?
Why can't I just unwind?
What are these strange, strange feelings in me?"

...the audience stood, clapped, and cheered for several minutes. His performance was phenomenal.

During the intermission, I expected Mom and Dad to continue the interrogation of the beautiful Miss Maria Bianchi, but she was nowhere to be found. "Oh, she had to go take care of something," Mike said. "She'll be back."

But when we went back in for the second half of the program, she was AWOL. Her seat remained empty for the remainder of the program. *Too bad. She's going to miss Troy's other solo.*

When it came time for his second solo, Troy came forward again, but the choir director stopped him and announced, "I know you are all looking forward to this final number, but I'm pleased to tell you that we have a very special guest here tonight who will introduce the song to you. She is a professor of voice and music theory and composition at the Juilliard School in New York City." (Mom and Dad glared at each other and mouthed the word 'teacher,' as if it were the understatement of the century.) "Please give a very warm welcome," Ms. Garcia continued, "to Miss Maria Bianchi."

We all swapped looks at each other and at Mike, who tried valiantly but fruitlessly to suppress smiling like the cat that ate the canary.

After the courtesy applause and all the women had jerked their husbands back to reality, Maria explained.

"Wolfgang Amadeus Mozart's 'La Ci Darem La Mano' from the opera *Don Giovanni,* is considered one of the most beautiful love songs in all of the opera world. It is a duet in which Don Giovanni attempts to seduce the beautiful Zerlina. Troy Mazure has been practicing this duet for weeks with a recording of Zerlina's part."

At that point, she surprised the audience by walking over to Troy and saying something to him that we could not hear, even from the front row. Then she stepped just to the side of downstage center and announced, "Ladies and Gentlemen, with Mr. Mazure's generous permission, I will sing the role of Zerlina while he sings the role of Don Giovanni."

Troy seemed a bit stunned himself, but being the consummate professional, he took a breath and began to sing to the recorded music. When Maria came in with Zerlina's first line, the entire audience was instantly captivated. Her voice was every bit as gorgeous as her face.

After another prolonged standing ovation, peppered with shouts of 'bravo' and 'encore,' the choir director gestured to Maria to again take center stage. "Thank you so much, ladies and gentlemen, and thank you, Troy, for allowing me the honor of singing with you. You have an amazing talent," which drew more resounding applause from the audience with our families leading the charge.

"Earlier this evening," she added, "Troy referenced the song 'I Don't Know How to Love Him' from the musical *Jesus Christ, Superstar*. It was written for Mary Magdalene to sing about her love for Jesus, but, as Troy said, with just a little tweaking of pronouns, it can be sung by either a woman or a man. So, again with your permission, Mr. Mazure, I would like to sing this song with you."

Troy smiled such a big smile that I thought his teeth would fall out. Once the music began, Maria let Troy sing the first few lines solo before joining him, and at certain points, she again stepped back and let him take the lead.

When he sang...

I never thought I'd come to this.
What's it all about?
Yet, if he said he loved me
I'd be lost. I'd be frightened.
I couldn't cope, just couldn't cope
I'd turn my head, I'd back away.
I wouldn't want to know
He scares me so,
I want him so,
I love him so.

...I thought he was speaking directly to me. I felt strange, confused, lost, scared, and overwhelmed. Was I losing my mind? Why couldn't I just unwind? Was I falling in love for the first time?

Of course, the audience demanded another encore, so after Troy quieted the audience, he said, "I know that Ms. Bianchi did not come here tonight to perform because she did not want to take away from the choir's night, but I can assure you, Ms. Bianchi, that we would all be very disappointed if you did not share another song with us," and the members of the choir proved his point by pleading with her to sing.

"Very well," she said. Then she chatted with Troy for more than a minute. We all assumed that they were trying to figure out which song to sing, and she surprised us again when she turned and approached Ms. Garcia and the choir. Troy cracked everyone up at that point when he shrugged his shoulders and rolled his eyes in mock frustration. After consulting with the choir for a minute, Maria came back downstage and stood with Troy. We all expected them to sing an opera duet, but imagine our surprise when the two of them, backed up by the choir, broke into "You're the One that I Want" from *Grease.*

Everyone in the audience laughed and then started clapping and singing along, which Maria strongly encouraged. She even led members of the choir down from the stage, and into the audience, where they danced and pulled members of the audience from their seats to dance with them. Maria even thanked one dance partner with a little peck on the cheek. I suspect that man did not wash his face for a week.

Toward the end of the song, Maria and Troy led the choir back on stage, and when the song ended, they turned and opened their arms to the choir, giving them the lion's share of the credit. Maria even directed the students to take a bow and led the applause for them. Talk about a class act. Mike had really picked a winner in this one.

As we waited in front of the auditorium for Troy and Maria after the concert, Troy's mother was besieged by parents and students alike who wanted to congratulate her on Troy's impressive performance. A few people who knew Mike well told him they were glad to see him again and asked him about Maria. I guess they figured that no one else in our town could catch the eye of such a beautiful woman, and, no doubt, more than a few probably wondered how a football player could meet up with an opera singer. We learned later that Mike had gotten smitten with Maria when she was invited to sing the national anthem at the 49ers' game against the Giants in New York.

"Well, go ahead," Maria prodded Mike. "Tell them the rest of the story."

Beginning to blush, Mike withdrew as if he did not know what she was talking about...or he knew and didn't want to tell. I had always been impressed with how composed Mike always was no matter the circumstances. That was the only time I ever saw him melt like butter.

Seeing that Mike was not going to spill the beans, Maria continued, "Later that week, I was performing the role of Mimi in Puccini's *La bohème*. At the end of the performance, I was presented with a bouquet of a dozen red roses, but there was no card, so I did not know who they were from. The following evening, I received two dozen roses, and the next night three, but that time when I asked the usher who had sent them, he pointed to the handsome man in the front row who had sat through three performances with his jaw on the floor and his eyes glazed over."

Mike turned redder than I had ever seen him blush, which caused all the rest of us to smile. The big strapping football player was turning to mush.

"I had the usher invite Mike backstage so I could thank him for the flowers," added Maria, "and our relationship blossomed from there."

We all gathered at the Andersen's house to sing the praises of Troy and Maria. I observed how remarkable it was that this professional opera singer would defer to a high school student, but I must say that Troy had earned the courtesy.

"She is indeed a remarkable person," concurred Mike, squeezing Maria's hand as he spoke. She just looked at Mike and smiled, and we all knew that there was indeed something remarkable going on between them.

"How long will you be in town?" Dad asked Maria, who replied that she had to leave early in the morning for an appointment in Austin before flying back to New York on Sunday. Mrs. Andersen asked where she was staying that night, and she replied, "I believe Mike has made some arrangements." *Yeah, I bet he has.*

Mom thanked Maria for coming and said she hoped to see her again and assured her that she was welcome to our home any time.

As we all said good night and went our separate ways, I felt the pain of parting. I so much wanted to take Troy home with me, but I knew that his mother would want family time that evening. And I knew that my time with Troy would come.

17 Strange Feelings

As if Troy weren't getting enough attention, his eighteenth birthday fell on the last day of school, the second Friday in May. Mrs. Mazure had planned a small party for the following day, but during his first year at our school, Troy had made lots of friends. Everybody on the football team as well as those in the choir and half the girls in school practically begged to be invited to the celebration, so Mrs. Mazure reluctantly accepted the Andersen's offer to host the party at their house.

Maria returned to Hilldale for Troy's birthday party, as did Mike, of course. He wasn't going to go anywhere without her.

The celebration was much like the ones Johnny and I had enjoyed on our birthdays. Kids swam in the pool, danced around it, ate burgers and other picnic food, and generally acted like teenagers. Troy got more presents than he had probably gotten in his whole life. He blew out the candles on the cake made by my mom and decorated by Mrs. Andersen with confectionary music symbols along with football gear. We all sang "Happy Birthday," which seemed incongruous given that the best voice in the crowd was Troy's ...and Maria's, of course.

After Troy blew out his candles—no problem given his breath control—there were shouts of "Speech! Speech!" Troy obliged with a two-word speech, "I'm gay."

Reactions ranged from shock to laughter to shrugs. You might expect that deep in the State of Texas, the reaction might be to run him out of town on a rail, but not so. Of course, I already knew that Troy was gay, but I hadn't expected this sudden announcement. Some people looked to me to say something, but Johnny beat me to it.

Johnny got up from the patio chair he was sitting in, stood next to Troy with his hand on his shoulder, and spoke. "Some people might praise Troy for the courage it must have taken for him to make this statement, but to me, that seems a bit condescending. Why should it take courage to be who we are? No doubt trying to keep this aspect of his life hidden has imposed tremendous stress on him, and I am happy for him that he no longer has to deal with this stress. I wonder how many of us could have achieved all that he has under that kind of stress.

"A German Gestalt psychiatrist named Fritz Perls once said, 'I do my thing, and you do your thing. I am not in this world to live up to your expectations, and you are not in this world to live up to mine. You are you, and I am I, and if by chance we find each other, it's beautiful.' Personally, I don't care if you are gay, straight, bisexual, or transcendental" (which drew snickers from the few people in the crowd who caught the nuance). "I am just glad and honored that you found me, bro. You have been my friend since the day we met, and you will, I hope, continue to be my friend for as long as we live—provided I don't do anything stupid to screw it up.

"I want to wish my friend a very happy birthday and many more." And with that, Johnny hugged Troy and said, "I love you, bro."

Mrs. Mazure, Mrs. Andersen, and Mom wiped tears from their eyes. Most of the kids, including all of the football players, came forward and shook Troy's hand or hugged him.

Then, quite a few eyes turned toward me. More out of frustration than anything else, I rose to speak. "Everybody here knows that Troy and I are friends, so some of you may be wondering in view of what Troy has just said if I am also gay. The honest answer is that I don't know. I like girls, as some of you in this crowd can attest." (A few snickers circulated through the crowd.) "I also like guys, especially this one right here," I said reaching for Troy's hand. "I don't know if that makes me gay, straight, bisexual, or, as Johnny says, 'transcendental'. I think it makes me human. Beyond that, I'm still exploring, and if I ever reach a conclusion, you can read about it in my best-selling memoirs."

Some people laughed, and others just scratched their heads. Johnny hugged me and said that he loved me. All of my teammates on the football team shook my hand or slapped me on the back as they had done with Troy. Some of the guys also hugged me, and a couple of them seemed to linger on the hug a bit, causing me to wonder if they were trying to tell me something. Some of the girls kissed me on the cheek, and several said something like, "You still have my phone number, don't you?"

When our classmates turned their attention back to partying, our parents came forward and embraced us. Not one of them said anything like, "I love you regardless." *Regardless of what?* Rather, they affirmed their love for us, and that's all we needed.

Mike and Maria, who had been sitting back observing all of this activity, came up and spoke to Troy and me both. I didn't hear what she said to Troy, but she gave him a kiss on the lips. It wasn't a sexual thing...more like an Italian thing.

She also kissed me on the lips in that cultural, big-sister way and said, "Yes, you are a human being, a very beautiful human being." *God, I hope you become my sister-in-law.*

Mike gave me a great big bear hug, and said, "I am so proud of you, Patrick Captain Fucking America Murphy." And as he started to walk away, he turned back, waved a finger in my face, and cautioned, "And keep away from my girl."

After everyone else had left, I said to my folks, "I'm staying with Troy tonight." When that definitive statement drew an odd look from them, I turned to Mrs. Mazure and said, "If that's all right with you, ma'am. I think he could use a friend right now." Mrs. Mazure replied, "Thank you, Rick. You're always welcome in our home."

In Troy's room, we debriefed the events of the day and decompressed. Yes, for Troy especially, a tremendous weight had been lifted off his shoulders, but it also left him wondering, "OK, what do I do now?"

"What can I do to help?" I asked.

"Make love to me," he replied.

"All the way?" I asked.

"All the way."

I kissed him tenderly and undressed him slowly, kissing him lightly as I worked my way down his body. Then I removed my own clothes and took him to bed. We kissed again, enjoying the taste and feel of each other. I needed no priming; I was instantly and completely hard. I asked if he had any lube, and he said, "Nightstand." I opened the one drawer in the only nightstand and retrieved the bottle of lube, which had never been opened. "I've had it for two years," he said. "Never had the occasion to use it before." I smiled and began to grease up my cock and his hole.

Even though I had lost my virginity to a couple of girls two years before, I felt like I was losing it now all over again, and I was about to make love to a virgin too. And this time it wasn't just about having sex. It was about making love.

I rubbed the tip of my penis gently against his hole but did not push it in yet. I traded my penis for my index finger, which I inserted slowly. Troy flinched. "Relax," I said. "Just relax." Once I had my finger all the way in, I slowly rubbed it around, teasing his prostate. I pulled the finger out slowly and then inserted two fingers. He flinched again. He was incredibly tight. I was beginning to doubt that he would be able to accept my huge dick, but I continued rubbing two fingers in and out, and he began to moan with pleasure.

"I want you," he said. "I need you inside of me."

I took my tool into my hand and directed it to his opening. I again massaged the tip against it. I primed his sphincter muscle until I was able to get the head of my penis past it. Troy winced in pain. I had read that pain was common until the rectum adjusted to the foreign invasion, but what the hell did I know? This was my first time too.

I paused to give his insides time to cope. When I felt his body relax, I inched my way deeper. In and back, in and back, in and back until I felt the tip of my cock against his prostate. I had no way of knowing what Troy was feeling, physically or emotionally, but my dick was feeling fucking incredible.

"How are you doing, babe?" I asked. He didn't speak. He just looked up at me with dreaminess in his eyes. I leaned forward and kissed him, just the lips at first and then with my tongue in his mouth. "I'm inside you," I whispered in his ear. "We are joined together. You are mine, and I am yours." Corny, I know, but it was also very genuine.

I rose up and began again pulling my penis almost out, but not completely, and pushing it back in again, going slightly deeper each time. I knew he would never be able to accept the full length of my giant penis, but I kept going until one of us could not take any more.

His moaning became more peaceful, more reflective of satisfaction. I took that as my cue to press on. I increased the speed of my insertions. In, out; in, out; in, out. Damn, it felt so good. I was trying so hard to take it easy for his sake, but my dick was screaming for more. "You OK, baby?" He moaned his approval, so I picked up the pace once more.

I didn't want to come. Not yet. I wanted to hold out as long as I could for his sake as well as mine. I slowed the pace, reached over for the bottle of lube and poured some onto his penis, which was as hard as mine. I pumped his cock in my hand with the rhythm of my dick in his ass. He began to squeal. "Oh, god!" he suppressed his scream. I could tell that he wanted to scream his head off but didn't dare because we were not alone in the house. I knew how he felt; I too wanted to scream and curse and praise the lord for this divine sensation.

I pumped harder, but I had to be careful not to push too deep, which would not have been pleasant for either of us. My cock began to throb, but I also felt his dick pulsating in my hand. I had to hold out and let him come first because I was afraid that if I came first, I would just collapse in exhaustion and not be able to finish him off.

I slowed the pace of my pelvic thrusts while accelerating the pumping of his penis with my hand. I willed myself to hold out. And it worked. He explodeed, spewing volley after volley of jizz over his head, across his face, and onto his chest and belly. His glorious love juices covered his beautiful, virile, hairy body. I found the contrast of the luscious white cream against his thick black fur to be beautiful and incredibly erotic.

It was too much for me to resist, so I shot into him like a cannon. "Ah. Ah. Ah. Fuck! Oh, god! Fuck! Fuck! Fuck!" I knew I had to keep my fucking mouth shut because his mother would inevitably hear us, but I could not hold back. Hell, I wanted the whole fucking State of Texas to hear our screams of ecstasy. I felt like his body was sucking my whole body inside of him, making us truly one being, united in the blissful pain of coital union.

I totally collapsed on top of him. There was almost nothing left of me, but, luckily, I could still feel his hard, hairy body beneath me and his life juices squishing between us. The feeling was indescribable.

I had had sex before—with girls—but there was something profoundly different about this experience, and not just for the obvious reasons. As overwhelmed as I was with the unbelievably intense physicality of this act, I was equally consumed by the epiphanous spirituality of it.

I wanted to kiss him to make sure that he was all right, to make sure that I had pleased him and not just used him for my own sexual gratification, but I could not even muster the strength to raise my head. I just rubbed my cheek against his and purred. He purred back, and that told me that all was well.

My dick stayed hard inside of him for the longest time, and every time I felt it start to slip out, I pushed it in farther. Even soft, it was bigger than many when they are hard, so I was able to stay inside of him for quite a while.

I panted and panted until I finally fell asleep on top of him and still inside of him. At some point, I know that he had pushed me off because I woke to find myself lying beside him with his head against my shoulder and his arm stretched over my chest.

"I love you, baby." Maybe it was too much, but it was the only thing I could think to say.

"Are we in heaven?" he asked.

"I don't know," I answered. "But last night sure as hell was."

We lay there in bed for quite a while, just enjoying the feel of each other before we finally got up and took a shower. I didn't know what was on his agenda for the day, but I felt that I should get home. I crept downstairs hoping that I would not run into his mother. I felt absolutely no shame for what we had done, but I did feel a little bad about having made such a ruckus. As I neared the front door, she came out of the kitchen and caught me. She kissed me on the cheek and looked me straight in the eye. "Rick, what I said last night, I meant it. You are always welcome in our home." *Such a sweet lady. Why can't every mother be like this?* I hugged her and went on my way.

When I got home, I expected to find that Maria had returned to New York and maybe Mike had gone with her, but I found everyone sitting around the den, almost as if they were attending a wake, it seemed at the time. "How is Troy?" Mom asked.

"He's fine," I said. "He's good."

"And how are you, son?" asked Dad.

"I'm good, Dad. I'm good. We're both good."

"Have you had anything to eat?" Mom asked.

"No, I'm...I'm...." I hadn't even thought about food. "Actually, I'm starving." That drew a noticeable snicker out of everyone.

"You run upstairs and change." I was still wearing the same clothes I had worn the day before. "I'll have some breakfast for you when you get back downstairs."

When I entered my room, I just stood there by the bed, still a bit dazed.

"Rick?" I heard the voice coming from the doorway. I turned to find Mike standing there. "From the way you're acting, I really can't tell if what happened with you last night was good or bad, but either way, I'm here for you if you need to talk about it."

I mustered up a faint smile and replied, "It was good, Mike. Very good. It's just...I don't know. It's like everything is different now. The whole world has changed, and I don't know what...I don't know how...."

Was I in love with Troy? Or was I just delirious from this new world that had suddenly burst wide open for me?

"I understand," he said. "Believe it or not, I really do." He sat me down on the bed, pulled up a chair, leaned in, and said to me, "It's a beautiful world, champ. Yes, there are bad things out there too, but there's more beauty than any of us can process. It looks to me like you might have gotten an overdose of that beauty last night, and there's absolutely nothing wrong with that. You'll survive." We both chuckled. "Keep your head up. Walk proudly. And grab all the beauty you can. You deserve it. You're Patrick Captain Fucking America Murphy."

At the time, I'm not sure I could process exactly what he was saying, but I could feel the love in it, and it almost brought me to tears. He leaned over and gave me a little hug, but I must have caught him off guard when I jumped up from the bed and squeezed him as hard as I could. When we broke that lock, he walked toward the door. But he stopped, turned back to face me, and said, "You don't have to tell me anything, but I'm here if you ever feel the need to talk. I'm always here for you. I love you, champ."

When he walked down the stairs, I closed the door, walked back to my bed, and collapsed in tears. They were tears of joy, tears of confusion, tears of accomplishment, tears of doubt, tears of angst, tears of hope. But mostly, they were tears of feeling overwhelmed with more love than I ever imagined could exist.

I gave Eddie and Carlos the next day off. I felt that doing the chores myself might help me clear my head. That afternoon, while I was sitting under the old oak tree out in the sheep pasture, Mike walked up and asked, "Mind if I join you?" I smiled up at him and gestured to the spot beside me under the tree.

After a long stretch of silence, Mike spoke, "Two weeks until our trip to Europe. You still up for it?"

"Of course," I said. "Why wouldn't I be?"

"Just checking." After another pause, he informed me that he and Maria would be leaving the next day. "I need to go back to San Francisco to prepare for the trip," he explained, "but I'll meet you guys at the airport in New York for the flight to Athens."

"OK."

As Mike got up to leave, I stopped him, "Mike?"

"Yeah, champ?"

"What is love?"

"Whoa. Philosophers and poets have been struggling with that question for millennia."

"I mean, how do you know if you're in love...if it's real?"

Mike sat back down on the ground, not next to me, but facing me. He took a deep breath and continued, "Despite what you hear in love songs and read in Hallmark cards," he continued, "love is not this universal, unitary thing. It has neurochemical aspects, physical elements, emotional and psychological components, and more, and people do not experience them all the same. Some people believe that they have fallen in love at first sight, but what they probably experienced was infatuation. Sometimes that infatuation evolves into real love, sometimes not. Other people develop strong friendships over time that eventually lead to love. When you're *in* love," Mike said, "you don't know. You're too confused to know. You can only know when you start to accept it or reject it."

"I must really be confused," I said, "because I don't even understand what you just said."

Mike chuckled and explained, “Do you remember that song that Troy sang at the concert last year, ‘Strange Feelings’?

Why does my heart beat so madly I barely can breathe?
Why does my head spin so wildly I can’t even think?
Why do my feet only stumble whenever I walk?
Why do my lips only mumble when I try to talk?

Why do I hear bluebirds singing sweet songs in the air?
Why do I see rainbows gleaming when nothing is there?
Why do the stars twinkle at me in broad daylight?
Why do I feel the sun’s rays in the middle of night?
Why does the river run backwards and time stand still?
Why does the world seem so crazy and yet seem so real?

What are these strange and mysterious feelings in me?
What do they want from me, why won’t they just let me be?

“It looks to me like that’s what you’re going through right now,” he noted. “Don’t try to analyze it, Rick. Just experience it. Let it wash over you. Bathe in it. At some point the fog will clear, and you will understand whether it was love or not, but either way, you will be a better person for the experience, a better man, and, eventually, a better lover.”

"Wow. I'm surprised that you remembered all those lyrics," I said.

"Well, that song had a tremendous impact on me because that's what I was going through at the time. I didn't know what was real and what wasn't."

"Maria?" I asked.

Mike grinned and acknowledged the fact.

"I can tell you this much. When you are in love, that person's life means more to you than your own, and when you're both in love, each of you will feel that he is the lucky one.

"There may be times when you can't quite hear the bluebirds singing," he said, "but they will always come back around, and when the noise settles, you *will* hear them again."

"Are you in love with Maria now?" I asked.

"I think I may be," he replied. "But I can tell you this: I'm the lucky one."

"Looks to me," I said, "that you're both pretty damn lucky. And I'm lucky to have the best damn brother in the whole wide world."

Mike smiled. "You're just saying that because you're really confused right now."

19 Greece

Less than two weeks remained before our departure for Europe. Troy and I spent much of that time with each other. Sometimes I slept with him at his house, sometimes he slept in mine, and every night we made love.

I told Troy about my conversation with Mike, and he confessed that he was feeling the same way. We agreed that what we had experienced was something beautiful and that we really cared for each other, but we also concurred that we weren't really sure if it was true love or not. We agreed that perhaps the best thing we could do at the moment was just to experience it, as Mike had advised. We also agreed that neither of us wanted to be possessive. We felt that continuing to experience sexual relations with other people might clarify our feelings and help us decide whether or not an exclusive relationship would be best for us.

On Memorial Day weekend, we packed our bags and boarded a plane for Athens, Greece. We were met at the airport by an executive and staff of people from Marriott, who welcomed us and escorted us in limousines to the hotel, where we were led directly to our rooms, bypassing the registration desk. All the adults got suites, and Troy, Johnny, and I got two adjoining rooms with two queen-size beds in each. The executive, who I had presumed to be the hotel manager or guest relations manager, said that he had prepared three separate rooms for us but that Mike had requested this arrangement. He apologized if it was not satisfactory and pledged to make everything right, but we assured him that the accommodations were just perfect. Johnny took one room, Troy took the other, and I was free to move back and forth depending on where the action was. I chose to spend my first night in Greece christening my bed with Troy.

At dinner, we were given a private room off the main dining room with a spectacular view of the city. Seeing the Acropolis all lit up at night just blew my socks off. I expected the photographer to join us, but Mike said he would meet us at lunch the next day, giving us a little time to adjust to the jet lag. We were, however, joined by an unexpected guest. We were surprised and, of course, thrilled to see Maria, who had arranged to spend the week with us. Naturally, we all understood that she was there to spend the week with Mike, but that was all right too.

I was also surprised when Mike invited the Marriott executive to join us and surprised still when he accepted. Mike seated him next to Mrs. Mazure, and all of a sudden, I began to suspect that Mike was up to something. I found out later that Mom had put him up to it.

The Marriott rep was Rob Palmer, an American, and it turned out that he was not the hotel manager, but the director of operations for all of Marriott's properties in Europe. We also learned that his mother, like Mrs. Mazure, was a nurse and that he was a big football fan and a lover of classical music. *What a coincidence, huh?* Oh, and by the way, he looked like a middle-aged Chris Evans with the sophistication of Cary Grant or George Clooney. He was a real DILF, and I would have jumped his bones in a flash given the chance.

Mr. Palmer, Rob, reminded us that all of our expenses were covered and that he was at our disposal for anything we needed. "Our concierge is at your service," he said, "but, of course, I am also here to assist you in any way I can." Maybe it was just my imagination, but he seemed to be addressing that comment more to Mrs. Mazure than to the rest of us.

Mike briefly went over our schedule for the week. We were to meet with the photographer tomorrow over lunch, but until then we were free the rest of the day to rest or to take in some of the sights of Athens.

Jet lag or not, most of us were too excited to sleep in, so we rose early and strolled the Agora, the ancient Greek shopping promenade still used by merchants and shoppers today. We bought fresh baklava from a vendor and thought we had died and gone to epicurean heaven.

At lunch, Rob, not Mike, introduced us to the photographer, Nicholas Dimitriopolis, who graciously and mercifully invited us to call him 'Nic.' Mike was meeting Nic for the first time along with the rest of us, but Rob had known him for a while. He explained that Nic had done some work for the Marriot Hotels in Greece and nearby countries as well as some of the chain's most prominent executives and guests. Nic chatted with everyone and made us all feel comfortable with him. His English was more fluent than

Claude's or Armando's, which made it a little easier to get to know him.

As lunch was wrapping up, Rob offered to give a brief tour of the hotel to anyone who was interested. At first, I wasn't particularly interested, but then he mentioned that many of Mike's photos would be shot in the hotel, not only in his suite, but in the hotel's sculpture gardens and ballrooms, where studios had been set up. I suggested to Troy and his mom that the brief tour might be worthwhile, but I guess that Mrs. Mazure had already made the same decision.
Hmmm.

After the hotel tour, we broke into groups and went our separate ways, some to the National Museum, some to the National Palace to see the changing of the guards, known as Evzones, and some went shopping. As we were leaving, Mike pulled Troy aside and told him that he and Nic would be spending the afternoon going through underwear and swimsuits to select the best ones for the photoshoots. Mike told Troy that there was no need for him to be there all day but that he was welcome to stop by an hour or so before dinner to get a feel for the process.

Shortly after five o'clock, Troy, Johnny, and I went to Mike's suite, and sure enough, Mike and Nic were still hard at work going through their many options. Since we had been outside exploring the city, we came into the room wearing shorts and comfortable shirts. Johnny and I wore tank tops, and Troy wore a loose-fitting beach shirt unbuttoned halfway, exposing his very hairy chest.

Even though Nic had met us at lunch, he had not seen us in these revealing clothes, and when he did, he nearly flipped out. "Oh, my god!" he exclaimed. "You men are so handsome. Are you sure you're not models?" He was particularly taken with Troy, whom he practically accosted. He went up to Troy and immediately put his hand on Troy's hairy chest. Then, with no preface, he quickly unbuttoned Troy's shirt the rest of the way and pulled it off him. He circled around Troy, sizing him up and down, rubbing his torso all over. "Greek women love virile men with hairy chests," he said. "You must model for me."

Mike asked Troy if he would like to be an extra as Johnny and I had done, and Troy agreed, but Nic seemed very disappointed that he could not use Troy more.

That night at dinner, Mike briefed Mrs. Mazure on the arrangement and told her that she was welcome to observe the shoot but that it was not essential since Troy would be properly clothed the whole time and would not be involved in anything too suggestive. Mrs. Mazure decided that it would be enough for Mike to be there.

The next morning, Johnny and I went with Troy to the shoot to provide moral support. Nic shot some rather traditional swimsuit photos by the pool. Nic had hired only four supplementary models, two male and two female, so he was grateful that Mike had allowed Johnny and me as well as Troy to act as extras, wearing super skimpy suits that Nic pulled out of a case he had brought with him.

In the fitness center, he took some photos that were along the lines of the ones Claude had taken in France but with a few creative differences here and there. It suddenly dawned on me that this was Troy's first time seeing Mike naked—in the flesh anyway. Johnny and I had to take turns standing in front of Troy to prevent others from seeing his boners, which never seemed to go down. I was reminded of that TV commercial, "If you have an erection lasting more than four hours...." It was wasted effort, though, because I'm sure that everyone, including Mike, saw Troy's bulges. Mike didn't react, though. I'm sure that was not the first time that his nude body had triggered an erection.

Around noon, Nic expressed some frustration with the way the shoot was going. He suggested that we break for lunch and re-convene in the Olympic Ballroom, where he had erected some sets.

The Olympic Room was aptly named because Denier had decided to adopt an Olympics theme for that year's shoot. Nic had brought in backdrops of scenes from Olympia and other historic spots in Greece. He had also constructed pedestals of various types and sizes. Three of the pedestals mimicked the bronze, silver, and gold pedestals used at Olympic medals ceremonies. Mike was to stand in the center with one of the models on either side.

The models were all attractive. The males were fit and in good shape, but they were not as broad-shouldered and muscular as the three of us. Since Nic had seen Troy shirtless and Johnny and me in tight tank tops, he begged Mike to let us flank him instead of the models. For the shots where we were to wear swimsuits, Mike agreed, and Johnny, Troy, and I rotated positions on the pedestals. Most of the swimsuits Nic selected for me were designed with extra-large pouches, which made me feel very self-conscious and very conspicuous. "That's the whole point," Johnny teased. "If you've got it, flaunt it."

In the original Olympic Games, the athletes competed in the nude, so Nic took some shots of Mike standing on the center pedestal naked, but Mike refused to allow us to be photographed in the nude, so the models got back into place. Their junk would be obscured by some digital techniques later. It didn't matter that they were not wearing any of the sponsor's clothing because those would be featured in sidebars to the photos in the ads.

Another set was supposed to mimic the inside of a sculpture museum with the models standing on pedestals in classic Greek poses. Museum visitors (extras) stood facing the models as if they were touring a museum. The backs of their heads obstructed views of the models' genitals. There again, Nic really wanted us three guys to be some of the statues, but again Mike prohibited it. The whole afternoon continued in that mood with Nic repeatedly cursing the gods for making his life so difficult.

When Nic found out that Troy was now 18, he nearly went ballistic. "He is not a child!" screamed Nic. "The man can decide for himself!"

That night after dinner, we all gathered back in the Olympic Ballroom, where Mike explained how the photo campaign was designed and what kinds of photos Nic wanted to take to carry out that theme. He explained how he had allowed us to serve as extras within certain limits. Then, Mike turned the floor over to Nic and let him make his pitch.

Our parents asked all kinds of questions, including whether or not there would be any nudity involve-ed. Nic explained honestly that Troy would sometimes be posing nude but that his genitals would be blocked by something either in the shoot or in the post-production.

"And no nude photos can be released to anyone without Troy's permission," added Mike. "I have that clause in my contract, and I can make sure it is in Troy's too."

Finally, Mrs. Mazure asked Troy, "Is this something you want to do?" and Troy replied that he was curious to try it.

"So, what do you think, Mom?" Troy asked.

"Troy," she replied. "You're a man now. If you want my opinion, I'll give it to you, but it's really your decision to make."

"I want your opinion," Troy confirmed.

"Let me ask Maria a question, if I may," said Mrs. Mazure. "If Troy does this, do you think it could damage his career prospects in the opera world?"

Everyone looked at Maria, who finally spoke, "There's no way to be sure, but if it's done tastefully and aesthetically, it probably won't do any harm...and it might even help."

"I had the same concerns when I started modeling," interjected Mike, still the responsible big brother but less constraining than before, "and my agent gave me the same opinion. Of course, opera is not the same as football, but I have no regrets, and I don't think my folks do either."

Mrs. Mazure looked to my parents, who nodded their confirmation. Then, all eyes turned to Mrs. Mazure again.

"Troy...son...I trust you, and I trust Mike. Like I said, it's your decision, and I will support you whatever you decide."

"Thanks, Mom," said Troy. "Nic," he said, turning to the photographer, "I think that I'll try it."

And when the confab started to break up, Troy questioned, as if puzzled, "Wait, what about Johnny and Rick? Nic wants them too."

"They're not 18," snapped Mike, reverting to his overprotective big brother mode.

"They will be in just a few months, and they know more of what to expect than I do," replied Troy. "I would feel a lot more comfortable about doing this if they were with me."

All the parents looked at each other for a decision until Dad asked, "Rick, is this something you want to do?"

"I've been wanting to do this ever since Armando asked us two years ago," I said.

"Oh," snapped Johnny, "you just want to make the rest of us feel inadequate." The parents took it as a reference to inadequacy in general, but I knew Johnny was referring to the comparative sizes of our penises.

Mr. Andersen asked Johnny if he wanted to participate also, and Johnny replied, "It really doesn't make any difference to me one way or the other, but Mike is going to need all the help he can get to keep these guys from ruining his photo shoot, so I guess I'm in."

"One last thing," said Mike. "As their parents, you have every right to observe the shoot."

Dad responded immediately, "I see no point in making the guys feel uneasy, and I think Rick is in excellent hands. Besides," he added, "I would much rather spend my time sightseeing with your beautiful mother than watching a bunch of guys strutting around naked."

That comment drew a little chuckle from everybody, and Mr. Andersen said he agreed with Dad, so it was settled.

The next day, Nic re-shot some of the scenes in the fitness center locker room and showers as well as in the Olympic Room with the three of us either replacing or supplementing the hired models. Some of the scenes in the fitness center involved us in gymnastics on the pommel horse, rings, parallel bars, or other equipment. Others had Mike wrestling with one of the models.

Everything went smoothly. The only problem was having to keep each other from popping a boner. We had to break a couple of times to deal with that problem, and the other hired models were more than eager to help us with the solutions.

That night at dinner, Mike gave a brief report on how we had done, and Nic expressed his appreciation and his delight that the shoot had been much better than the day before because of our participation. Our parents beamed with pride, and the three of us ate up the praise.

"Tomorrow," announced Rob, "the show moves to the island of Mykonos. We have arranged for a boat to cruise the southern islands on the way to Mykonos. Anyone who wants to stay in Athens is, of course, welcome to do so, but I strongly encourage you to experience the amazing beauty of these islands."

Rob went on to explain that deluxe accommodations would be available for anyone who wanted to remain on Mykonos for the duration of the trip but that the boat would make daily runs for those who wished to return to Athens at any time. "If you would like to visit Olympus, Delphi, or any of the other fabulous sites in the country," said Rob, "a motor coach will take you wherever you want to go, and reservations will be made for you."

The "boat" that Rob had secured turned out to be a 100-foot yacht. I couldn't clear my mind of the thought of making love to Troy on that yacht, but it was a fantasy that I never got to realize.

As soon as we laid eyes on the Santa Marina Resort & Villas, everyone decided to stay at least one night. Located on the southern tip of the island, the resort provided unequalled views across the Aegean Sea. Johnny, Troy, and I were lodged in a two-bedroom villa while everyone else was housed in hotel suites.

The next morning, Mom and Dad announced that as much as they were enjoying the resort, they did not want to miss the opportunity to see more of the country, so they opted to return to Athens, and Rob said he would have a guide meet them at the dock and take them wherever they wanted to go. "And if you would like help working out a travel itinerary," he said, "please see one of the concierges at the hotel."

The rest of us opted to stay on the island. Of course, Mike, Johnny, Troy, and I had no choice since we were there to work, but we were more than content to remain in the Aegean paradise.

We began the day with Nic distributing the swimsuits he had selected for us. He took us to another part of the island with a more secluded beach. He explained that we would have to be changing out in the open, and he wanted to protect our privacy. As before, Johnny, Troy, and I rotated with the hired models on most of the shots.

In one scene, Nic had us walking out of the ocean waters toward the beach. Our swimsuits were down to the bottom of our pubic hairs, and we posed as if we were pulling them up, suggesting that they had been pulled down while we were in the water. In another scene, Mike wrestled with one of us. It was a repeat of the scene in the gym except that this one was on a sandy beach.

Denier had come out with a new swimsuit and underwear line for the Olympics, but because the company was not an official sponsor of the Olympics, we were not allowed to use the name or any of the symbols of the Olympics in the shoot, so we had to find ways to skirt around the problem.

One suit in the new line featured red, white, and blue stripes with gold stars and another carried the blue and white colors of the Greek flag. One suit had red, white, and blue stripes around the waistband and a gold star right in the middle of the pouch.

Denier was very interested in promoting its Ring Up™ line of swimsuits and underwear that have a built-in cock ring, so they designed one with four rings across the waist band. Nic took pictures of each of us stretching our swimsuits out and looking down into the pouch. He also took pictures of us standing next to each other and looking into the other guy's pouch. In another pose, he had one guy standing next to another, pulling on the waist band, and looking into that guy's pouch. Finally, he had one guy on each side pulling at the waistband and looking down. When the ad ran, it carried the caption, "See only four rings? Look again."

Being very new to this business, I admit that I really didn't know how to use the cock ring at first, but the other male models, Theo and Alex, were not at all shy about showing me. While Mike and Nic were off in a corner discussing business, Theo walked up to me, pulled down his swimsuit, and demonstrated how to use the cock ring. Not to be outdone, Alex walked up and stuck his hands down my suit to "adjust" me. Feeling challenged, I guess, Theo insisted that it did not look right, so he circled around behind me, wrapped his arms around me tightly, and stuck his hands inside my swimsuit to "fix it." When Nic turned around and saw what was happening, he scolded the boys to get back to work.

Another pose used with both underwear and swimsuits had one model's hand reaching toward another model's crotch with the caption to be "Go for the Gold." In some shots the reaching hand was female, in others it was male. In one variation, the reaching hand was actually partially inside the waist band. The same scenario was also shot with two models reaching, one on either side. In a variation of the two-model set-up, one of the models was reaching from the top or the side while the other was kneeling or lying down on the beach and reaching up to the package. In the final variation, one or two of the models were actually grabbing the swimmer's package. Some were full-body shots while others were close-ups of the swimsuits and hands.

Mike let Troy take either the role of the guy modeling the swimsuit or one of the reachers in all the various combinations, but he restricted Johnny and me to those shots that did not expose our faces.

We wrapped up that session around 1:00 p.m., just in time for lunch. Because Mom and Dad had taken the yacht back to Athens, Nic had arranged for Jeeps to transport us overland back to the resort, but only one vehicle arrived, and the driver explained that the other one had broken down and he would have to transport us in shifts. We all agreed to let Mike, Johnny, and Nic take the female models, Zoe and Thalia, back to the hotel with the camera equipment while we waited for the driver to come back to get us.

Troy and I spent the next two hours learning more about Greek "culture" from Theo and Alex. With our driver out of sight, Alex, approached me and grabbed my basket, as he had done in the pose. He said something provocative about the size of my cock. I looked over to Troy, who grinned and gave me a nod that said to me, "Go ahead. Enjoy it."

Just as Alex was reaching inside my swimsuit Theo buried his face in Troy's chest. Apparently, it was not just Greek women who went crazy over hairy chests.

Theo was on a marathon to lick every hair on Troy's magnificent body. When he got down to Troy's dick, he sucked for a bit and then licked down his perineum all the way to his asshole. Troy seemed unsure at that point; he had never been rimmed before; but he quickly decided that he liked it. It became obvious that Theo was prepping Troy to receive his cock. Troy looked to me as I had looked to him, and I just gave him a thumbs up.

19 Dressing Up

Back at the resort, Nic informed us that we would not be needed again before noon the next day because he wanted to take some solo shots of Mike in the morning. Totally exhausted, Johnny, Troy, and I fell asleep as soon as our heads hit the pillows. In the morning, though, Troy and I made love again and decided to take a walk on the beach.

As we walked, we talked. We talked about our new modeling experiences, including how we felt about them and whether we would ever agree to do them again. We also discussed our "culture lessons" with Alex and Theo the day before. In the two weeks since Troy's birthday, we had made love with each other—and no one else—every day, often several times a day. Now, we had knowingly and willingly had sex with different partners, and we had even done it in each other's presence. What implications did those acts have for our relationship going forward?

We agreed that our feelings for each other had not been diminished. We had enjoyed sex with the other models and would do it again because it had given us a chance to experiment and learn new things about sex and sexuality—things that we might then share with each other. Perhaps that experience and others we might have in the future could actually strengthen our relationship. Airing all these issues lifted a cloud from our heads and made us feel more confident and optimistic about approaching the future.

Mike and Nic met our team back at the resort for lunch, and we all boarded the yacht for the return trip to Athens. Mom and Dad met us on the dock, where Rob informed us that he had planned a big farewell for our final evening in Greece. On a private patio that Rob had reserved for us, we got caught up with our parents and vice versa. We answered all their questions about our first modeling gig—without giving all the extraneous details, of course—and they told us how much they had enjoyed their excursions.

"Before our star models leave," said Mike, handing us some papers, "I need you guys to sign these contracts. They're pretty routine," he said, "and include the provisions we previously discussed."

Looking over the documents, I spotted something before Johnny and Troy did. "Uh, Mike, is this a typo? "This says that I'm to be paid $2500."

"Yeah," said Johnny, "mine says the same."

"Isn't that enough?" Mike asked.

"Oh, my god, Mike," I exclaimed. "I didn't expect to get $250, let alone $2500.

"Well, Nic offered $1000. I demanded $2500. So, we compromised, and we got $2500." Johnny and I practically squeezed Mike to death, and everyone complimented him on being such a fantastic negotiator. As we did, Troy just stood as still as a Greek statue.

"Are you OK?" I asked.

Looking like a deer caught in the headlights, Troy finally managed to say, "Uh...my contract doesn't say $2500." Then, in response to our puzzled looks, he added, "My contract says $10,000."

When everyone looked to Mike for an explanation, he instructed, "It's basic supply and demand. Nic really, really wanted you, and he was willing to pay top dollar. Frankly, if he ever asks for you again, you can probably get double that."

I thought Troy was going to faint. Regaining his composure, he said, "Mom, we can get that car you wanted."

"You're replacing the Lexus?" Mrs. Andersen asked Mrs. Mazure.

"Well," she replied, "the loaner from Lexus was for one year, which will be up in a few months."

"If you're looking to buy a good used car, I might be able to help you with that" offered Mr. Andersen. "My company has a fleet of cars that we rotate every year. We give employees a chance to buy the ones we're releasing and sell the rest to a broker. I can get you a one-year-old car that has been maintained in excellent condition for a very good price."

Mrs. Mazure looked thrilled and agreed to take Mr. Andersen up on his offer. "But Troy," she said, "since I haven't had any bills to pay on a car for the past year, I've been able to put aside a good bit, so you keep your money. Save it for college."

With everyone floating on cloud nine, Rob explained the surprise he had planned for our final evening there. "Please gather in the Olympic Ballroom for a formal reception. Then, after dinner, we're going to the theatre."

When Johnny, Troy, and I got back to our villa, we found tuxedos lying on our beds. Troy wanted to meet up with his mom before going to the ballroom, so Johnny and I went ahead. Mr. and Mrs. Andersen arrived next, he in a tux and she dressed in a lavish formal gown. Mom and Dad came in next, dressed similarly, Mom also wearing an emerald necklace with matching earrings. Mike and Maria were the next to arrive, looking stunning as usual. Finally, Troy entered with Rob and Mrs. Mazure.

I had always thought Mrs. Mazure was a pretty woman, but that night she just blew me away in her Georgio Armani gown, accentuated by a sleek platinum necklace with matching bracelet and a sparkling tiara, which gave her the look of a Greek goddess. Naturally, Troy stepped proudly as he escorted her into the room.

All of the men looked very handsome in their tuxedos. I had never seen my dad in a tux before, and I almost didn't recognize him without jeans and a plaid shirt. Mr. Andersen looked like the international businessman that he was, and it was clear to see where Johnny had gotten his good looks. From the moment I first met Rob Palmer, I had always thought that he was a very handsome middle-aged man, but in his tuxedo, he looked like a movie star on Academy Awards night.

Mom explained that they had found the clothes in their rooms with a note that Rob had arranged to rent them for the evening.

Before we could finish ooh-ing and aah-ing over one another, the guests began arriving for the reception. The guest list included some of Greece's most prominent citizens from the worlds of sports, the arts, academia, science, and business. Our parents were thrilled to have their pictures taken with Olympia Dukakis, John Stamos, and Jennifer

Anniston, all Greek-Americans who were in Athens to film a movie and visit their Greek relatives.

You might expect that we football players would be most excited about meeting some of the hunky athletes, like star soccer players Georgios Samaras and Kostas Manolas, but Troy spent most of his time talking with baritone Dimitris Platanias while Johnny seemed captivated by Professor Nicholas Peppas, one of the world's leading authorities on biomedical engineering and who, ironically, was then teaching at the University of Texas at Austin.

Mike parlayed with the American ambassador and the Greek foreign minister, and I just cruised the ballroom hitting on all the hot hunks—waiters as well as invited guests.

Thank goodness that Rob had ordered plenty of food for the reception because there was not enough time for a sit-down dinner. We had to get to the National Theatre for a production of Aristophanes' classical Greek play *Lysistrata*, a comic account of a woman's plan to end the Peloponnesian War between Greek city states by persuading the women to withhold sex from their men. It made me relieved that I had not closed any options as far as sex was concerned.

By the time we got back to the hotel, we were all tired, but sated, and we still had to pack because we had a morning flight to Rome. We were instructed to call the front bell desk as soon as we were out of our borrowed clothes and jewelry to have them picked up before we went to bed. Troy and I were naked when the bellboy arrived to collect our clothes, and...well... that's a story for another day.

20 Rome

When we arrived at Rome's Leonardo da Vinci Airport the next morning, we were shocked to be met not only by Armando, but also by Rob Palmer, who had apparently taken a red-eye flight to confirm that everything was ready for us at the hotel. Hotel limousines took us to The St. Regis, a five-star Marriott hotel just about a block from the National Gallery of Ancient Art. Just as in Athens, we were led directly to our suites, bypassing the registration desk.

Our suite was designed like a roommate apartment, albeit a very luxurious one. An elegant sitting room separated two spacious bedrooms, each with a king-size bed and private bathroom, which was bigger than most people's living room. Each had a spa-like tub and a walk-in shower with room for six people and multiple sprays. A large terrace was accessible from any of the rooms.

We were given 30 minutes to freshen up and report to the hotel's Lumen restaurant, where we enjoyed a delicious lunch. Since most of us had skipped breakfast, we were famished and ready for a hearty meal. At the conclusion of lunch, Armando previewed the week's agenda.

Tomorrow was designated as "Family Portrait Day," when Armando would photograph each of the adults individually, as couples, and with their sons. There was no need to photograph Johnny, Troy, and me separately because Armando had already photographed us at Christmas.

The next two days were to be what Armando called "Commercial Photo Day," which seemed to be much like the Addicted photo shoots we had participated in but with different products. Finally, the last two days were to be "Special Photo Days." Armando explained that for years he had been collecting photos of men all over the world and wanted to include our photos in a book to be published as *Men of the World*.

"Family Portrait Day?" whimpered Mom. "I'm a fright. I can't be photographed looking like this." The other ladies commiserated. They weren't prepared to pose for the camera either.

"Not to worry," said Rob. "I have booked reservations for each of you this afternoon in the hotel's spa. You can have whatever spa treatments you would like, and that includes the men too."

"But I have nothing to wear," said Mrs. Andersen.

Rob sighed demonstrably, "Oh, Emily. Have I ever let you down?" The men chuckled; the women didn't, but they knew that Rob could be counted on to have a plan.

Right after our conference was over, everyone reported to the spa. The moms got the full treatment, from hair to toenails, and the dads got massages. Since Johnny, Troy, and I were not scheduled for our massages until later in the afternoon, we three *paisanos* decided to hit the gym first for a long-overdue workout.

The masseur assigned to me in the spa was a real stud muffin. I couldn't help but get aroused when he rubbed my body, especially "down there." I kept hoping that he would offer me a "special massage," but he just smiled and never went that far. When I got back to our suite, I expected to see Troy there, but he didn't show up for another 45 minutes. When I asked where he had been, he told me that he had gotten a "special massage."

"Damn!" I complained. "How come you got one and I couldn't?"

"I dunno," he said. "Maybe your masseur is straight." And then Troy pretended to get excited, "Or maybe he's a top, and he was just waiting for you to ask him to fuck you."

"Har har har," I growled. "In either case," I said, "you owe me one." I pulled down my underwear and waved my hard dick at Troy, who immediately took the cue.

We had been instructed to gather at a private room next to the restaurant at 6:00, so after the blow job, Troy and I got dressed and headed to that floor.

The room was impeccably designed and furnished like a luxury drawing room. "I wanted to show you this room," said Rob because it's a great place to relax, read newspapers or magazines, or just chat. You can also get snacks or beverages here, and a breakfast buffet is available every morning."

From that private room, Rob led us to the Lumen Restaurant. Over a delicious Italian dinner, Rob announced that a hotel motor coach would pick us up at 8:30 in the morning to take us to Armando's gallery and studio, where the family portraits would be taken. "Clothes will be waiting for you there," said Rob.

The next morning, our destination was quite a surprise. Armando's studio was essentially a warehouse stocked with all kinds of sets and props as well as photographic equipment. It was situated behind a gallery containing four large rooms. Armando explained that he owned and operated the gallery with two other artists: a painter and a sculptor. Each artist had his own separate studio, and the fourth was for special events featuring joint exhibits or works by outside guest artists.

The pieces on display were incredibly impressive, and they all carried hefty price tags, in the thousands and above...way above.

Nic directed our attention to opposite sides of the studio where there were dressing rooms. In front of each was a clothes rack, one containing tuxedos for the men and the other containing the same evening gowns that the women had worn to the theatre in Athens. It seemed that Rob had collected all the formal wear, brought it with him on his red-eye flight, and sent it out for cleaning. Trays on the ladies' rack also contained the jewelry they had worn.

While the women took turns changing into their gowns, Armando photographed the fathers separately in their tuxedos. "What about Rob?" asked Mrs. Mazure.

"Don't be silly, Sarah," said Rob. "This shoot is for family."

"Well, I don't care," she snipped. "I want a photograph of you."

Rob looked at Troy, and Troy smiled and nodded his approval.

"But I don't have—"

"There," said Armando, pointing to a stock room. Rob walked to the stockroom and found a whole rack of clothes, including a large selection of tuxedos.

After Rob's sitting, Armando began photographing the mothers individually. Then he photographed the parents in couples, and Mrs. Mazure again insisted that Rob join her in the picture. Finally, Armando photographed the parents with their sons. The whole session took all day.

That evening, Rob treated us to dinner in the Cavalieri Hotel's La Pergola, universally rated the best restaurant in Rome and one of the four best in all of Italy. The wine, food, ambience, and service were *magnifico*.

The next morning, we all gathered in our private room for the buffet breakfast. Mike reminded the parents that they all had the right to observe the day's shoot, but they agreed unanimously that they had trusted Mike to monitor the sessions in Athens and did not feel the need to change course now. Besides, they were all dying to see the many historic and artistic sights in The Eternal City.

When the four of us arrived at Armando's studio, we were met by one of Armando's two assistants. Armando had also brought in two male models (Lorenzo and Pietro) and two female models (Sofia and Angelica) for the shoot.

In the studio, we found props of all sorts positioned everywhere. Armando explained that he would be taking two types of photos. Some would contain the target product in the actual pose. Some would just be eye-catching photos with the product superimposed on the photo after the fact or featured in a sidebar to the photo.

Since this was not a Denier-sponsored shoot, Armando had collected underwear and swimsuits from more than a dozen different companies—mostly companies I had never heard of until Troy introduced me to gay websites—but also a wide variety of men's clothing and accessories, toiletries, watches, wines, electronics, etc. Armando's plan was to approach a multitude of companies for possible sponsorship. In other words, keep fishing until we reeled in one (or more).

For starters, he directed the three of us to put our tuxedos back on, and then he led us to the alley behind the studio, where we found a parking lot full of Porsches, Maseratis, Ferraris, Alfa Romeos, Bugatis, and Lamborghinis. But the inventory was not limited to Italian cars. There were Rolls Royces, Bentleys, BMWs, Jaguars, Corvettes, and Lexuses. Armando photographed each of us modeling with each automobile in various poses and various degrees of undress.

When we went back inside the studio, we found a mock fountain set up in front of a Roman backdrop and one of the female models, Angelica, dressed like Audrey Hepburn in *Roman Holiday*.

"You can sing 'O Sole Mio,' no?" Armando asked Troy.

"*Si, signore,*" replied Troy.

"In *Italiano*?"asked Armando.

"*Ovviamente,*" replied Troy. "Of course."

"Over-a-minty," mocked Johnny.

"You serenade girl," instructed Armando. "Move around fountain, dance, improvise."

"*Capisco,*" said Troy, turning to stick his tongue out at Johnny.

"*Un momento*," said Armando, turning to one of his assistants manning a video camera and asking if he was ready.

"You're going to film this?" asked Troy.

"Miss Bianchi request it. I no ask questions. Ready?"

"Anything for Miss Bianchi," said Troy.

Armando had Angelica sit on the rim of the fountain and also told her to improvise along with Troy. Then, he cued Troy to sing *a capella*. Troy eased into the song, approaching Angelica, circling the fountain, walking on the rim, kneeling before the model, pulling her up seductively, and dancing with her—just like you would expect to see in a musical. It seemed thoroughly rehearsed, though it wasn't.

"*Eccellente*!" proclaimed Armando. Then, he removed Troy's coat, untucked and unbuttoned his shirt to expose his hairy chest, and said, "*Ancora*."

Armando cued the cameraman for the encore, and Troy repeated his flawless performance. He wasn't just a singer; he was an entertainer.

Next, Armando took still photos of Troy posing with his shirt unbuttoned or completely removed—some with the coat on and some with it thrown over his shoulder. In some of the shots, there was a bottle of wine or other featured product on a nearby table.

Then, it was my turn. Armando had his assistants change the set. They brought in a rather plain-looking dresser with a mirror. Armando had the other model, Sofia, stand in front of the mirror dressed in a very sexy evening gown. It was flaming red and strapless with a plunging neckline. Sofia wore a necklace with three strands of diamonds and a teardrop hanging between her half-exposed breasts. Mike and I recognized it as a parody of the picture that Claude had taken of Mike in France.

"But why the plain dresser?" Mike asked, "instead of an ornate one like we used in France?"

"Distraction," replied Armando. "The eye must focus on people," he said. "We are selling sex, not furniture."

Whereas Claude had positioned Mike standing behind the beautiful model helping her with her perfume, Armando had me helping my lady with her diamond necklace. We began this set with me dressed in a full tuxedo. Later, I wore only briefs, changing to a different brand with each shot.

So as not to waste time running back to the changing room for every new scene, I just changed right there. I was already acclimated to changing in front of other people, male and female, in Greece, so it didn't seem like any big deal. *Wow! It seems like only yesterday when I was too shy to undress in front of the guys in the gym.*

Armando repeated the set with Johnny and then with Troy, telling each of us to remain naked after our turns.

Upon completion of that set, Armando directed the three of us to go over to a table and select a pair of socks and a watch from the wide selection. While we did that, he had his assistants remove the dresser and bring in an ottoman. He had each of us in turn stand with one foot resting on the ottoman at just the right angle to cover our junk. We posed as if we were pulling up our socks with the watch prominently displayed.

In a variation, he had two of us facing each other with a foot on the ottoman. Then, he added the third man sitting on the ottoman with his back to the camera. He also shot one of us sitting on the ottoman facing the camera with legs crossed to cover his crotch and a second man standing behind, hands reaching around to cover the sitting man's eyes in a kind of "see no evil" motif.

Armando also had us pose facing the camera, legs spread approximately two feet apart, hands cupping our dick and balls to conceal them. We each posed individually, then in pairs, and then as a trio—some shots with female or male models, some not. That pose might work with the other guys, I thought, but not with me because my dick was just too big to cover up. Armando acknowledged that fact and said that he would touch up the photo later.

In all these ads, the intent was to draw attention to the watch. I could just imagine a caption in the ad saying something like, "If you're not wearing a Rolex (or Cartier or Piaget), you're not wearing anything at all."

Many of the sets carried a theme. Armando had his assistants switch the backdrop to a scene from the inside of the Coliseum. They also brought in a Roman chariot and a horse. With these props, we simulated a Ben Hur theme. Sometimes we stood alone in the chariot, sometimes with one or both of the female models. The horse was a mannequin, not a real animal, but Armando said that did not matter because the photos would probably not include the horse's head. And if they did, he would modify the pictures with adjustments to the lighting (*chiaroscuro*) or blurring the edges (*sfumato*), techniques perfected by Leonardo da Vinci.

Another set depicted a cowboy theme. At first, I thought Armando decided to do that because we were all from Texas, but he said that many Italians have a fascination with cowboys. *Who doesn't?* And then I remembered reading somewhere that Clint Eastwood got his big break in so-called "spaghetti westerns," cowboy movies filmed in Italy—films like *A Fistful of Dollars; The Good, the Bad, and the Ugly;* and *Once Upon a Time in America.*

Armando had us dress in cowboy hats, western-style shirts, jeans, leather belts with silver buckles, and leather boots. Sometimes we wore a badge on our shirt or a gun belt strapped across our waists. Strapped at an angle, the gun belts drew attention to our bulging crotches. Mike reminded me that many of these items are actually made from Italian leather.

Mike's comment triggered my memory of the bandana he had given me years before, so I suggested to Armando that we include bandanas in our costumes, and he liked the idea. We wore them over our faces (like outlaws), around our necks, and hanging out of our back pockets or, with underwear, out of our waistbands.

He posed us on and off the horse. Mostly, we posed alone, but there were also poses where one of us sat on the horse behind the rider, holding onto him with an arm around his waist. In some of these scenes, the rider wore nothing but hat and boots. On the horse, our private parts were blocked by the saddlehorn. In another scene, we straddled a bench with a boot blocking the view.

The contracted models, male and female, tried not to stare at our naked bodies, but we could tell they were looking. Either they were taken with Johnny's blondish hair and blue eyes, Troy's hairy chest, or my big dong.

The rest of the day continued in similar rotations with different products prominently featured, some with the female and male models, some with just us. As we were getting ready to go back to the hotel, we thanked Armando and his assistants as well as the hired models, and I handed each of the models a card from the St. Regis with our suite number written on the back.

21 Making the Rounds

At dinner, our parents shared their experiences touring the Vatican, the Coliseum, and other local sites. They asked, of course, about our day, and we played it down, telling them it was just another workday. Since Mike had been our “chaperone” for the photo shoot, they all asked his opinion, expecting a more forthright answer, and he reported that everything had gone well.

Following dinner, we had just enough time to get into comfortable clothing when the front desk called to say that we had visitors in the lobby. I cursed under my breath that I would have get dressed to go down and get them, but the desk clerk said that he could have a bellboy escort them to our suite.

When the knock came on the door, I opened it to welcome the four models from our day’s shoot. I tipped the bellboy, who was terribly cute, and when he saw what was dangling inside my sheer lounge pants, he leaned forward and told me that he would be happy to take care of anything we needed.

”Anything!” he emphasized. I learned that he would be getting off work in less than an hour, so I invited him to join us then.

Johnny led Angelica and Sofia to his room, and Troy led Lorenzo and Pietro to our room. I bounced back and forth.

After an hour of "working out," I got up to go to the bathroom when I heard a knock on the door. When I opened the door in all my anatomical splendor, the bellboy stepped in and a couple of 30-something men walking past in the hallway caught a good look at my schlong and gasped. I just grinned and said, "Thank you," and closed the door.

I led the bellboy to our room, where everyone was still on the bed, some just resting, and some raring to go at it again. He told me that his name was Leo (short for Leonardo). I was really turned on at the sight of a man in uniform—even if it was just a kid in a bellhop uniform. When I expressed this pleasure to Leo, he offered to introduce me to one of the hotel's security guards and a cousin who was in the Italian Navy.

After a marathon session that lasted all night, Troy was still horny in the morning. *When are you not horny?* As Lorenzo and I were trying to satisfy Troy's needs, Johnny popped his head through the door to caution us not to be late for the morning's session. After we hurriedly showered and got dressed, we met Johnny down in the lobby. He had collected some breakfast for us from the restaurant and brought it for us to eat on the way to Armando's studio. *God bless you!*

The driver dropped us off at the corner of Armando's street, and we had to walk past several shops and businesses on our way to the studio. We noticed that the place next door to the studio had once been a health club but now all the windows were covered with black drapes or black paint.

As we entered the studio through the gallery, Armando led us to a door which, much to our surprise, led to the health club next door. Armando explained that the owner of the establishment had died, and the heirs were desperate to get rid of it, so he was able to buy it for a steal. He said that he used it as the setting for some photo shoots and permitted his models to use it to keep in shape. The showers also came in handy sometimes for the models and himself.

Armando, with Mike's help, described for Troy the shower scenes that Claude had shot in France. Of course, Johnny and I had been there, but Mike's review refreshed our memories. Armando was determined to do the photos better than Claude.

He had Lorenzo and Pietro put on sexy jockstraps that he had selected for them, and he had the three of us strip naked. He began by positioning Troy in the shower facing forward. Lorenzo and Pietro stood outside of the shower facing each other. Their bodies created a foreground frame for Troy's naked body in the background. Claude had used steam from the shower to cover Mike's genitals, but Armando had a different approach. He had re-engineered the shower heads so that two from opposite sides of the shower room clashed in front of Troy's genitals, obscuring them from view. What's more, the shower bursts clashed in such a way as to force their streams upward. Anyone with a filthy mind (i.e., anyone breathing) might construe the water spray as emulating an ejaculation.

In a variation, Armando had Johnny and me standing two steps to the side of Troy and two steps behind but also facing forward. Lorenzo and Pietro sat on opposing benches facing each other so that their heads blocked the view of our crotches.

The gym also had a fairly large hot tub and a steam room. The photos that Armando took there reminded me of a painting by Michael Breyette called The Baths, a painting that I loved and was determined to purchase as soon as I had enough money.

As before, we rotated positions so that each of us had a chance to be the focal point, and that meant that we had to dry off between rotations. Armando's assistants were constantly—and enthusiastically—bringing us fresh towels and helping us dry off, even when they probably should have left the task to us.

After the shower scenes, Armando announced that he had made lunch reservations at one of the best pizza restaurants in the city. He had rented a van to take us there and another van to follow behind with wardrobes for the afternoon shoots, which would take place in and around various famous landmarks in the city. These shots would involve no nudity, but there would be frequent changes of clothing, and the second van would serve as a changing room.

The pizza was out of this world, and after eating it, I really just wanted to take a nap, but there was no chance of that.

For the rest of the afternoon, we drove from one site to another, changing clothes in the wardrobe van frequently. Around 4:00 p.m., Armando announced that he needed Troy and Angelica to stay for some shots at Trevi Fountain and the Spanish Steps, but that the rest of us were free to go. I said goodbye to Sofia and Leonardo since I would not be seeing them again, and I practically dragged Pietro to my suite at the St. Regis.

22 Rough Stuff

In my room, I ripped our clothes off—Pietro's and mine—and threw him on the bed. I had to release all the pent-up frustration I had been feeling all day. I was out of control.

After an hour or so of some of the most vigorous sex I had ever experienced, I was so totally spent that my brain was completely devoid of life-essential blood. I had zapped myself into a different dimension. When I finally came out of my delirium, I checked to see if Pietro was still alive or if I had killed him in my frenzy. Apparently, he was just coming out of the same stupor that I had been floating in. I got up, went to the bathroom, and returned with a glass of water for him.

"I'm so sorry, Pietro. I don't know what came over me. I never meant to get so rough. Please forgive me."

"Forgive you, signore Rick? That was fucking amazing. I had no idea that sex could be so powerful. I doubt that I will ever experience anything so exhilarating as long as I live."

"Oh, really?" I asked. "If I weren't so exhausted, I might take you up on that challenge."

Just then, we heard the door to the suite open and Troy call out, "Rick, there's someone here to see you," and before I could ask who it was, Troy entered the bedroom with a hotel security guard on his heels.

"Mr. Murphy," said the guard, "we have been receiving some complaints from other guests about the noise coming from this room."

"What? I thought these walls would be soundproof. I guess we'll have to tone it down a bit."

"I'm afraid that won't be enough," said a city policeman following Troy and the guard into the room. "You'll have to come with me, sir."

"Come with you where?" I asked somewhat defiantly.

"You'll have to come with him inside of me," said Leo, showing himself.

Throwing a pillow at Leo, I chided, "You nearly scared me to death."

Laughing, Leo said, "He (the guard) is Alfredo, and this (indicating the policeman) is his friend Ricardo."

"And don't forget me," said a voice coming from the sitting room.

"And this is Carlo," said Leo, indicating the sailor entering the room. "I hope I'm not too late," said the sailor. "I really need to drop my anchor," he said, grabbing his crotch.

And just when I thought it could not get any better, in came Lorenzo, one of the models, dressed in one of the cowboy outfits we had worn for the shoot.

Having sex proved to be a bit cumbersome at times because I insisted that the uniformed men not remove any more of their clothes than absolutely necessary. I delighted in watching them go at each other...and at me. I just love a man in uniform.

At dinner, our families recounted our experiences of the day—well, some of them anyway. Our parents talked about their sightseeing, and we talked about our modeling, not about the hot sex. At the conclusion of the meal, Mike said, "We need to discuss a couple of things."

Opening a folder, he held up several sheets of paper and announced, "These are the contracts for the next two days' shoots."

"Contracts?" asked Troy. "I thought we were not being paid for this gig since there is no sponsor."

"That's true for the three days so far, but the next two days are different. The photos that Armando wants to take the next two days are for a book that he plans to publish. In my opinion, and I have told him this, the guys are entitled to a percentage, like royalties."

Rob and Mr. Andersen, both of whom had substantial business experience, nodded their concurrence. "It won't be much," Mike continued, "but you're entitled to it however much or little it is."

Everyone voiced agreement and thanked Mike for his diligence and for looking out for us.

"Now, before you sign these contracts, we have to talk about something else." Everyone sat up in their seats, curious as to what Mike was talking about.

"This book that Armando is preparing...the photographs...they're nudes."

"I don't understand," said Dad. "Haven't they been posing nude in Greece and again here?"

"Yes, Dad, they have occasionally been photographed nude, but their private parts have always been concealed, either in the shoot itself or in final production, so they were never exposing themselves publicly. If they follow through with this contract, that's exactly what they will be doing. The photographs that appear in the book will show them in all their glory."

Dead silence. No one, including the three of us, quite seemed to know what to say.

"That might be OK for Troy," said Mom. "He's 18, but Rick and Johnny aren't."

"True," acknowledged Mike, "but they will be 18 before the book ever comes out, which won't be for several months at best."

"And we sort of discussed this before the shoot in Athens," I said. "We'll be 18 in just three months."

Mom sighed as if to say, "Don't confuse me with facts. I'm wrestling with this."

"Are you saying that you're OK with this, son?" Dad asked me.

"Well, yeah, Dad. I guess I am saying that."

"Mike," said Mr. Andersen. "You raised the issue. What do you think?"

"Well, I'll admit that I had some strong reservations about it at first, but after talking it over with Maria, I think I'm inclined to support it."

All eyes shifted to Maria. "Maria?" asked Mrs. Mazure with a touch of surprise in her voice. Everyone was looking for an explanation.

"First, let me say that I do understand your reservations," offered Maria, "and it's not my place to tell you what you should do with your own sons, but if you want my opinion, I'll tell you what I told Mike." Everyone indicated by their non-verbal communication that they were ready to hear what Maria had to say.

"You've all seen Armando's work. He sent you albums of the photos he took at your house (indicating the Andersens), and you all were very impressed with them, right?"

"They were absolutely gorgeous," said Mrs. Andersen, and everyone else chimed in their agreement.

"And you've all seen the work in his gallery, and I heard some of you being effusive in your praise of his artistry." More nods of agreement.

"And some of the works in that gallery are nudes, and I didn't hear anyone express disgust or disapproval...because they are absolutely magnificent. They are artistic masterpieces." More nods.

"Armando likes to say that he does not photograph people. He photographs souls as they are revealed in faces and bodies. I think you can see that in the photographs you have seen in his gallery and the photographs he took of your sons. He captured their souls in those photographs, and I'm biased, I admit, but when I look at your sons, including this one," she said, squeezing Mike's hand, "I see four of the most beautiful souls I could ever imagine. I don't have a son," she continued, "but if I did, I would be eternally grateful to have Armando capture his soul for all the world to see."

Maria's words took everyone's breath away. It was virtually impossible to argue with her premise.

Finally, Dad spoke, "Rick, son, do you want to do this? It's your call."

I didn't speak. I just walked up to Mike, took my contract from his hand, and signed it.

"Show off!" Johnny chided me, as he walked up to Mike and signed his contract too.

"Well," said Troy, "I don't know what all the fuss is about. Once Armando photographs me, he's not gonna wanna waste his time with these two." As everyone chuckled, Troy too signed his contract.

For the next two days, it would be just Johnny, Troy, and me, the three amigos, the *tre amici nudi*.

You might wonder why it should take two whole days to photograph three naked men. Armando was as meticulous as he had been when he photographed us at the Andersen's house at Christmas. He photographed us at every angle in all kinds of light and all kinds of positions. He took full-body shots, close-ups, and extreme close-ups of every part of our bodies. He photographed us flexing our muscles and completely relaxing. The photographs were not meant to be sexual, but sexuality was clearly a significant part of our souls, as it is for all living creatures, so it had to come through along with all other facets of our being.

Naturally, at the end of the first day of the "Special Photography Day," our parents were exceptionally curious about the session. We told them how professional Armando had been and how confident we were that the pictures would be good. We also told them that modeling had been much harder work than we could possibly have imagined. They seemed pleased...and relieved...that we had approached the entire experience so maturely.

We had one more full day in Rome before we all went our separate ways. The three of us decided to spend that time exploring the wonders of The Eternal City together. We met our parents at the Pergola Restaurant for a veritable feast. It was like our last meal before being executed.

As much as I had enjoyed our sexual exploits with the groups, I wanted to spend this night alone with

Troy since I would not be seeing him for a whole month. We made sweet, passionate love three times that night and once again the next morning. After breakfast, we said our goodbyes. The Andersens were off to explore the Scandinavian countries; Mrs. Mazure, Rob, and Maria were going to accompany Troy to Milan for one more week before Mrs. Mazure had to return to work; and our family, Mike included, was off to Ireland.

23 Ireland

We soon discovered that one week was just long enough to fall completely under the spell of the Emerald Isle, but not nearly long enough to embrace all of its beauty. In Dublin, of course we had to visit Dublin Castle and St. Patrick's Cathedral, where Jonathan Swift had served as dean when he wrote his famous essay "A Modest Proposal" and his classic *Gulliver's Travels*. At the top of my list were also the Writer's Museum and the *Kells* exhibit at the Trinity College Library.

When we came out of the library and back into the college courtyard, Mom and Dad said they wanted to go back to the hotel, and I told them I wanted to stroll around the historic campus for a bit.

The college courtyard proved to be a treasure trove of eye candy. There were lots of hot college students walking or racing from one class to another, and others sitting around reading or chatting with classmates. I noticed a couple of redheaded guys who kept staring at my crotch. They walked past me but then turned around and were about to walk past me again when I said to them, "In case you're wondering, yes, it's real—every inch of it."

Their green eyes nearly popped out of their heads. Once they got over their initial shock, they came closer, and one of them asked, "How many inches?"

"Almost eight," I replied, "about twenty centimeters," to which they gasped, smiled, and licked their lips.

"I'd be happy to show it to you if you'd like," I said. "Your place or mine?" They suggested that we go back to their frat house.

On our way to their place, I learned that one of them, the taller one, was named Conor and the other was named Dylan. I also learned that they were more than just frat brothers, they were biological brothers.

Several of their frat brothers were sitting in the front parlor when we got to their house. Conor introduced us and told them that we were going to the party room. At the same time, Dylan kept pointing at my crotch.

As we walked down the hall toward their party room, we could hear the moans and squeals of their frat brothers having sex with their girlfriends (or boyfriends). Most of the doors were closed, but a couple were cracked just slightly. "That means that they are open to having any of their brothers join them," said Conor.

Once we reached the end of the hall, they led me down the stairs to a large room in the basement. "Our party room," said Dylan. It was fitted with couches that folded out to make beds and end tables that supported bowls overflowing with condoms and lube.

The three of us stood in the middle of the room waiting for the other guy to make the first move. "Well, help yourselves," I said finally.

Dylan moved first, rubbing his hand over my crotch. Then, Conor walked up and unbuckled my pants, allowing them to fall to the floor. Dylan also dropped to the floor and rubbed his face against my crotch. "Enough!" proclaimed Conor as he reached over and pulled my briefs down, freeing my cock to fly up and slap Dylan under his chin. Dylan flinched and then just stared at it.

"Go ahead," I said. "You can touch it. It'll get bigger if you do."

Dylan began rubbing his open palm over my dick and balls, and Conor followed, wrapping his hand around my cock. At that moment, I heard the sound of footsteps descending the stairs. It was the frat brothers from the parlor. They paused on the stairs briefly and looked to Conor for permission to proceed. I was beginning to think that Conor might be the fraternity president.

"Do you mind?" Conor asked me.

"The more, the merrier," I replied, so the other guys came closer, taking turns feeling my cock. They made all kinds of comments about its size, some tactful and some vulgar, but all complimentary.

"It's not even completely hard yet," I pointed out.

"Make it bigger!" one of the over-eager pledges practically shouted.

"*You* make it bigger," I said, and when he walked forward, I grasped his shoulders and pulled him down on his knees. He wasted no more time grabbing ahold of my dick and sticking it in his mouth. One of his frat brothers placed his hand on the back of the sucker's head and pushed him forward, and the others started goading him to take more and more of it. When he started to gag, they all laughed.

"I think he did a pretty good job," I said. "I doubt that any of you guys could take any more of it than he did."

Dylan took the challenge, got down on his knees, and went at it. He actually did manage to slide more of it into his mouth than the previous kid, but he still couldn't get it all.

"Go get a measuring tape," commanded Conor, and one of the frat boys immediately ran to a cabinet and retrieved the item. That guy measured my cock and confirmed, "Twenty centimeters." Everyone laughed and expressed their amazement, if not disbelief.

"The bed!" commanded Conor, and immediately a couple of the guys hopped over to a board against one wall and pulled it down. It was a Murphy bed. (Not named after me, but I was about to give it my blessing.)

A couple of the guys escorted me over to the bed, and what followed resembled a tag-team wrestling match. I could tell that Dylan wanted more, so I grabbed him by his shirt and pulled his face toward mine. Our mouths locked together as we tongue-fucked. Seeing that, another frat brother joined us in a three-way kiss. He then unbuttoned my shirt and started sucking one of my nipples as another guy took possession of the other one.

Another brother came up and tore off Dylan's shirt, exposing his beautiful, hairy chest. He was an adorable little cub with red fur extending from his pecs all the way down to his pubic area. I had to bury my face in that red forest.

When it seemed that everyone had had a turn at whatever he could get, the frat brothers paired off, sucking or fucking each other, sharing the most foul language in their Irish brogues that really turned me on. They begged me to spend the night or to come back another night, but I told them I was on a tight schedule and had to leave in the morning.

Just as I was pulling up my pants, though, three more frat bros came down the stairs, and they weren't alone. They had their girlfriends with them, so the party started all over again. Though I had told the guys that I was tired, and I was, the arrival of our new guests gave me another boost of adrenalin. I couldn't wait to tell Johnny about it...to rub it in, that is.

My family and I took the train to Cork, Ireland's second largest city, which is just a short ride from Blarney Castle. Dad enjoyed the castle's history and architecture, Mom practically went crazy taking pictures of the lush gardens for her garden club, and Mike and I really did kiss the Blarney Stone, though we argued over which one of us really didn't need its purported power.

"You're already full of blarney," Mike teased.

"Oh, yeah? Well, you're full of shit!"

And so it went.

From Cork, we boarded the train for the Burren National Park on the magnificent west coast, but I insisted that we stop in Limerick, which was directly on our way. Not only is Limerick famous for a unique form of poetry, but it is also the setting of most of Frank McCourt's memoir *Angela's Ashes*. I even took a walking tour that stopped at significant points mentioned in the book.

As much as I loved our Irish adventure, I missed Troy terribly, so at the last minute, I asked my folks if I could return to Italy with Mike for the remainder of Troy's stay there, and they relented. They flew back to the States to meet up with Mrs. Mazure and the

Andersens at Kennedy Airport, from which they all flew together back to Austin in route back to Hilldale.

24 Milan

Mike flew back to Italy with me, and we were met at Milan's Linate Airport by Troy and Maria, who took us to the STRAF Hotel, a Marriott Design Hotel, where they had been staying while our family was in Ireland. Maria had chosen that hotel because it is centrally located between Teatro alla Scala (the opera house) and the Academy for the Performing Arts, where Troy had been studying.

Troy and I spent the rest of the afternoon getting caught up—in bed—and I'm quite sure that Mike and Maria did as well.

At dinner, Mike and I told Troy and Maria all about our week in Ireland, and they told us about their week in Milan. Every morning, Troy had spent three hours studying advanced Italian with his tutor, but most of those lessons took place as they toured the city. His afternoons were spent taking voice lessons and studying music theory and music composition at the Academy. These were all subjects that Maria taught at Juilliard, but she told Troy that he should take advantage of the opportunity to study under other experts while he had the chance.

Since the next day was a Sunday, Troy had no lessons, and as much as I wanted to spend the whole day having sex with him, I was dying to go to Santa Maria delle Grazie, where Leonardo da Vinci's *Last Supper* and other great works of art are housed. Santa Maria delle Grazie, a church and Dominican convent recognized as a UNESCO World Heritage site, is a work of art in itself.

Rather than meet back up with Mike and Maria for dinner, Troy and I decided just to walk around Milan, enjoying the ambiance.

With 1.2 million people, Milan is Italy's second largest city. Though Italy as a whole sits low on the rankings of gay-friendly countries (32nd, just below Slovakia), Milan is the notable outlier, perhaps influenced by the presence of all the fashion houses. Milan is the fashion capital of the world and the home of Italy's stock exchange.

Troy and I found ourselves on Via Sammartini, where we stumbled across several gay bars. "I wish I were 18," I said. Overhearing me, a young man coming out of one of the bars said, "The legal drinking age in Italy is 16. Some bars have higher limits, but many will let you in." Then, handing me his drink, he said, "*Pino* (cheers)!"

I've never been much of a drinker, but it was really special to be in a place with other gay men and not have to feel uneasy. Troy and I got hit on a lot, but we also met many guys who just enjoyed talking with a couple of gay Americans. One group of four guys invited us to join them at their table. They had given each other nicknames: Sorcio (Dirty Boy), Galleto (The Flirt), Zio (Dude), and Ciliegino (Little Cherry). As a group, they called themselves *I Fuorilegge* (The Outlaws).

We learned a lot from The Outlaws. Not only did we learn that the drinking age in Italy was indeed 16, but we also learned about rainbow flags. I had seen them on several buildings, but I had not known that the flag indicated a gay-owned or gay-friendly business. We learned too about the handkerchief code, and when they began explaining what each color meant and how the meaning varied depending on whether the handkerchief hung out of the left pocket or the right, I flashed back to the bandana that Mike had given me and how Armando had used them in our photo shoots, and I wondered if he and Mike had known about the code.

The Outlaws made us honorary members of their gang and dubbed me *Gigino* (Cute Young Guy) and Troy *Biondo* (Blondie, Clint Eastwood's nickname in *The Good, the Bad, and the Ugly*), which was ironic since Troy was anything but blond. They had a big laugh when I told them that Troy was not a cowboy since he was from Chicago and had probably never even seen a horse until he moved to Texas a year ago. I also told them that I was not actually a cowboy, just a farm boy, to which Dude said, "Cowboys, farm boys. No matter; both sexy. And I bet you are a lot of fun in the hay loft."

I thanked him for the compliment, and he leaned over and kissed me on the lips. When I flinched, he apologized, but I explained, "I'm just not used to being kissed by another man in public, but I like it." So, he kissed me again, and then each of the guys got up, walked around the table, and kissed Troy and me both. Dirty Boy stuck his hand inside Troy's shirt and rubbed his hairy chest as he kissed him.

The Flirt even asked us to dance, which was another first for us, dancing with a man in public.

When my dance partner held me close and began grinding, I told him that if he kept that up, I'd get hard. He stepped back, pointed at my crotch, and said, "That's *not* hard? Damn!" And he said it loud enough that quite a few of the guys on the dance floor stopped to look. Troy, who was dancing with Dirty Boy, looked at The Flirt, pointed his own finger at my crotch, and then, licking his lips, gave a thumbs-up. I was embarrassed but also flattered and turned on.

When Dirty Boy complimented Troy on being such a fantastic dancer—which he was—I said, "If you think that's talent, you should hear him sing." On that cue, Little Cherry went over to the DJ, who announced that the club had a guest singer, and the crowd goaded Troy onto the stage. Troy did an impromptu and saucy rendition of "Rhinestone Cowboy," and when he got to the line, "Riding out on a horse in a star-spangled rodeo," he did a pelvic thrust that had the crowd screaming for more. So, he gave them more. He finished the song with a strip tease. The crowd cheered, stomped their feet, and demanded an encore. Some of the guys shook their booties at him and slapped the butt cheek that displayed their handkerchiefs.

For his encore, Troy decided to change the pace. He sang "The Prayer" from the movie *Quest for Camelot,* and when he finished, half the people in the club were in tears.

When Troy started to step down from the stage, the DJ pulled him back and told him that he couldn't leave the audience in that mood; he had to pick it up. So, he performed a rendition of Faith Wells' classic rock-and-roll hit "My Guy" that lifted the crowd off their seats and had them pouring onto the dance floor. Not only did the crowd give him uproarious applause at the finish, but some tossed their handkerchiefs onto the stage, and a couple of guys even stripped and tossed their underwear at Troy. Troy picked up a jockstrap and put it on his head like a headband, and he walked off the stage with the waistband of a pair of rainbow-colored briefs between his teeth. Strolling back to our table, he was mobbed by guys who wanted to touch him, kiss him, or grope him.

When Troy mentioned to The Outlaws that we had been modeling for a photographer named Armando in Rome, we were quite surprised that they all were familiar with his name and his work. They said that his art was famous all over Italy and around the world and was particularly popular in ads in gay magazines and on gay websites. "There has been some debate about whether or not he is gay," said Dirty Boy, "but I heard that he has a boyfriend in France, another photographer."

"Wait," I said. "Not Claude?"

"Yes, that's his name."

"No, that can't be. They hate each other."

"They are professional rivals," said Dirty Boy, "but they actually love each other."

"Wow! I never would have guessed it," said Troy.

"Maybe your Italian is not as good as you thought," I teased.

When we told them about some of the juicier features of our modeling experiences at one time or another, they all had to reach under the table to adjust themselves. "Fuck," said Dude, "I would love to watch you model." Little Cherry advanced, "I would love to have you model for me." So, we invited them back to our hotel room to show them what it's like to ride a cowboy.

The next day, Monday, Troy had to go back to school—Italian lessons in the morning and music lessons in the afternoon. He introduced me to his language tutor in our hotel lobby. Giuseppe, a doctoral candidate in linguistics at Pavia University, was very good looking and even sexy in a nerdy sort of way. Although he was fluent in English and several other languages, he spoke only Italian. It was his way of forcing Troy to speak the language. Guiseppe had a lesson planned for that day, but he said that for the rest of the week, we could integrate the lessons into visits to tourist attractions and landmarks in the city and that I could go with them as long as I didn't distract Troy from his lessons. *It's not Troy I would like to distract.*

Not only was I left free for the day, but so was Mike since Maria had commitments at La Scala and the Academy for Performing Arts. We decided to stroll around the neighborhood, stopping a couple of times to enjoy a cup of coffee at some of the many outdoor cafés. It was also the first opportunity that Mike and I had had to chat one on one since we had left Texas. He asked me if I was still feeling confused, and I confessed that I was, but not as much. He told me that he was impressed with the way I had handled the photo sessions in Athens and Rome, and I thanked him for giving me the opportunities.

Troy met up with us for a quick lunch and invited us to go with him to the Academy. He said that Maria had something special planned. At the Academy, Maria took us to a recording studio and asked Troy to sing "O Sole Mio" just the way he had for Armando. She had even set up the video taken in Rome so that Troy could sync his voice with the lips in the video.

"What's this all about?" Mike asked.

"You'll find out," Maria replied. "Trust me." Of course, we all trusted Maria completely. She had given us every reason to trust her and no reasons not to.

The recording took less than half an hour, and Troy went off to his next lesson. Maria and Mike slipped away to some place where my presence was neither needed nor wanted. I told Troy that I wanted to go back to Via Sammartini and would meet him back at our hotel later.

Most of the gay bars on Via Sammartini, the ones with the rainbow flags, were not open so early in the afternoon, and the ones that were had almost no customers. As I walked down the street, though, I found several other businesses displaying rainbow flags. I went into one that appeared to be a clothing store. I told the cute young salesman that I was just looking. He smiled at me and said, "So am I." I smiled back and thanked him.

The store was much bigger than it appeared from the outside. There was one large section for sexy underwear and swimsuits and another one for shirts and pants. I began looking at the pants when the cute salesman, who introduced himself as Gabriele, came up, put his arm around my shoulder, and took the pair I was holding away from me.

"No, no, no," he chastened. "Your body is much too sexy for that one. Let me help you." He practically dragged me over to another section of the store and began flipping through the pants until he came to what he was apparently looking for. "Come," he commanded, as he led me to the fitting rooms. He handed me the pants and said, "Try on."

As I took off the pants I was wearing, Gabriele did not turn away but stood next to the stall watching me with the curtain half open. When he saw my sexy Addicted underwear, he said, "Very nice. Perfect for you."

The white pants he had given me to try on were made of a stretch material, somewhat like sweat-pants, but much nicer. They fit my body like a glove, making my package look even bigger than usual. I asked if he had the same pants in black, he said, "Not for you. Ugly man wear black. Beautiful man like you wear light color. It make your zucchini stand out," he proclaimed, as he cupped my balls and bounced them. "You want black, I show you sexy black."

Gabriele led me into another room at the back of the store that featured leather clothes from AD Fetish—jackets, pants, arm bands, and what he called "fetish gear." Glass cases displayed sex toys, cock rings, condoms, lubes, and other paraphernalia. In one corner, he pulled a pair of leather pants off a rack and handed them to me. "Here," he said, pointing to another, closer fitting room.

After I removed the white pants he had previously selected for me, I began to put on the leather pants when he stopped me, pointing to my briefs. When I indicated that I did not understand, he yanked my briefs down and demanded, "Off." I stepped out of the underwear and put on the leather pants commando style. The outline of my dick, hanging down my leg, stood out even in the black pants. Gabriele reached for my cock and began rubbing it through the material. "Very nice," he said. "You will be very popular in gay bars."

Gabriele also showed me a pair of chaps and said I could wear them with a leather brief or jockstrap... or nothing. I was skeptical, but curious, so I said I would try them on. He fetched me a pair of chaps and leather briefs with fold-down flaps in the front and back.

I heard someone else enter the store, and Gabriele went and spoke to that person and returned just as I was getting the chaps on over the briefs. Looking in the mirror, I had to admit they were hellaciously sexy. Gabriele thought so too. He asked me to turn around so he could see how well they fit. As I turned, he ran his hands up and down the chaps, asking me how they felt—the way Armando often did. I wasn't sure if he was asking me how well the chaps felt or how my body felt having his hands all over me.

Before I knew what was happening, Gabriele had pulled down the flap on my briefs and let my cock fly. "See," he said, "very convenient. You will always be ready for any opportunity. Like now." And he was down on my cock in a flash.

I shot my wad into his mouth, and he took every drop of it. I know this, because he rose up and kissed me. I heard the bell over the front door ring as customers entered the store—again and again and again. Fearing that we would get caught, I snapped the flap on my underwear shut, grabbed up my things, and dashed for the exit, where I was met by another clerk (presumably the person Gabriele had gone to speak to earlier). He grasped my shoulders and said, "You missed a spot," whereupon he licked my face. Once I got over the shock, I clutched my clothes tighter and rushed out the door.

When I got to the nearest subway stop for my ride back to the hotel, I reached into my pocket for a token, and it suddenly hit me that I wasn't wearing my pants. I was wearing the leather chaps with the leather brief. No wonder I was getting so many stares from people on the sidewalk. I fumbled through the clothes in my arms to find a token in my pants pocket. I continued to get stares on the subway and again as I walked through the lobby of the hotel.

25 Underwear Night

"Oh, my god!" exclaimed Troy as I stumbled my way into our room. "What the fuck have you been doing?" Embarrassed as hell, I began apologizing profusely, which only caused him to laugh hysterically. "Stud," he said, "you look fucking hot! I want you to fuck me right now in that suit." Well, how could I refuse a request like that?

When we stopped panting, I said, "Thank god that Mike and Maria didn't see me in the lobby."

"Yeah, but I know who would love to see you in that outfit," he said. "The Outlaws." We had exchanged phone numbers with them last night, so Troy called The Flirt and invited the guys to come over for a little show and tell.

The guys whistled and gave me catcalls as I modeled the outfits for them and recounted my experiences with Gabriele. "Everyone in Milan loves Gabriele," said Dirty Boy. "That is why we all shop there." When I got to the part about Gabriele pulling down the flap on my leather briefs, The Flirt said, "You mean like this?" and he dove for my cock just as Gabriele had done. Well, that started it, and the six of us ended up in an orgy.

"You should wear that outfit to Dante's this weekend," said The Flirt when we lay around in a heap of man flesh.

"Dante's?" I asked. The guys explained that there were different kinds of gay clubs. The one where we had met them was a dance club that attracted mostly young people. There were also neighborhood bars, where friends of various ages got together to socialize, and cruise bars, where men went to pick up other men for a good time. Most bars have "theme nights" such as karaoke, underwear night, naked night, and leather night, but there were also a couple of bars that focused exclusively on the leather and denim fetish, and Dante's is one of them.

"And the place will be packed this weekend because it's Pride Week. You will be very popular there," added Little Cherry, "especially if you wear those chaps."

I had read about Pride Week on the internet, but I really didn't know much about it, so the guys educated me on that point. We also decided to go to Dante's on Friday night because on Saturday it would be packed and difficult to get in.

"That sounds hot," I said. "Troy would probably love that, but I'm sure I couldn't get in since I'm not yet 18."

When The Flirt learned that I was only a couple of months shy of my eighteenth birthday, he said, "No problem. We can get you an ID." He took a picture of me (with clothes on) and said he would have the ID for me by Friday.

"The bars tend to relax their rules on Pride Weekend," added Little Cherry, "but when you show up in that outfit, nobody's going to be focusing on your ID anyway."

We began to discuss which of the clothes I should wear and which Troy should wear, and then it hit me like a Mack truck. In my frenzy, I had rushed out of the store without paying for my merchandise. Once the guys had regained their composure from the uproarious laughter, Dude said, "No worry. We will meet you there tomorrow evening to settle up. Gabriele will be delighted to see you again. Besides," he said, "you have the pants now, but we will help you select some shirts to complete your outfits."

The next morning, Tuesday, Troy had his Italian lesson as we toured Sforzesco Castle, a 15th century fortress that is one of the largest citadels in Europe. Renovated several times, it now houses many of Milan's museums and art collections, including Michelangelo's *Rondanini Pietà*, and Leonardo's *Codex Trivulzianus* manuscript as well as works by Mantegna, Canaletto, Tiepolo, Titian, Tintoretto, and Vincenzo Foppa. The castle also contains museums devoted to ancient art, musical instruments, Egyptology, prehistoric archaeology, applied arts, antique furniture and wooden sculpture, as well as the Achille Bertarelli Print Collection. It was impossible to cover everything in one morning, so we committed to come back when we had more time.

After lunch, Troy had his music lessons at the Academy, and I just roamed the neighborhoods around the hotel and worked out in the hotel gym. When Troy got back to the hotel, we made love, of course, and went out for dinner before meeting The Outlaws at Gabriele's store.

As soon as Gabriele saw me, he rushed over, gave me a great big hug, kissed me, and teasingly licked my face as his associate had done when I was fleeing the store. "I knew you would be back," he gloated.

Dirty Boy introduced Troy to Gabriele, who nearly melted at the sight of him. With no hesitation or compunctions whatsoever, he lifted up Troy's shirt and rubbed his hands all over his hairy chest and even stuck one hand down his pants to rub his pubes. "You want to buy some pants, I hope," he said to Troy.

"Actually," said The Flirt, "they have enough pants. Now they need shirts to complete their outfits."

"I know just the thing," asserted Gabriele, as he grabbed Troy's hand and pulled him over to where the shirts were.

"Take off your shirt," he commanded, and when Troy did, Gabriele rubbed his face all over Troy's furry chest and abs, purring like a pussy...er...a kitten, that is. "No shirt," said Gabriele. "You must show the world that magnificent chest." And with that, he pulled a black leather vest off a rack and put it on Troy. "No button. Leave open."

All of the gang concurred that the leather vest was a perfect complement to the leather chaps and briefs. Gabriele dragged Troy to a mirror, and as Troy fell in love with the sexy look, Gabriele stepped away and came back with a black leather cowboy hat, which completed the outfit perfectly.

"Accessories?" asked Gabriele.

"Like what?" asked Troy, so Gabriele led him to another area where he showed us chain-linked belts, handcuffs (to hang from a belt loop), leather wrist bands, and more. Troy accepted the wristbands and passed on the rest, though he looked very tempted, and I got outrageously turned on at the thought of him in all that gear.

"Now what for you, *la mia piccola faccia da sborra?"* Gabriele asked me, squeezing my face like a baby's. The guys practically fell on the floor laughing.

"What did he call me?" I asked.

"He called you 'my little cum face,'" said Troy.

"Fuck," I said to Troy, "You've been working much too hard at your Italian lessons. You're gonna have to teach me all those dirty words you've been learning."

Gabriele led me over to a table stacked with all kinds of shirts. He pulled many off the table, tossing them in the air like the day's discards. Finally, he pulled out one, yanked off my shirt, and helped me on with a sheer black sleeveless muscle shirt.

"Perfect with leather pants or white pants," he said, referring to the items I had bought (or run out of the store with) the day before. And everyone agreed that he was right. It was the perfect shirt to go with either pair of pants...or with the chaps, for that matter.

I also accepted a bicep band to accentuate my muscles. When Gabriele selected a black band with blue piping, I asked him if a colored arm band had the same significance as a colored handkerchief, and he just said, "Maybe...if you are lucky...but you, handsome man, will not need luck."

"Boots," said Gabriele. So, Troy and I each got a pair of shin-high black lace-up leather boots.

"Anybody want to go over to *Costolo di Adamo* (Adam's Rib) tomorrow night?" asked Dirty Boy after we paid for our new clothes. "Wednesday is underwear night there."

Dude explained that on "underwear night" the bartenders all served drinks in their sexy underwear, and customers who stripped down to their undies could get drinks at a discount. It sounded interesting, so we all agreed to meet there the next night.

When we got to the bar, which everyone just called "Adamo" for short, we all stripped down to our underwear and put the rest of our clothes in bags that we marked with our names. Those bags, along with our shopping bags from Gabriele's shop were tucked safely behind the bar.

All of the bartenders and most of the customers also wore nothing but underwear, most of which were sexy, but not overly daring, which pretty much describes what The Outlaws were wearing. Apparently, there are regulations as to how revealing the underwear could be, but some of the men cavalierly flaunted the regs, especially during Pride Week.

For example, some guys wore jockstraps or undies with open bottoms, which were against the regulations. Some wore regular undies, but they were pulled down low to expose their pubes and butt cracks. Some wore sheer undies that left nothing to the imagination. And some wore undies with flaps, like my new leather ones, but with one of the snaps undone. Troy was wearing a red thong, and I wore a pair of my Addicted Push Up briefs, the kind for guys with extra-big cocks. As expected, we drew lots of stares and quite a few gropes.

"Groping is allowed," said The Flirt. "If you don't want it, just politely say, 'no grazie,' and they will usually respect your wishes."

Troy got as many guys who wanted to rub his hairy chest as grope his package. Some guys just wanted to feel our muscles. But, of course, most of the guys who approached me wanted to feel my cock. Some even pulled out my waist band or even unsnapped my flap to get a good look at the merchandise.

Around 10:00 p.m. the lights in the back of the bar dimmed, and many of the guys drifted in that direction. "What's going on?" I asked. "Come," said Dirty Boy. "I show you."

Back in the darkened area, guys were groping each other openly, by which I mean that they pulled down one another's undies and, in some cases, removed them altogether. Some guys were getting blow jobs, and some were even getting fucked. Naturally, everyone wanted to get a good look at my Texas-size schlong, even in the dim light, so it wasn't long before I was surrounded by guys tugging at my briefs and groping my cock and balls. They lined up to take turns sucking it, and they even placed bets to see who could swallow the most of it. And when they weren't sucking my dick, they were kissing me, licking my neck, or nibbling on my tits.

"You have the right to stop it if you want," said Dirty Boy, "It's your body."

"My body is enjoying it just fine, thank you," I said.

After a dozen or more guys had sampled my meat and gotten it stiff as a bone, one backed me up against a wall and gave me a kind of lap dance before he spread his ass cheeks and covered my cock with his eager hole. I didn't have to fuck him; he did all the work. After about 10 minutes or so, he pulled away and made room for another guy to ride my throbbing dick. This parade went on for nearly an hour. Normally I would have shot my wad before that, but having the guys pull off every 10 minutes or so was like edging.

All the while, I was so preoccupied that I never even thought about where Troy was or what he was doing. As it turned out, he was getting his ass worshipped by a parade of *cazzos* (cocks) and getting blow jobs at the same time. "There's nothing better than fucking somebody's face while another guy is fucking your ass," he told me later.

By midnight, Troy and I were both completely spent, and Troy had to go to class in the morning.

"Tomorrow night is naked night at *La Casetta,*" said Dude. I knew immediately that *La Casetta* meant The Little House because it is almost identical to the Spanish *La Casita,* which is what Carlos calls our guest house/bunkhouse.

"Sounds wonderful," said Troy, "but I don't know if I'll be able to walk tomorrow."

All the guys laughed, patted him on the back, and told us to rest up for our big trip to Dante's on Friday night.

26 Eat it! Eat it! Eat it!

For Troy's Italian lesson on Thursday, we toured Duomo di Milano, Milan Cathedral, the largest cathedral in Italy and the fifth largest in the world. Nearly 600 years in the making, it is a masterpiece of Gothic architecture.

Thursday afternoon, I just went back to the hotel to work out and rest while Troy had his music lessons at the academy.

On Friday, the Italian lesson had a different venue. We took a cruise along Navigli Lombardi, Milan's 12th century canal, and took a leisurely stroll back to the hotel. Troy's lesson focused on commerce and the various items we saw for sale along the way.

That evening, Troy and I dressed in our new leather outfits. He wore the chaps with the black leather brief, vest (unbuttoned, no shirt), cuffs, and cowboy hat. I wore the tight black leather pants (commando), the sheer black T-shirt, and armbands. And, of course, we both wore our black leather boots. I hung a blue handkerchief from my left rear pocket to signal that I was cruising for hot Italian *culo*, and Troy draped one from the D-ring on his right side, indicating that he was cruising for *cazzo*.

To say that I was self-conscious walking through the hotel lobby and out to the street would be a humongous understatement, but it was Pride Weekend, which meant that the streets were filled with people dressed much more brazenly than we were. There were men in drag, men in dog collars being led around on leashes, and guys walking around in nothing but their underwear, much of which left hardly anything to the imagination. And whereas Troy wore briefs under his chaps, we saw a couple of guys wearing chaps with no briefs at all, only cod pieces, thus exposing their bare butts. Troy's briefs had a zipper in the back (for easy access), but at least his butt crack was covered—for the time being anyway.

When we arrived at the subway stop we were directed to, The Flirt met us, handed me the ID he had procured for me, and escorted us to the bar, where we met up with the other Outlaws. Just as Little Cherry had predicted, the doormen barely even glanced at our IDs. They just ogled us salaciously and waved us on through.

Dante's was packed like a can of sardines—sardines in spawning season. It was impossible to go anywhere without getting groped, but I guess that's the idea. There was also no shortage of men offering to buy us drinks.

Dirty Boy led us like a teacher leading a class of first-graders, hand in hand, to the back of the bar, where we found a stairway leading down to a basement, and over the stairway was painted a sign that read *l'Inferno*. OK, I finally got it: Dante's Inferno. Were we about to descend into the Nine Circles of Hell? I didn't have to wait long for an answer.

It was almost pitch black when we entered the Inferno, but once our eyes adjusted, we could make out what was around us—barely. As we walked through the maze of narrow corridors, I got the feeling that I was losing my compatriots one by one. Feeling my way through, I realized that there were corridors off of corridors leading to all kinds of mysterious places.

Some of those places were rooms with men sitting on benches masturbating as they watched porn on TV—masturbating either themselves or someone else. Some rooms had walls with what I came to learn were called glory holes. Other rooms contained cushioned platforms capable of accommodating anywhere from two to ten men. Another room housed a *crux decussata* (St. Andrew's Cross), cages, and an array of BDSM furniture and gear, most of which I had never seen or heard of before. And a couple of rooms contained contraptions that I now know as slings.

As I fumbled my way through the darkness, I found myself constantly being groped, intentionally or unintentionally, just as I inevitably groped other men. Eventually, I came to a room with a large wooden frame with padded tops, not altogether dissimilar to some of the padded exercise equipment in gyms. Men bent over the padded beams with their asses up in the air, inviting pedestrians to take a stab at them. It appeared that about half of them had docked while the other half were still waiting for their ships to come in.

Suddenly, I was approached by one big hairy stud in biker's gear who backed me up against a wall. Actually, he backed me up against another big hairy stud with his back to the wall. "Sandwich?" whispered the man behind me into my ear as he massaged my crotch. "*No grazie*," I replied, as The Outlaws had taught me. I was certainly not averse to playing, but before I did that, I wanted to get my bearings.

I decided to try to retrace my steps and see if I could find Troy and The Outlaws. I found Dirty Boy naked with half a dozen other naked men on one of the padded platforms. The Flirt was sandwiched between the two guys who had propositioned me. I saw Dude entering the BDSM dungeon, but I didn't hang around to see if he was to be the master or the slave. And Little Cherry was handcuffed to a chair and getting bathed in an avalanche of cum in an activity that I learned is called bukkake. And Troy? I finally found him in one of the slings with men lined up to take their turns fucking him.

"Does it bother you seeing your boyfriend getting fucked by so many other guys?" a man next to me asked.

"How do you know he's my boyfriend?" I asked.

"I saw you together at the dance club," he replied. "So, does it bother you?"

"Not at all," I answered. "I'm just glad to see him enjoying it. As long as he's happy, I'm happy."

I crossed paths once again with the two hairy studs who wanted to sandwich me. I tried to explain to them that I wanted to lie naked between their hairy muscled bodies and that I would like to fuck one or both of them, but that I was not a bottom and didn't want to get fucked myself.

Stud #1 bent over the padded frame and pulled down his leather pants. I loved feeling his hairy chest with my hands wrapped around him, and I enjoyed the feel of stud #2 rubbing his hairy chest against my back as I entered his buddy. He wrapped his arms around me and rubbed my chest, playing with my nipples. As I continued to pound stud #1, stud #2 began rubbing my butt cheeks, even slipping his hands beneath the leather to rub my butt raw. Before I knew it, he had one finger stroking my butt crack and teasing my ass lips.

I had never been anything but a top, but I had to admit to myself that the finger probing felt pretty damn good. I had occasionally fantasized about the possibility of taking a dick up my ass when the time, place, and person were right, but this just wasn't either. So, when I felt his dick rubbing against my ass, I stopped him, pulled out of stud #1, and directed stud #2 to take my place in his hole. He did so reluctantly, but not angrily. I moved around behind him and began rubbing my cock against his hole, as he had done with me, only he didn't try to stop me.

I pushed my dick into him and began pumping him as he had pumped stud #1. Yeah, we ended up sandwiching, but I didn't end up in the middle as they had hoped. When the three of us came, we locked in a three-way kiss.

When we entered The Inferno, we had agreed that we would meet back at the bar upstairs in two hours. I had lost all track of time, as I'm sure the others had too, but I thought it best to drag myself back upstairs to see if any of the guys were there. Everyone was there except Little Cherry, who, of course, was still handcuffed to that chair. I offered to go get him, but Dude said I should just leave him. "He's in *paradiso*," he assured me.

"Before we leave," said Dirty Boy, "everyone check to make sure you've got everything you came in with." We all inspected one another and everything seemed to be in order...except...one thing. My handkerchief was missing. Oh, well.

On Saturday, central Milan was a beehive of activity. An estimated 200,000 people poured into the city from all over the country and from every corner of the world. The big Pride Parade was not scheduled to begin until 4:00 p.m., so Troy and I slept late and had The Outlaws meet us at our hotel at 3:00, which gave us plenty of time to find a good spot along the parade route.

Milan's Gay Pride Parade is much like those in other major cities around the world except that Milan is the fashion capital of the world, and that heritage is obvious in the parade. All of the big fashion houses sponsored extravagant floats, exhibits, or events, and the parade featured some of the best-dressed drag queens ever.

The parade lasted a good two hours, just in time for an early dinner—early by Milanese standards anyway. So, we found a nice café with a rainbow flag flying over the door and enjoyed a leisurely dinner, after which we navigated the streets, looking for anything interesting, and there was plenty of that.

Gay bars that normally didn't open until the evening were still going full blast from the night before; shops, cafés, and other businesses were offering specials. Tents were set up for vendors to hawk their wares and for non-profit organizations to promote their services. Some gave out free condoms and lube to promote safe sex. There were also music pavilions all over the area. Where else but Milan would you find opera music featured at a Pride celebration?

As we strolled the streets, Troy and I both drew seductive looks from men we passed in the crowds, and we even got groped a few times. I attributed the actions to our sexy outfits, but then several people came up to Troy to ask for his autograph. He was as shocked as the rest of us. "Why would anybody be asking for my autograph in Milan, Italy?" he asked.

"Maybe they saw you sing the other night at that club where we first met," suggested Dude.

"Or maybe they recognized your ass," teased The Flirt.

Whatever the reason, Troy took it all in stride and graciously signed every autograph requested.

When we passed one of the pavilions, the band that was performing stopped right in the middle of their song, and the lead singer announced that he had spotted Troy in the audience. The crowd didn't exactly go wild, but there was definitely a stir among them. Speaking Italian, of course, the singer asked Troy to go up and sing something, and the crowd didn't need much coaxing to urge Troy to the stage. He finally gave in, went up, and greeted the lead singer and every member of the band individually—in Italian, of course. Then, much to my surprise, he broke into a rendition of Michael Jackson's "Beat It," a perennial favorite among gay crowds. I suppose I should not have been surprised that he chose that song, but I was.

The phrase "beat it" occurs 47 times in the song, and Troy had the crowd joining in on every utterance of it. Even though the phrase is meant to be synonymous with "scram," many gay people like to superimpose a masturbatory connotation on it. So, every time Troy sang "beat it," many in the crowd mimed jerking off, and a few guys actually pulled out their dicks and pumped to the rhythm. A couple of dudes knelt before two other men in leather and began blowing them, whereby the crowd around them began chanting:

Eat it! Eat it! Eat it!
Eat it! Eat it! Eat it!

At the end of the song, the crowd erupted in applause, cheers, whistles, and even some well-meaning catcalls. Troy thanked the band and the crowd and walked to the portable steps when the crowd started chanting "opera" and "aria," at which point the lead singer pulled him back to the microphone. In keeping with the theme of debauchery often associated with Pride events (last night was a good example), Troy chose a song about drinking and philandering, *"Fin ch'han dal vino"* from Mozart's *Don Giovanni* (libretto by Lorenzo Da Ponte). He began by asking for two volunteers and selected a very butch lesbian and a bearded drag queen, and as they approached the stage, he asked someone in the crowd to hand each of them a beer. (The actual song is about champagne, but nobody in that crowd was drinking the bubbly.)

Troy positioned a volunteer on each side of him, took a deep breath, and launched into the short, rapid-fire, tongue-twisting song, acting out the scene as he sang. The aria concludes with the following lines:

In the meantime I shall have my own fun
Making love to this or that girl
Ah, my list tomorrow morning
Shall have at least ten new entries.

When he got to "making love to this..." he grabbed the drag queen's crotch, sang an arpeggio up to a very high note, and held it for what seemed like an eternity while rolling his eyes at the crowd, who laughed so hard it's a wonder they didn't wet their undies—those who were wearing undies anyway. Then, with a short pause, he finished the line "...or that girl," pointing to the lesbian with fear and trepidation. And when he sang, "...at least ten new entries," he pointed to various "girls" in the audience—only he repeated the line over and over and over, pointing to a hundred different people.

When Troy finished the song, he thanked his two volunteers, directing all the attention to them instead of himself. I wondered at the time if he had learned that kind of modesty from the way Maria had deferred to the students at his annual high school concert or if it was something that just came naturally for him. Either way, it was very impressive.

As Troy began to descend the stairs again, the crowd shouted, "Encore! Encore!" Troy tried to beg off, but neither the crowd nor the band would have it, so Troy got back on the stage, conferred briefly with the members of the band, and sang Queen's "We Are the Champions," another favorite of gay crowds everywhere. Rather than perform solo, though, he pulled the lead singer up to the microphone with him, sometimes singing harmony and sometimes just backing off and letting that guy take the spotlight. Of course, many people in the crowd knew the lyrics and sang along, and everybody sang along with every repetition of "we are the champions."

When the crowd again burst into applause and cheers, Troy once again had the members of the band take the bow and he went around singling out each one in turn. Never before and never since have I seen an entertainer absolutely steal the show by stepping out of the spotlight in deference to others.

When Troy finally managed to get off the stage, he was mobbed by people asking for his autograph. Since most of them did not have paper with them, he ended up autographing T-shirts, bras, briefs (mostly at the crotch), and even a box of condoms.

By the time we all got away from that gathering, Troy was so wrapped up in the experience that he seemed to have forgotten all about why he had become so famous all of a sudden. As we hopped from bar to bar, passing music stage after music stage, Troy continued to be approached for his autograph, and the scene on the bandstand was repeated three more times, and each time, Troy sang a completely different set, often segueing seamlessly between Italian and English and back again. He sang songs from Culture Club to Andrew Lloyd Webber, from Enrique Iglesias (in Spanish) to Wagner, from Hughie Thomasson ("Ghost Riders in the Sky") to Gershwin. Altogether, we estimated that he had just given a three-hour concert.

By the time Troy and I got back to our hotel, it was well past the witching hour. The night manager told Troy as we walked through the lobby that he had received several messages. "I'll collect them in the morning," Troy said.

As we lumbered into our hotel room, Troy asked, "What's that?" A note had been slipped under the door.

"Oh, boy," I said. "Looks like we may be in trouble." The note read:

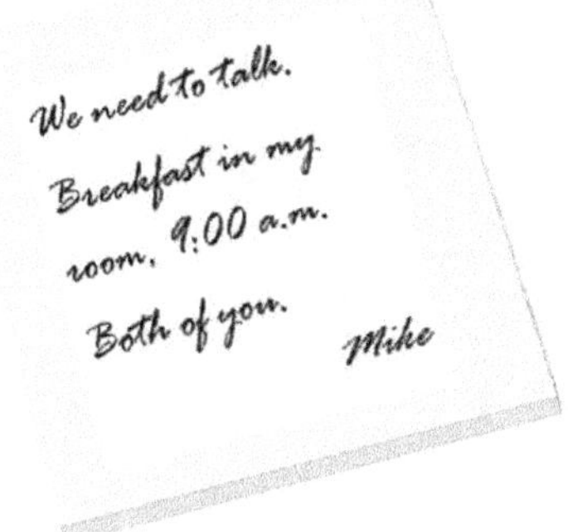
We need to talk.
Breakfast in my
room, 9:00 a.m.
Both of you.
Mike

Despite being very tired after a long day, I tossed and turned wondering what could have gotten Mike upset. Maybe he had found out that I used a fake ID to get into a gay club, or maybe he had heard from someone what I did in that club. *Oh, my god. I'm a dead man.*

27 Facing the Music

Just as Troy and I were getting ready to leave our room Sunday morning, Troy recalled that he had messages at the front desk, so he called down and asked the desk clerk to send them up to Mike's suite. We arrived at Mike's door at 8:54 and paced the hallway waiting for the minute hand to reach 8:59. I knocked on the door with six seconds to spare.

Mike answered the door in his underwear, suggesting that he had only just woken up. Though I had seen him in nothing but underwear countless times, I never ceased to be impressed with how hot he looked, especially when he was just being natural, not posed. "Have a seat, guys," he said, indicating the two sofas facing each other across a coffee table. "Be right back." When he returned a few minutes later dressed in comfortable slacks and T-shirt, Maria followed him to the sofa across from us.

"I'm so sorry," I started to say. "I never meant to...."

"What are you talking about, Rick? Have you done something wrong?"

"Well...."

"Squelch it. You haven't done anything wrong...not as far as I know anyway."

"So, I'm the one who's in trouble?" asked Troy.

"What the fuck, guys? Nobody's in trouble here. We've just got some unexpected business that we have to take care of. We've got to deal with these videos."

"Videos?" I asked.

"Videos?" Troy asked.

"Oh, my god. You haven't seen them?"

"What videos? What are you talking about?"

Mike didn't speak. He just punched a few keys on his laptop sitting on the coffee table and flipped it around for us to watch. It was a video of Troy singing at the dance club on Monday night. "Remember? 'Rhinestone Cowboy,' 'The Prayer,' and 'My Guy.' This was posted Friday night."

That explains all the autograph seekers.

"And then this morning," continued Mike, "we saw these." They were videos from Troy's cameo appearances on the bandstands at Milan Pride.

"I'm so sorry, Mike. I didn't mean...."

"Dammit, guys. I wish you would just quit apologizing. You're starting to make me think that you've really got something to apologize for. How many times do I have to tell you? There's nothing wrong. All I see on these videos are a bunch of people having a good time, and it's obvious that the crowds are absolutely eating it up."

Troy and I breathed deep sighs of relief, and then I said, "I don't understand, Mike. If you don't see anything wrong, what are we talking about here?"

Mike punched in a few more keys, turned the laptop toward us again, and asked, "What do you see?" The video wasn't running, so I was at a loss again.

"Look here," said Mike, pointing to a box in the corner of the screen. "Three million hits and counting."

"Holy shit!" exclaimed Troy. "That's gotta be a mistake."

"It's no mistake," said Mike. "The other videos don't have as many hits, but they were only posted this morning. My guess is that they are going viral so fast because this is Pride Week in cities and countries all over the world, so LGBT people are seeing them and sharing them with their friends, who are sharing them with their friends, and so on."

"And some of the comments from associated chat rooms," chimed in Maria, "have indicated that people are seeing them on TV screens in gay bars from Toronto to Tokyo and from Johannesburg to Helsinki. You may not be a star yet, Troy, but you are quickly becoming an international phenomenon."

Troy fell back in his seat to collect his thoughts as Mike got up and walked over to the breakfast cart he had ordered from room service. In addition to pots of hot coffee and tea, the cart contained not only an assortment of breads, butter, and jams typical of the Italian breakfast, but also eggs, sausages, bacon, ham, yogurt, granola, and other items that might appeal to international travelers, especially Americans. After the workout we had had last night, I was famished. "So what are the rest of you going to eat?" I joked.

Mike sneered but then realizing that I was only half joking, quipped, "We can order more if we need to."

"So," Troy finally spoke again. "I'm still confused. What's this business we have to take care of?"

Maria leaned forward and spoke in that heavenly voice of hers. "Mike, Mike's agent, Armando, and I have been working on a plan to help you launch your music career and maybe a modeling career—if that's what you decide that you really want, but we were going to pace it. We wanted to let you finish high school, maybe do a little modeling and make a few small appearances, let you ease into things gradually, but these videos have changed everything. What we had planned to do over 12 months we now have to do in 12 days."

"I'm so sorry," said Troy. "You've done so much for me, and now I've just created more work for you."

"Goddammit, Troy, if you say 'I'm sorry' one more time," snapped Mike, "I'm going to come over there, grab you by your balls, and throw you off this fuckin' balcony." (We were on the top floor of an eight-story building.)

Maria threw Mike a look that said, "Let me take care of this." She rose up from the sofa she was sitting on, walked around the coffee table, and sat right next to Troy.

"Troy," she said, "This is not a problem for me. I've been in this helter-skelter business for a while now. I can handle the pressure. We're just worried about you. Only a year ago you were adjusting to a new home, a new school, new friends, and so much more. You've adapted remarkably well, and we didn't want to see you lose any of that. We aren't concerned about ourselves, sweetheart." *She never called* me *'sweetheart'*. "We're concerned about *you*."

I leaned across the breakfast cart and whispered to Mike, "I hope you realize what a one-in-a-million woman you've got there."

Mike smiled and said, "I think I do."

"You'd better," I said, "Because if you don't hurry up and ask her to marry you, I will."

Mike raised his eyebrows and nodded to the balcony, suggesting that I might be the one he'd throw over.

Then came a knock on the door. Mike set down his cup of coffee and went to answer it. It was a bellboy saying, "Messages for Mr. Mazure."

"Oh, I asked them to send those up here," said Troy. "I hope you don't mind."

As Troy turned his back to walk over to the breakfast tray (he had to be even more famished than I was), Mike tipped the bellboy and walked back to the coffee table with a very large shopping bag. Troy turned back around and gasped as Mike dumped the pile of messages, dozens—maybe hundreds of them—on the coffee table.

"May I?" Maria asked Troy as she gestured toward the pile of notes.

"Uh...yeah...please," Troy stammered.

Maria quickly flipped through the papers like a shipping clerk sorting bills of lading for shipments destined for widely dispersed ports.

"Some of these are repeat calls from the same people," she said. "They're persistent, if not desperate."

"But what do they want?" asked Troy.

"Some are talent agents eager to represent you. We'll get to those in due time. Some," she continued, "are TV producers who want you to appear on their shows IMMEDIATELY! We'll prioritize those."

"What kind of shows?" Troy asked.

"Mostly talk shows...like *Good Morning, America* and the *Tonight Show*, shows not only in the States, but also here in Italy, Great Britain, Australia, and Greece, where they say they 'just missed you.' Actually, we already have an appearance lined up for...." She stopped, dropped the papers into her lap, and walked over to Troy by the breakfast cart. "Sweetheart...." *Damn! She said it again!* "Eat some breakfast. We still have a lot to cover, but let's not do it on an empty stomach."

Over breakfast, Maria asked us about how we had been enjoying our time in Milan. Of course, we couldn't tell her about our experiences in the gay bars or at Michele's shop, and I suppose she was mostly asking about Troy's lessons, but instead he launched into a detailed account of his musical performances on the bandstands. He sounded like a six-year-old describing all the fantastic presents that Santa Claus had brought him. He lit up like a Christmas tree.

During the rare moments when he stopped to catch his breath, he scarfed down his breakfast and went back for seconds. Every once in a while, Maria or Mike turned to me to ask about my experiences, but I think they only did that to give Troy time to eat.

When we had finished clearing off the entire breakfast cart, Maria picked up where she had left off.

"I need to ask you a very serious question, Troy. Is this whole music thing just a hobby for you, or is it a career goal? Is it something that you really want to pursue and are willing to make sacrifices for?" I already knew the answer to that question. When Troy was performing on those bandstands, he was in his element. He was in heaven.

"I love music," said Troy. "I can't imagine my life without it. But I don't just enjoy listening to it. I enjoy sharing it with people. At the risk of sounding mushy or crazy, it feels like a calling to me."

"If that's crazy, Troy, they're going to have to lock us both up," said Maria.

I can think of lots worse things than being locked up with you, Maria, but I get your point.

And then Mike stepped in. "And what about the modeling? How do you feel about that?"

"I enjoy it," said Troy. "It's fun. I would like to keep doing it if I can, but I would never let it get in the way of my music."

"I know what you mean," said Mike. "Football has been my life, and modeling has been a very enjoyable—and lucrative—sideline. I know that someday they will both come to an end, but I'm grateful for the opportunities they have both given me."

Troy smiled at Mike like he had discovered a fellow traveler, a kindred soul.

"And what about you, Rick?" *Oh, so I am a part of this conversation after all?* "What are your goals for the short term and the long term?"

"Hmm. I'm looking forward to going back to school this fall and playing football again. If I have the chance, I may continue to play in college, or I may not. I like it, but it's not the center of my life. As for the long term, I intend to be the best damn Irish-American writer since Eugene O'Neill." Mike laughed at the reference, but I'm sure he got the point.

"All right then," said Maria. "Now that that's settled, let's get to work." After reaching down next to the sofa and retrieving a notebook, she continued. "Before we stopped for breakfast, I started to tell you about something I've already done. Does either of you know what Rai is?"

"Is that the Italian TV network?" I asked. While Troy was in his classes, I occasionally had time to turn on the TV, and I thought I had seen that name.

"Yes," confirmed Maria. "It's the government-supported network, kind of like your PBS, and they have five channels, each one devoted to a different specialty. Channel 5 focuses exclusively on culture and the arts. They have a weekly program on Saturday nights that deals with current events in the arts. The format is a bit like *The Tonight Show* and similar programs in the U.S. The host, Silvana Serafini, has made it her mission to bridge the gap between 'high culture' and 'popular culture,' kind of like what the Boston Pops tries to do with music."

"And she and Maria were classmates at the Academy," interjected Mike, as if he were revealing some top-secret information.

"Yes," said Maria, "so as soon as I saw the first video yesterday, I called Silvana and asked her if she had seen it. She said, 'Seen it? It's all that everyone at the studio is talking about.' When I told her that I knew the young man in the video, she got so excited and insisted that I bring you to her show this Saturday. She even offered to cancel other scheduled guests to make room for you."

Troy fell back against the sofa as if someone had gassed him with heavy-duty euphoria. To use a technical term, he was blown away.

"Isn't that show broadcast from Rome?" I asked.

"Usually, yes," replied Maria, "but sometimes they take the show on the road, and it just so happens that Silvana had already planned to broadcast this week from Milan, from La Scala, in fact."

Troy was still too stunned to talk.

"So," continued Maria, "this afternoon, you and I have to get together to decide on which songs you should perform on the show, and all of your lessons at the Academy this week will focus on rehearsing those songs for the show. I'll talk to your instructors, and if they give us any flack, I'll just take over as your instructor."

Troy didn't speak, but I know he felt reassured that Maria had his back.

"Your language lessons," Mike announced, "will take you out into the community in ways designed to promote your image with an eye toward courting potential sponsors." Seeing the confused look on Troy's face, Mike said, "I'll explain more later. But right now, we need you guys to go back to your room and pack. We're moving over to the Marriott Hotel."

"Moving?" I asked. "Why?"

Mike explained that while the STRAF was very nice and conveniently located between the academy and the theatre, it did not have some of the amenities we would need: a conference room where we could work out our strategy and tactics as well as access to a business center, to name just two.

"Do we know that they have vacant rooms right now?" I asked.

"I called Rob Palmer last night," said Mike, "and explained to him what was happening and what we would need, and he said he would take care of it. We'll meet in the lobby in one hour. You can leave your bags in your room; the staff will collect them and take them over to the Marriott."

How did Mike know that we would need those facilities when he hadn't even confirmed that Troy would want to proceed with the plans? Either he was just trying to prepare for possibilities, or he knew Troy and me better than we had thought.

Troy and I headed for the door, and Maria walked to their bedroom to pack. As she passed Mike, I heard her say under her breath, "Your brother is even more charming than you are."

When Mike turned to see if I had overheard the compliment, I just gestured toward Maria and then myself and then to my wedding finger. Mike dashed to the sofa, grabbed a pillow, and threw it at me, but it only hit the door as I was closing it behind me. Before we reached the elevator, I heard Mike calling my name. He indicated that he wanted to talk to me alone, so Troy went on ahead to our room, and I went back to Mike's room.

Mike didn't invite me to sit down. He just placed one hand on my shoulder and gazed into my eyes in his "big-brother-talk" stance. "Rick, you know I love you, don't you?" I didn't want to get all mushy, so I just nodded in the affirmative. "I'm not overlooking you," he continued, "and neither is Maria. And we never will. But right now, Troy is the one who needs our help. Whether you realize it or not, you are much more self-sufficient than he is. Even so, Maria and I have discussed ways we might be able to help you achieve *your* goals, and we *will* be working with you on those plans. I just wanted to make sure you knew that, OK?"

I gave him a great big bear hug and just said, "I love you too."

When I finally broke my grip, I walked back to the door, but before I could leave, he spoke again, "Rick?"

"Yeah?"

He walked toward me, closed the door, and said, "All these apologies this morning...is there anything I should know about?"

"Not really," I replied.

"So, you haven't done anything illegal?"

"No...well...mmmm..."

"Have you killed anybody?"

"No," I chuckled.

"Robbed a bank?"

"No."

"OK, so you used a fake ID to get into a bar?"

"How did you know?" I asked, shocked.

"Lucky guess. That's all."

"Am I in trouble?"

"That depends," said Mike. "Did you get hurt in the process?"

"No."

"Did you hurt anybody else?"

"Of course not."

"Did you learn anything in the process?"

"Quite a bit, actually."

"Hmm. Did you have a good time?"

"Yeah, I did," I said, with perhaps a little more enthusiasm than I should have expressed.

"OK, then. Bless you, my child. Go forth and sin no more."

Gawd, I loved my brother. I gave him another great big bear hug and squeezed until he finally said, "This isn't getting your bags packed."

28 Reunions

When the courtesy van deposited us at the Marriott Hotel, we were met by, of all people, Rob Palmer. "I was in Brussels when Mike called yesterday," he told us, "so I caught the first plane I could get and flew over to make sure that everything would be in order. Before you go to your rooms, could I show you the conference room we've arranged for you?"

The room was spacious, with a conference table containing multiple jacks and electrical outlets for laptops. At each end of the room were two other long tables, one for coffee and snacks, and another one for sorting and collating papers. There were phones, two printers, and a cabinet containing printing paper and an array of office supplies, including pens, markers, and multiple pads of differently colored Post-It™ Notes. There was an electronic white board, and the walls were plastered with local, country, and world maps with a variety of colored push pins marking significant cities. A door led to an adjacent room set up like a parlor with comfortable chairs arranged in pairs or small clusters for chatting or just relaxing.

"This is fantastic," said Mike, "even better than we could have hoped for."

"Well, if you need anything else," said Rob, "just ask."

And just then, the bell captain approached Rob and said something to him. "Your rooms are ready," Rob announced. When we walked out of the conference room, we were met by a platoon of bellboys, who escorted us to our respective rooms—suites actually—where we found our luggage already delivered.

The very cute bellboy who escorted Troy and me to our suite called us by name and said how honored the hotel was to have us as guests. He asked if we needed anything and assured us that he was available to meet our every need. When he reached the door, he stopped. "What is it, Matteo (the name on his tag)?" Troy asked.

"Forgive me, sir," he said to Troy. "I hope I am not too forward. My boyfriend and I saw you perform at the Pride Festival yesterday, and he can't stop watching your videos. Would it be possible to get your autograph for him?"

"What's his name?" asked Troy.

"Tommaso," he replied.

Troy asked Matteo to wait for just a minute while he went into our bedroom. A minute or so later, he came back with two pairs of designer underwear, one autographed for Tommaso and one for Matteo. "Will these do?" asked Troy as he handed the souvenirs to the bellboy.

Matteo went almost apoplectic with joy. He thanked Troy profusely until Troy finally said, "And stop calling me 'sir.' My name is Troy."

"Yes, sir...I mean, thank you, sir...I mean, Troy. Thank you. Tommaso will be thrilled."

Troy grabbed Matteo and gave him a hug. "Thank you, Matteo. I really appreciate your support. And please give this to Tommaso for me," he added, just before he planted a big kiss on Matteo's lips.

Matteo was too stunned to even move, so Troy opened the door for him and said, "Please bring Tommaso by sometime. I would like to thank him too."

After Matteo left, I said to Troy, "Jeez, man. You didn't have to do all that. He would have jumped into bed with you at the drop of a blue handkerchief."

"That wasn't about sex," said Troy, almost scolding me. "He and his boyfriend are fans. I am grateful to have fans."

We had one hour for lunch before Troy had to meet with Maria again to select the songs they would perform on Silvana's show, but we were still stuffed from breakfast, so we decided to skip lunch and just snack on the fruit the management had placed in our suite until dinner. Troy went downstairs to meet with Maria at 2:00, and I didn't see him again until dinner. I called The Flirt to let him and the rest of the gang know that we had changed hotels.

Rob joined us for dinner on Mike's invitation, and we were all glad that he did. I liked Rob right off the bat, but I think Troy was a bit skeptical since Rob seemed to be taking an interest in Troy's mother. Troy had come around, though, and I think he was actually hoping that his mother would find new happiness with Rob.

"This is going to be our time every night to get together, review what's happened, and share our plans for the next steps," said Mike, "so don't make other plans, guys. You're needed here. In fact, don't make plans to go out after dinner. If you're not needed here, you'll be free to go, but this is now your number one priority."

"Not to sound stupid or insensitive, but did it really take you guys all afternoon to pick out three songs?" I asked Troy and Maria.

Maria explained that they had brainstormed dozens of titles from a wide variety of genres. They had to consider who might be in the audience, but they also wanted to demonstrate Troy's range and versatility, and they had to plan for contingencies. What if they want an encore? What if they get cut short for some reason? Eventually, they settled on three songs: "*O Sole Mio*," the traditional Italian favorite, "All I Ask of You" from *The Phantom of the Opera*, and Lonestar's pop-country hit "Amazed."

"You had Armando film Troy singing "*O Sole Mio*" during our photo shoot in Rome," I observed.

"Yes, and we also recorded it here last week," Troy reminded us.

"It was part of my long-term plan," said Maria. "I wanted to put together a very nice video that we could use to introduce you to the world, but I had planned to take our time and do it very professionally. We may still do that, but for now, we need to throw it together and get it out on the internet before Saturday night. It may look a little amateurish, but so do all the other videos that are out there right now."

"But why that song?" I asked.

"The other songs appeal to very specific demographics," explained Maria. "This song has very wide appeal, especially in Italy. If we can get it out there before Saturday, it may help drive up the TV audience."

"What's more," added Mike, "that song and that video are likely to appeal to lots of potential sponsors."

On Monday morning, at Maria's request, Guiseppe, the language mentor, joined us for breakfast. She had already called to brief him on the change in plans for the week, but his participation was now needed in working out the details. "We want to get these guys out in public," said Maria. "We want them to be seen, especially by people who might have watched the videotapes or seen Troy sing at the Gay Pride Festival."

"One place you'll find young people," said Guiseppe, "is colleges and universities—not just on the campuses, but in the cafés and shops around them."

"That's an excellent idea," said Maria. "Let's do that today."

"We also want to link them to potential sponsors," said Mike.

"We could go to *Quadrilatero d'Oro*," suggested Guiseppe.

"What's that?" I asked.

"It's a shopping district," said Guiseppe, "where all the fashion houses have their flagship stores. It's also called *Quadrilatero della Moda*, Rectangle of Fashion."

"Perfect," exclaimed Mike. "Let's plan on that for Tuesday morning," and he asked Guiseppe to join us for dinner again Monday night to work out more details.

"What can I do today to help?" I asked.

"You go with Troy and Guiseppe this morning," instructed Mike. "Meet me back here for lunch. I have something I need your help with this afternoon." Naturally I was curious about what that something was, but before I could ask, Maria spoke up.

"Mike, Rob, and I will go through all those messages you got yesterday—"

"And there were more this morning," interrupted Rob. "Lots more."

"...and I'll meet you at the Academy this afternoon to start working on the songs for Silvana's show Saturday."

As we walked the neighborhoods around the University of Milan and Bocconi University, Troy was approached for autographs from a number of students (and even professors) who had seen his videos or watched him perform at the Pride Festival. Fortunately, being students or faculty, they inevitably carried papers of some sort, so Troy didn't have to take off his underwear to autograph for them—though I am sure many of them would have welcomeed that gesture or taken off their own.

I left Troy and Guiseppe at a café near the University of Milan and went back to the hotel to meet up with Mike. When he ushered me into the hotel shuttle, I asked where we were going, and he simply replied, "Reinforcements. You'll see."

"What about lunch?" I asked.

"Patience," he said, "Patience."

I was surprised when the shuttle dropped us off at the airport. *Are we going somewhere or picking up something—or someone?* After checking the arrivals board, Mike led the way to a baggage carousel, and as he scouted the crowd for someone, I heard a voice over my shoulder, "Forgotten me already, huh?" I turned and was shocked to see Johnny standing there. It had only been three weeks since we went our separate ways from Rome, but it seemed like a lifetime. I attacked him with a ferocious bear hug and squeezed until he begged me to let go.

"What are you...I mean, why are you...how did you....?" I fumbled.

"Mike called and said someone needs to come and rescue you from your sudden onset of aphasia, so here I am."

I wanted to get Johnny back to the hotel so we could get caught up, but Mike said we had to wait for one more person. Just as I was about to ask who that was, I spotted a familiar face approaching from the baggage carousel.

"Armando, what are you...how did you...?"

"Oh, don't start that again," Johnny scolded.

As we rode the shuttle back to the Marriott, Mike explained that he wanted Johnny to participate in the show on Saturday night as well as some other promotional activities and that Armando was here not only to see that we were properly dressed, but also to call on his extensive network of influential contacts to assist in our publicity efforts.

When we got back to the hotel, Rob greeted us and had Johnny's and Armando's bags taken to their rooms. Then, he led us to a private dining room off of the main restaurant, where we had a delicious lunch of *Cotoletta alla Milanese* (veal with risotto). Before taking Armando and Johnny to their suites, Rob showed them the "war room" that had been set up for us, and along the way, he pointed out some of the works of art that he had purchased for the hotel from Armando's gallery, not only photographs, but also sculptures and paintings.

Johnny's suite was right next to the one that Troy and I shared, and, as before, Rob had already had his bags delivered to his room. Johnny and I spent the rest of the afternoon getting caught up. He wanted to hear all about the week that my family had spent in

Ireland as well as the past two weeks in Milan, and I wanted to hear about his trip to Denmark, Sweden, and Norway. When Troy came in from his afternoon at the academy, he was as thrilled as I was to see Johnny, who had to repeat for him everything he had just spent four hours telling me.

Johnny told us about going to Tivoli Park in Copenhagen and seeing the statue of *The Little Mermaid* in the harbor. He said he was surprised at how little it was. "Wait," I said, "are we still talking about the statue or about your dick?"

Johnny described the cruise they had taken from Copenhagen to Oslo and how impressed he was with the fjords as they cruised into the Norwegian capital. He also raved about the Viking Ship Museum there and the one in Stockholm. And he told Troy that he would love to go back to Oslo and take him to the magnificent Opera House, which sits right on the harbor.

Johnny also described his visits to *Gamla Stan* (Old Town) in Stockholm and the Nobel Museum, where he said he expects to see my name on a plaque someday after I win the Nobel Prize for Literature.

I asked him if he came across Britta and Inga, the two Swedish college students we had met in Hawaii, and he said he did not but that he found "no shortage of shield-maidens (female Viking warriors) who were eager to do battle with my Viking spear. They liked to call me 'Thor,'" he boasted.

I told Johnny about my delightful trip to Ireland, including the afternoon I spent at the frat house. He listened politely as I described the red-headed frat boys, but he really perked up when I mentioned that some of them had brought their girlfriends into the party room. I could just see the wheels in his head spinning as he imagined all the possible configurations.

Johnny asked Troy about his three weeks thus far in Milan, and Troy told him all about his language and music lessons. "But what about the sex?" Johnny asked.

"Oh, I've joined a monastery and become celibate," he claimed, which compelled Johnny to tackle him and wrestle him to the floor. At one point, I was afraid that Johnny was actually going to fuck Troy to prove that he wasn't celibate. Johnny let him up only when Troy promised to spill the beans about his sexual adventures, and there was a lot to spill.

Troy and I told Johnny about The Outlaws and our visit to the gay bars, including Dante's Inferno. Johnny had already heard from Mike and Rob about Troy's Italian debut as a sexy singer, which is what brought him back to Italy, but he seemed to enjoy hearing the first-hand account from Troy and me.

Johnny reported that he had been in touch with many of our teammates even though football practice hadn't started yet. They had grilled him about Greece and Rome and wanted to know if we would be back in time for football camp. He assured them that we would, but "I told them that I can't guarantee that Troy will be able to walk.

"They kept bugging me about seeing pictures from our modeling gigs and any new underwear we might have accumulated, both of which arrived about 10 days ago, by the way," he told us. "So, I invited the guys over to have a look, and after I set aside the underwear that I wanted to keep, I let them pick over the rest.

"Oh, and there's gonna be a new guy on the team," said Johnny. "His name's Sam, and he's a sophomore whose family just moved to Hilldale from Chicago. Never played football before—at least, not on a team anyway—but Coach says he has potential. He's not sure which position he wants to put him at, so he wants to try him out as backup for each of us, and I assured him that we would help the kid any way we can."

"Cool," said Troy.

"And I think he plays for your team, Troy."

"My team?"

"Yeah, when he was looking at the new modeling pictures from Greece, he seemed more interested in checking out us than the girls. And when the guys started trying on the various underwear, I think he started to get a boner. I didn't want to see him get embarrassed, so I pretended to get a hard-on myself, and it wasn't long before all of us were stroking."

"Is he cute?" Troy asked, only half joking.

"Nah," replied Johnny with all the irony he could muster. "He just looks like I imagine Denzel Washington looked at 16."

"God, I miss those circle jerks," I interjected, and all of a sudden, all three of us started chanting, "Circle jerk, circle jerk, circle jerk."

29 Cars and Jocks

After dinner, we all moved to our work room to debrief and plan for the next day and the rest of the week. Armando brought clothes for us to wear for our visit to the high-fashion shopping district in the morning. Mike instructed us to skip breakfast at the hotel since we would eat at a restaurant over there. He suggested to Johnny that he sleep late in the morning to get over any jet lag he might experience.

The next morning, Troy and I met Guiseppe and Mike in the lobby as planned, and when we stepped out of the hotel, Mike handed the valet a ticket and told us to wait for the car. "You rented a car?" I asked.

"Yes, the stores don't open until 10:00, so we're going to just drive around the district for a bit and hopefully be seen. That's why I got us a convertible," he said.

And some convertible it was too: a Maserati Gran Turismo. "The whole point is to be seen," said Mike, "and you should definitely be seen driving this car."

"You mean, I'm going to drive it?" Troy asked, almost in shock.

Mike didn't even answer. He just dangled the keys in front of Troy.

Mike and I sat in the back seat so that Guiseppe could navigate for Troy. We just drove around for almost an hour, occasionally waving back at people who waved to us or snapped pictures of us. When we parked, we were besieged by autograph seekers.

"Pop the trunk," Mike told Troy, and from that trunk, Mike pulled out shopping bags from Dolce & Gabanna, Versace, Gucci, and several other fashion houses with shops in the area. The bags contained some clothes, but nothing special—just something to make them look full. Mike told us to walk around the district, stopping at any store we might want to check out, carrying the bags to give the impression that we had already bought merchandise from those stores. As we "shopped," more people stopped us to ask for Troy's autograph or to take pictures, and some even took pictures of Mike and me. And each time, we told Troy's fans to be sure to watch him on Silvana Serafini's show Saturday night.

After our morning in the fashion district, we dropped Troy off at the academy, and Mike let me drive the Maserati back to our hotel. I called Johnny, who had just gotten up, just to make him jealous about the Maserati.

Instead of eating in the hotel restaurant or one of the nearby cafés, we took the Maserati around town (with Mike's approval) and ended up on Via Lecco, one of two major streets in the gay district. I pointed out to Johnny the bars and clubs we had been to and, of course, Michele's shop.

Wednesday morning was largely a repeat of Tuesday morning except that we went to regular shopping malls instead of the exclusive shops. In the afternoon, while Troy was at the academy, I took Johnny to some of the attractions that Troy and I had seen. Many of the local papers carried stories and photographs of our shopping spree. The society pages focused on where we had shopped, the entertainment pages talked about our fans and the fact that Troy would be on TV Saturday night, and the sports pages concentrated on the novelty of having three young American football players in Milan. (I guess they must have figured that Mike was over the hill at that point.) Most of the photographs focused on Troy, but Mike and I were in some of them too.

That night, our debriefing/planning session was jam packed with news. Rob announced that with the help of his staff, Troy's website was up and running with some of the photos that Armando had taken, and Maria announced that the "O Sole Mio" video had been posted to that page and had already gotten over 750,000 hits.

Mike announced that we would be spending most of the next day, Thursday, in Turin, a town about two hours away from Milan. When I asked why we were going there, Mike turned the meeting over to Armando, who asked, "Does anyone know what Juventus is?"

"Soccer team," snapped Johnny, almost like he was trying to beat the other contestants to the buzzer on a quiz show.

"*Si*," said Armando, "and Juventus is based in Turin. We are going to Turin to get a tour of the Juventus stadium, and our tour guide will be none other than Alessandro Del Piero, one of the greatest soccer players of all time and practically a national hero here in Italia."

We were all very impressed but not totally surprised since Armando seemed to know everybody who was anybody in Italy.

"Right after breakfast," added Mike, "we will caravan down there."

"Caravan?" I asked.

"Yes, Rob, Maria, and Armando will be going with us, and we can't all fit into the Maserati, so I've rented a couple of other cars. Guiseppe, Maria, and I will ride with you, Troy, in the Maserati. Rick, Armando will ride with you in the Alfa Romeo that I have rented, and Rob will ride with Johnny in the Ferrari."

"Holy shit!" shouted Johnny. "I'm driving a Ferrari? Hot damn! How did I rate that?"

"You see," said Armando, "Ferrari is owned by a company called Exor, and do you know what else that company owns?"

To a roomful of blank stares, Armando answered, "Juventus. Exor owns the Juventus team and the Ferrari company. And do you know what else is in Turin—besides the Holy Shroud?" Armando asked, again to blank stares. "Fiat is based in Turin."

"So why aren't we driving Fiats to Turin?" I asked.

"Because," said Armando, "Fiat owns Alfa Romeo and Maserati, among others. We thought it would be a good idea to have you driving around—and hopefully being seen—in luxury cars owned by the Fiat company, which, as I said, is based in Turin. It's good for publicity."

"So, are we going to be meeting with folks from Fiat?" I asked.

"Not yet," replied Armando, "but it is all part of our grand scheme."

So, the next morning, we all piled into our luxury sports cars and headed for Turin. Alessandro met us at the entrance to the stadium and gave us the royal tour, which Armando photographed all along the way. Troy was delighted to learn that Alessandro was not only a world-famous soccer player, but also a singer who had recorded several albums of mostly rock songs.

As we were wrapping up the tour, Alessandro announced, "I hope you don't mind, but I asked a friend to join us for lunch." *Any friend of yours has got to be a friend of ours.*

I just about fell over when I recognized that friend as Ben Cohen, the hunky rugby player from England. "He's a big fan of yours," Alessandro said to Troy. "We've both seen your videos and were very impressed." I thought I would have to scrape Troy off the pavement with a shovel.

Over lunch, we talked about football—American style and the-rest-of-the-world style (soccer) as well as rugby. And then Ben dropped a bomb on us. "A couple of years ago, I established a foundation called the StandUp Foundation."

"It's the only foundation in the world set up specifically to combat childhood bullying," I jumped in. "Sorry, Ben."

"That's quite all right, Rick. I'm glad to know that you're familiar with our work."

"And since LBGT kids are bullied more than most, the foundation has made that population a priority of its work," I added.

"Wow, Rick. I should hire you as the head of publicity for my foundation."

"Sorry again, Ben. It's just that you're doing such remarkable work, and it's something that no one else has tackled before."

"What did I tell you guys about apologizing?" Mike scolded. "So, Ben, the StandUp Foundation... what can we do to help?"

"I'm glad you asked, Mike, because that's why I invited myself today. I was planning to come down to meet with Alessandro tomorrow, but when he told me that you guys would be here today, I moved up my plans."

For us? Oh, my god!

"My foundation has several projects for raising funds, and one of them is a concert we're working on for next year. I came here originally to ask Alessandro to sing in that concert, and now that I have you here too, I want to ask you, Troy, if you would also participate?"

Since we were all speechless, Alessandro saved our asses. "I would be honored to do that, Ben. Actually, I'm planning to put out a new album, and I wanted to ask Troy if he would be willing to record a duet with me for that album."

Sitting next to Troy, I had to brace him to keep him from falling off his chair. That time Mike saved us. "He would be delighted to accept both of your invitations."

Finally, Troy acknowledged, "You heard my manager. I'm in."

"That's great," said Ben, and Alessandro agreed.

"Now, there's one more thing," said Ben. Our eyes all widened further in anticipation. "One of our traditional fundraisers is our annual calendar. So far, the calendars have featured only me—in different poses and various settings—but we're exploring the idea of mixing it up next time. I would be the featured model for half of the months, and we would invite other celebrities to fill the other six slots. Mike, I would like to ask you to be one of those six."

Mike seemed genuinely surprised, but Mike never lost his composure, so he quickly accepted. Then, Ben turned to Troy again, "And I'd like you to be in the calendar too," he said. "You could do it solo, or we could work Johnny and Rick into the shot. Armando has sent me some samples of the shots he took of you guys recently in his studio, and I think they are dynamite. In fact, I think you could put out your own calendar and corner the market. It would sell like hotcakes."

Once again, we all looked to Mike for a decision. "Let us talk it over, Ben, and get back to you, but at this point, I'd say it's a strong possibility."

"Fantastic," said Ben.

All the while, Armando was constantly snapping candid shots, and when we stepped out of the restaurant, we were faced with a small cadre of paparazzi and reporters. Ben, Alessandro, and Mike were thoroughly experienced in dealing with the press, so it was no big deal to them, and Troy and I had recently experienced the phenomenon, but it was a totally new experience to Johnny.

As the cameras flashed away, the reporters asked us a barrage of questions. "What are you guys all doing here? Are you old friends, or have you just met? Are you planning some new initiatives? Who? What? When? Where? Why? How?"

The three veterans handled the questions deftly, and Armando managed to steer us toward the cars so that the photographers would capture the Maserati, Ferrari, and Alfa Romeo in the backgrounds.

Troy, Johnny, and I were too excited to drive, so Mike drove the Maserati back to Milan so that the three of us could go ape shit over what had just happened. By the time we got back to the hotel, our pictures were all over the evening newscasts and the internet, including Troy's own newly established website.

I couldn't wait to call home and let my folks know what was happening, but there was no answer, so I left a message and called The Flirt to invite him and the guys to come over later to celebrate.

After dinner, we gathered in our little conference center to hear Mike's plans for the next day, Friday. Whatever the plans were, they couldn't be any better than what we had just experienced. "Tomorrow morning," he said, "we're taking all three cars to the airport." He didn't elaborate, and we were all still so focused on our trip to Turin that we didn't even bother to ask.

I was thrilled that Mike dismissed us early so that we could get together with The Outlaws. They were all excited to meet Johnny even if they weren't going to get him in bed with them, and Johnny enjoyed meeting them too, especially after all the stories he had heard us tell. No, they weren't going to get Johnny into bed, but Troy and I were a totally different story.

Troy and I spent the rest of the evening celebrating with The Outlaws in as many different sexual positions and configurations as we could come up with. Johnny, of course, did not participate, but he did watch for a few minutes before he got bored and went down to the pool to find his own outlet, which, we learned later, consisted of two Italian sisters and their mother visiting from Sicily.

The morning after our visit to Turin, we assumed that we were going to the airport to return the cars to the rental agencies, but Mike led our caravan instead to short-term parking near the arrivals gates. *Are we here to pick up someone else?* Once inside the terminal, Mike directed Johnny and me to go with Rob to purchase every newspaper we could get our hands on.

When we completed our errand and got back to the baggage claim area where Mike told us to meet them, we literally dropped all the papers we had collected. All of our moms were standing there to greet us. We were absolutely thrilled to see them again. Dad and Mr. Andersen had to stay behind to tend to the farm and the business, but Mom explained that our mothers "wouldn't miss the big TV show for anything."

We loved showing off the sexy sports cars Mike had gotten for us to drive, and we practically talked their ears off about meeting Alessandro Del Piero and Ben Cohen, and, of course, they all listened just like mothers are expected to do even though they had no idea who these sports celebrities were.

When we got to the hotel, Rob, of course, met us and had bellboys take their things to their suites, where Armando had displayed the dresses they were to wear to the studio on Saturday night.

At our debriefing/planning session after dinner, Rob had spread the newspapers we had bought at the airport across our conference tables. We were on the front pages of the Turin and Milan newspapers, and Rob had learned from his worldwide network of hotels that we were in many other papers around the world as well. In some papers, we were in the sports pages with headlines like, "Who is the best ball player?" The entertainment pages focused on

Alessandro and Troy as singers. Other papers followed the "next generation" theme, with Troy, Johnny, and me as the up-and-coming young stars of sports and entertainment, and we even appeared in the automotive section of some papers with speculations about the cars we had driven. Some of the photos were from the paparazzi, and some were unmistakably Armando's. It was becoming crystal clear that Armando was a major force in our publicity campaign.

30 Show Time

Saturday was the big day. Maria told us that we could take our mothers sightseeing as long as we didn't overdo it. We had a late lunch because we wouldn't get to eat again until after the show. Maria pronounced Troy ready for his TV debut but cautioned him to save his voice for that evening.

At La Scala, where the show was being broadcast from, Troy waited in the green room with Maria and Armando, who would also be on the show. Our mothers sat in the front row along with Johnny, Mike, Rob, and me, and right behind us were Guiseppe, Troy's language teacher, who had also become a good friend, as well as the four members of The Outlaws.

After a brief musical introduction, the announcer called Silvana's name, the curtains opened, and she walked out to the center of the stage. As the music and the applause subsided, she announced that "we have a spectacular show for you tonight. We have an amazing lineup of guests who are going to help us explore the intersections of sports and the arts. My first guest tonight is none other than Alessandro Del

Piero." That came as a shock to most of us since he had said nothing about being on the show.

After Silvana went through Alessandro's qualifications as a soccer star as well as a singer, she then named Maria Bianchi as another of the night's guests with appropriate praise. "We also have with us tonight," she said, "perhaps the world's greatest photographer, Armando." The naming of each guest was met with strong audience applause.

Silvana then stated that the audience would see the debut of the new internet sensation, Troy Mazure, which just about burst the amps with audience applause and shouts of "Troy! Troy! Troy!" When Silvana was finally able to regain control of her show, she explained that Maria and Armando both had a hand in discovering this new phenom and would tell us how they had done it.

"As if that weren't enough," said Silvana, "we have some big, big surprises on tonight's show, so let's get started."

With a little "walking music," Silvana strode over to her Johnny Carson-style desk, sat down, and introduced Alessandro as her first guest of the evening. Alessandro first talked about his soccer career and then about his albums before announcing that he was working on a new album to be released next year. Silvana mentioned Troy, and Alessandro confirmed that he had just met Troy two days before and was very pleased to announce that Troy had agreed to record a duet with him for his new album, which drew huge applause from the audience.

Silvana then told the audience that it was time to meet the woman who had discovered this amazing new talent. Introduced as an old friend and frequent guest, Maria looked positively angelic in her white chiffon dress with black pearls and matching earrings. Silvana asked Maria to explain how she had discovered Troy, and Maria told the story of how she had gone to Texas to visit her boyfriend.

"Wait," said Silvana. "Is that your boyfriend sitting in the front row?" with the camera pivoting to zoom in on Mike. "So, Mike Murphy, famous American football player, world-renowned model, and the sexiest man alive is your boyfriend?"

"Yes, I do believe that he plays football now and then," Maria joked and then added coyly, "but he does have other talents as well." The audience snickered, Mom blushed, Dad tried in vain to suppress a devilishly prideful smirk, and Mike pretended not to have the slightest idea what she was referring to, which just endeared him to the audience even more.

Maria then went on to tell how she had heard Troy sing in his high school's annual spring concert, and "even though all of the students were very talented, Troy had completely stolen the show."

Silvana then told the audience that Troy was not only an amazing singer but that he was starting his own career as a model and that he had been discovered in that capacity by none other than Armando, who took his cue and entered through the curtain.

Armando explained that he had done a photoshoot for Denier (he had to get that plug in) with Mike in Hawaii where he discovered Mike's younger brother, Rick, and his friend Johnny. Before he could proceed, Silvana stopped him and singled out the two of us in the audience before revealing that she had seen some photographs of the young men in question. So, as Armando continued his tale, pictures of Mike, Johnny, and me flashed on the screen, some showing us very well dressed next to luxury sports cars and some showing us in underwear and swimsuits, which drew gasps, cheers, and whistles from the audience. I felt very self-conscious at that point, but Mike told me just to roll with it, so I did.

Armando continued to tell how he had met Troy when he came to the Andersen's house to photograph Johnny and me, and as he talked, the screen showed photographs of the three of us in tuxedos, business suits, and close-ups. Armando then described photographing the three of us at his studio in Rome.

"And that's when you filmed Troy singing 'O Sole Mio,' right?" And with that segue, she showed a short clip of the video. "Oh, but why watch the video" she asked, "when you can see and hear the real thing?"

Troy emerged from behind the curtains to uproarious applause. He was wearing a black-on-black jacquard tuxedo, and from the way his package bulged out, I could tell that he was wearing one of those pairs of underwear with the built-in C-ring.

In lieu of the standard stiff shirt, he wore a white silk form-fitting pullover that highlighted his rippling abs when he unbuttoned the coat. The deep V-neck featured a red-and-silver brocade strip trimming the Mandarin collar and plunging neckline, which accentuated the cleavage between his hairy, muscular pecs and pointed like Cupid's arrow toward his family jewels.

On his head, he wore a black leather cowboy hat with a black silk band around the crown. He simultaneously projected the formality one would expect at La Scala with the sex appeal of a country-rock star. He looked so fucking hot that I wanted to storm the stage and ravage him right there on national television—and I'm quite sure that I was not alone in that thought.

The music started, and Troy sang three or four bars of "O Sole Mio" before Silvana interrupted. "Wait, wait," she said. "In the video you were serenading a lovely young lady, were you not?" Troy acknowledged that he was, so Silvana pulled out a card and called the name of Ciara D'Amico, a teenager in the audience who shrieked at the sound of her name. When Silvana failed to coax her down to the stage, Troy walked out and offered his hand to lead her to the stage, where the crew had placed a stool for her to sit on.

Silvana cued the music a second time, and once again, she interrupted after Troy had sung just three or four bars. "You know," she told Troy, "we believe in equality on this show, so it would only be fair to have you serenade a young man as well as a young woman," and she called the name Victor Forte, a handsome young man about Troy's age who needed no coaxing. He sprang from his seat and sprinted to the stage even before the stage crew could bring out another stool.

Troy made a show of asking Silvana if he could "finally" sing now, and it suddenly hit me why he had spent so much time rehearsing with Maria for the show. This whole scene, though it all seemed totally unscripted and extemporaneous, had actually been thoroughly rehearsed—Troy's part anyway.

Troy sang the first verse of "O Sole Mio" in traditional Italian directly to Ciara. Many people in the audience sang along silently and fell in love with the handsome young rising star. As Troy serenaded Ciara, he pulled from his coat pocket a silk scarf that matched the brocade design on his shirt and draped it across her body and face before finally tying it loosely around her neck.

At the end of the first verse, the band stopped abruptly and then launched into a high-speed rock version that Troy sang in English to Victor. As he sang, he danced seductively around Victor, running his hands from Victor's knees up to his thighs, which left Victor panting for more. Troy yanked Victor's legs apart and vibrated between them. As he swung around Victor, he shimmied against his body and ended up behind him, sliding his hands over his captive's shoulders, across his chest, and down to his waist. Troy purred in Victor's ear and ruffled his hair before removing his cowboy hat to place it on Victor's head. At the end of that verse, Troy snatched the hat off of Victor's head and tossed it into his lap, which was a very clever maneuver since Victor looked like he was about to spooge through his pants on Italian national television.

Troy alternated this pattern between Ciara and Victor, in Italian and English (and occasionally in French and Spanish) until he came to a rapid-fire, tongue-twisting finish that evoked memories of *"Largo al factotum"* from Rossini's *The Barber of Seville* or Twista's "Overnight Celebrity."

At the completion of the song, the studio audience roared their approval as Troy kissed Ciara and Victor both on the cheek and whispered something to each of them. Ciara and Victor offered the scarf and hat back to Troy, but he insisted that they keep the souvenirs. He then led the two star-struck assistants to the front row and asked Johnny and me to escort them back to their seats.

Silvana met Troy center stage and invited him back to the couch next to her desk. Troy greeted Alessandro, Maria, and Armando before sitting down. As Silvana asked him about his background and his recent experiences as a singer and model, Troy responded like a pro, not only answering the questions, but drawing the audience into the interaction, just as he had done at Gay Pride.

"Well," said Silvana, "I could sit here and listen to you talk in that devastatingly sexy voice all evening, but I think our audience wants to hear you sing again," and the audience erupted with their approval.

"I would love to," said Troy, "but I also know that the audience is dying to hear Maria, so with your permission, I would like to ask her to join me in singing 'All I Ask of You' from *Phantom of the Opera.*" And with that, Troy took Maria's hand and led her center stage, where they killed it with their rendition of the Broadway classic.

Following the song and after Maria and Troy had re-taken their seats on the couch, Silvana began asking Troy about school, football, and his friends. "I think our audience would like to meet these friends of yours," said Silvana, much to my shock and Johnny's, "and while we're at it, Maria, why don't we bring that gorgeous boyfriend of yours up here as well." So, with the audience's unrelenting prodding, Mike, Johnny, and I went up and took seats on stools that had been set up behind the sofa.

Silvana took note of how nattily dressed we were and asked us to tell "who we were wearing," which was our cue to plug the designers who had loaned Armando the suits for us to wear. Later, our mothers would do the same for their dresses.

"Don't be fooled by the ugly jock faces," teased Troy. "They are much more than just three dumb jocks."

Silvana took that as her cue and questioned me about my goals of becoming a writer. She asked who my favorite writers were, so I named Oscar Wilde and George Bernard Shaw as my favorite playwrights, W. B. Yeats and Seamus Heaney as my favorite poets, and Jonathan Swift as my favorite satirist along with several contemporary writers.

"And novelists?" probed Silvana. "Joyce?"

"A great writer indeed," I concurred. "The closing paragraphs in 'The Dead' are among the most beautiful and poignant in all of English language literature, and *Ulysses* and *Finnegan's Wake* are masterpieces, but Joyce...well, he can be very challenging to the average reader."

"He?" interjected Johnny, looking like someone had just told him that the tooth fairy isn't real. "Joyce is a guy?"

Half of the audience gasped at his apparent stupidity, and the other half cracked up at his feigned naïveté.

"OK," said Troy, "so two of them are not just dumb jocks," which drew more laughter from the audience, and in no time, we were right into our usual form, completely forgetting that we were on a live national television show.

"So, you're not into the arts?" Silvana asked Johnny.

"Actually," said Johnny, "as I am sure you know, there has been a very long history of interplay between sports and the arts. All one has to do is to look at the sculptures of the Olympic athletes in Greece. Most people don't realize it, but when the Modern Olympics were initiated in 1896, medals were awarded for painting, sculpture, architecture, literature and music, along with those for the athletic competitions. For the first 40 years, a total of 151 medals were awarded to entries in the fine arts."

Johnny had wrapped Silvana and the entire audience around his little finger.

"But you don't have to go all the way to Greece to see the influence of sports on the arts. Just go to the Museo del Settecento Veneziano in Venice (The Museum of the Venetian Eighteenth Century) and take a look at Tiepolo's *Pulcinella and the Tumblers* or Umberto Boccioni's *Dynamism of a Cyclist* in the Guggenheim Collection."

Everyone was mesmerized, including me.

"Not only do sports influence the arts, but the arts influence sports," he continued. "Knute Rockne got the idea for the Notre Dame shift from watching the dancers in a burlesque show, athletes everywhere use music to help them focus, and what better amalgamation of sports and art is there than figure skating?"

I had the feeling that Johnny was just getting started.

"Oh, my," said Silvana. "Much more than a dumb jock indeed. We must have you come back and devote an entire show to this topic. Would you please do that?" Johnny agreed that he would, and the audience applauded their approval.

"So," she asked in a quick change of topic, "which one of you is the best football player?" Without skipping a beat all of us replied in unison, "Alessandro," which caught the soccer player by surprise and endeared the Italian audience to us forever.

Silvana said that she could easily see why Maria and Armando had been so taken with the four of us, and she segued, "Armando, I believe you were about to tell us about your new project."

"*Si*," said Armando, and as he began to describe his *Men of the World* project, the screen showed examples of photographs to be included in the new compilation. Close-up face shots alternated with full-body nudes of men from around the world, including Mike, Johnny, and me, and the final picture was of Troy posing in all his natural glory.

The camera alternated quickly between that photo and shots of Troy's mom sitting in the front row. Silvana grabbed a hand mic and walked toward Mrs. Mazure and asked her, "How do you feel seeing this picture of your son broadcast across Italy on nationwide television?"

Mrs. Mazure took a moment to collect herself and then said, "I feel as proud today as I did the day the doctor placed him in my arms for the first time." Half of the audience was almost moved to tears.

"You have a beautiful son," said Silvana, "and Armando has done him as much justice as any artist possibly could." Addressing the audience, she continued, "Earlier, I referred to Mike Murphy as "the sexiest man in the world. Sorry Mike," she said, "but I think you've got three very strong competitors for that title here."

Music from the band cut into the mood and cued Silvana. "Before we run out of time," she told the audience, "how about one more song from Troy and Maria?" and the audience cheered.

As the stage crew placed two stools again center stage, the band continued to play the intro to Lonestar's "Amazed," and Maria took Mike by the hand and led him to one of the stools as Troy took my hand and led me to the other. I don't know about Mike, but I was taken completely by surprise.

The band repeated the intro until we were in place, and then Maria sang the first verse to Mike with Johnny occasionally providing harmony. Then, Troy sang the second verse to me with Maria backing him up. They sang the third verse together and started to do the same with the fourth verse, but when they got to the second line, "I'm so in love with you," Troy got down on one knee and took my breath away. As he continued to serenade me, Maria faded back and left the spotlight to Troy, who, in turn, reflected it onto me as he finished the song. He left me on the verge of tears and the audience in dead silence. Mike broke the trance by clapping slowly, and then everyone else slowly joined in, crescendoing to a thunderous standing ovation.

As all the guests got up from their seats and gathered around us, Silvana announced that she had one last surprise for everyone, and on that cue, out walked Ben Cohen to uproarious applause. Ben greeted everyone and said that he had just invited Alessandro and Troy to participate in a fundraising concert he was putting together and that he hoped to convince Mike and Troy to pose for his fundraising calendar, much to the audience's pleasure. Troy grabbed the opportunity to plug Ben's foundation and urge everyone to support it. Silvana thanked Ben for coming and then thanked her other guests as the music took us out.

As everyone congratulated Troy on his incredible debut, Mike put his arm around my shoulders and spoke softly into my ear, "That's a remarkable man you've got there."

"Yes, I know," I said, fighting back my tears.

"If you don't hurry up and ask him to marry you," he prodded, "I will."

31 Dessert

As the ushers herded the members of the audience out of the theatre, I detected a bit of commotion at the exit. Ciara and Victor were trying to hold back as the ushers pressed them to leave. Since Troy was surrounded by family and friends, I slipped away and strode to the back of the theatre to see what was going on. The ushers told me that Ciara and Victor refused to leave, and Ciara and Victor told me that Troy had invited them to remain after the show. That must have been what he whispered to them after he sang to them. I assured the ushers that everything was all right, and I led Ciara and Victor down to the stage and seated them on the couch.

As soon as I was able to free Troy from his admirers, I nodded toward the couple sitting on the couch. Troy immediately called them over to join the crowd. He again thanked them for their participation and took Ciara by the hand. He called Johnny over and introduced the two of them. Johnny seemed pleased to have the attention of a young lady instead of all of his queer friends, and Ciara practically gushed at the opportunity to meet such a handsome American athlete who was now a TV celebrity.

Then, Troy took Victor by the hand and introduced him to The Outlaws, who, ironically, fawned all over Victor because he got to be serenaded by Troy. They kept telling him how envious they were of him.

We had eaten only a light lunch and were all starving, so when Rob announced that a private dining room was waiting for us back at the hotel, everyone was eager to jump into the limousines that Rob had arranged to take us back. Ben and Alessandro made their apologies and took a rain check, but Ciara and Victor nearly jumped out of their skins when Troy invited them to join us.

As we exited the building, we were mobbed by adoring fans as well as reporters and paparazzi from international outlets as well as across Italy. Troy and I had begun to get used to such attention, but for our moms, it was a new experience, and they seemed impressed with how well we handled the situation. Eventually, most of us managed to slip into the waiting limousines.

Ciara and Victor had come to the opera house in their own respective cars, so Johnny rode back to the hotel with Ciara in her Alfa Romeo, and Little Cherry rode with Victor in his Maserati. Since Ciara lived in Turin, and Victor lived in Modena, a two-hour drive at best, Rob offered to secure rooms for them at the hotel for the night, but both politely declined. They evidently had other plans.

In the private dining room, the hotel staff had indeed laid out an Italian feast complete with sparkling prosecco along with a dangerous dessert buffet offering (among other things) several varieties of tiramisu, cannoli, panna cotta, and gelato.

Even as hungry as I was, what I really wanted to do was to drag Troy to our suite and make love to him like he had never been loved before, and as soon as dinner was over, that's exactly what I did.

Johnny invited Ciara to take a stroll with him, and they ended up in his room. The Outlaws invited Victor to go bar hopping with them, and they all eventually ended up...well, more about that later.

I began ripping off Troy's clothes even before we got back to our room—on the private elevator, in fact. He was still wearing that sexy outfit that he wore on the show—minus the cowboy hat, which, of course, he had given to Victor as a memento. Before I peeled off those tight black pants, I just had to rub my face all over that fucking hot bulge. And, of course, I had to run my fingers and tongue across the hairs flaring out of the V-neck shirt.

Once I got him stripped, I dragged him into the shower. As much as I enjoyed licking the sweat off his now-famous naked body, I understood that he was impatient to get clean so that we could work up a new sweat. I was torn between bathing him slowly and lovingly or scrubbing him down as quickly as possible. I toweled him off quickly and ushered him into bed, where I resumed the tongue bath I had commenced earlier.

I wanted to take my time showing him how much I loved and worshipped him, but I couldn't help myself. I was on fire with passion and just had to take him and fuck him like a wild animal in heat. I pumped hard and fast—harder and faster than I had ever fucked anyone before. To the extent that I could think at all, I rationalized that I could take it slowly and lovingly the next time. And so, I shot my wad deep into him and crashed on top of his fuckingly sexy, hot, hairy body.

Half an hour later, when I had painstakingly become somewhat human again, I apologized for my impatience, but Troy just laughed and assured me that he had thoroughly enjoyed my manic attack. "You can fuck me like that anytime," he assured me.

Now, however, it was time to give him the sweet love that I wanted to give him and that he had so thoroughly earned. I kissed him gently on the lips and then moved quickly to the other end. I licked the bottoms of his feet and sucked each toe one by one. Then, I licked all the way from his ankles to his perineum, which I swabbed to his delight as much as mine. I bathed his balls with my saliva, gently taking each nut into my mouth one at a time.

I lifted his muscular legs over my shoulders and probed his treasure trove with my eager tongue. It seemed that I might bring him to a climax with that maneuver alone, but there was more to come.

I licked the length of his cock with one slow, tormenting stroke. The twitching of his dick told me that he wanted more, much more, but it was not yet time.

I brushed my cheek against his beautiful cock and buried my face in his luscious bush. I so badly wanted to fellate every single hair on his hirsute body, drawing electric shocks to every follicle until his entire body exploded into a delirious stupor.

Moving upward, I sucked and nibbled on each nipple, which I had learned were hard-wired to his cock.

I painted his face with an abundance of butterfly kisses, licked them all off, and then painted a second coat. I kissed his sweet lips and tasted his delicious tongue until I thought our lips and tongues would melt into one.

"Are you ready?" I whispered devilishly into his ear.

"If you don't hurry up and fuck me," he almost screamed, "I'll roll you over and fuck the shit out of you."

Hmm. Maybe I'll take a rain check on that offer.

I slid back down to his crotch, took his cock into my mouth, and savored the taste and feel of it until Troy simply couldn't take it anymore.

With his ass lips already wet with my saliva and his juices, I slid my big cock into his desperate hole. Unlike the last time, I didn't just fuck him. I made slow, intense love to him, pausing occasionally to lean forward and kiss his sweet lips again. Periodically, I interjected fast, aggressive thrusts just to keep him on his toes, which, by the way, remained curled up through the entire episode.

Continuing to massage his prostate, I slowly brushed the back of my index finger along the thick vein running the length of his penis.

As I approached my own orgasm, I reached for his cock to jerk him off, but he beat me to the punch, erupting hands free like a volcano, spewing the contents of his nut sack all over his face and body. I followed immediately with a series of eruptions of my own, blasting my love seed deep into his gut.

Seeing stars (as I'm sure Troy was too), I collapsed on top of my lover, squishing his thick cream between us and resting my face next to his cum-coated cheek. As I began to fall asleep on top of him with my manhood still nested inside him, time and space evaporated, and our bodies, our minds, and our souls morphed together into a single, sanctified essence.

When I awoke the next morning, I desperately wanted to make love to Troy again, but I really had to pee, so I decided to take care of that urge first. As I was walking back to the bed, I heard a faint thud in the adjacent sitting room. When I went to investigate, I discovered Victor sprawled out naked on one of the couches and a mass of naked bodies piled into a heap on the floor, resembling a homoerotic Rorschach or something out of the *Kama Sutra*.

I counted six additional bodies, four of whom were The Outlaws. I didn't recognize the other two, but it began to make sense when I spotted two bell-boy uniforms mixed in the pile of clothes in the corner, which might explain how they all got into our room in the middle of the night. One of the creatures had evidently rolled over in his sleep, knocking an ashtray off the coffee table and onto the carpeted floor, which was the thud that had caught my attention in the first place.

I instantly popped a boner, and it seemed that I wasn't the only one. One body in the pile, most likely the one who had knocked over the ash tray, began to squirm like a worm in search of a hole. When he found one, he inserted his penis, but nothing more happened. I don't know if he was just too far gone or if he had forgotten his mission.

I needed to find a hole myself, but where to choose? Should I go back to my bed with Troy...or Victor...or should I just take advantage of the opportunities that lay before me? Decisions, decisions.

I decided to go back to my lover in the bedroom when I tripped over one of the bodies on the floor, falling with my stiff dick and itching balls smashed into someone's face. The shock was enough to rouse the poor victim, but he didn't seem too aggrieved since he instinctively took my cock into his mouth and began sucking like a starving calf. Before I even realized what had happened, my balls emptied their load into his mouth and all over his face. I retrieved what I could from his mouth and licked up the rest from his face, but rather than swallowing it, I made the rounds of the bodies on the floor, apportioning drops onto the face of each man. I thought it would be a hoot to have them wake up and wonder how they had gotten cum on their faces and whose it was. I also couldn't help but laugh at the thought of the hotel maids walking in and finding all those naked men sprawled out on the floor with dried cum on their faces.

32 Murphy's Law

Troy was so far out of it when I got back into the bedroom that I practically had to carry him to the shower. When he finally woke up, I reminded him that our mothers would be going home the next day, so we had only one day to show them the sights of Milan. Of course, we couldn't let them leave Milan without seeing Leonardo's *The Last Supper*, and we spent the rest of the day at Sforzesco Castle.

Later that afternoon when we got back to the hotel, I asked the concierge for recommendations on where to spend a fun evening. "Do you know Murphy's Law?" she asked me.

"Of course," I replied. "Whatever can go wrong will, but wh—"

"Not that Murphy's Law," she laughed. "It's an Irish pub just a few blocks from here."

So, we went to Murphy's Law Pub and had a grand time before going to dinner at Cracco, one of Milan's finest restaurants.

The next morning, before saying goodbye to our moms, we had the pleasure of their company at our morning planning session, where the news was fast and overwhelming. *What day is it now? Oh, yeah. Monday. I think.*

"It seems that our efforts are paying off," proclaimed Mike.

"Yes," chimed in Maria. "Silvana called me this morning to inform me that the show Saturday night not only won the ratings race for that time slot, but it was the highest rated episode her show has ever recorded. What's more, her website almost crashed because so many people logged in to view clips from the show and register their comments, which were overwhelmingly positive."

Of course, we were all thrilled, but we suppressed our giddiness so as not to cause our mothers to think we were letting the notoriety go to our heads.

"That's not all," added Rob. "Armando has some news to share as well."

"*Si*," said Armando. "We are going back to Turin tomorrow. The executives of Fiat and their subsidiaries want to meet with you to discuss possible endorsements."

At that point, we could no longer contain our excitement. High fives all around. "I'm calling dibs on the Maserati contract," teased Johnny.

"Jonathan!" cautioned Mrs. Andersen.

It was all I could do not to chide, "Yeah, cool it, Luuu Ellen."

"Don't worry, Mom," he boasted. "I'll get you one too."

Everyone had to laugh at that, but Mike quickly brought us back down to earth. "Don't count your Maseratis before they hatch. We're going to hear what they have to say. They may or may not make any of you an offer, but if they do, we'll discuss it and decide how best to proceed." That comment reassurred our mothers but felt like a bucket of cold water on us guys. It was like being edged to the brink of an orgasm only to have the hand slapped away. Still, we all trusted Mike to navigate us through the negotiations.

Following the strategy session, we took our mothers to the airport for their flights back home and returned to the hotel to plan what we were going to wear, say, and do for the trip to Fiat Headquarters in Turin. By the time we got back to our hotel rooms, all the party guests (Ciara, Victor, the Outlaws, and the bellboys) had left, so we just chilled and dreamed of luxury sports cars.

When we arrived at the Fiat Headquarters the next day, we were met by quite a surprise—two of them actually.

"Victor! Ciara! What are you doing here?" we all asked, almost in unison.

"When we found out that you were coming today, we asked Security if we could escort you to your meeting."

"That's great," said Troy, "but how—"

But before they could explain, security guards began ushering us toward a conference room. Victor introduced Troy and me to his mother, and Ciara said to Johnny, "I want to introduce you to my grandfather when he—"

And with that all eyes turned to the distinguished-looking older gentleman who breezed into the room and sat at the head of the conference table. The other executives claimed their respective seats, and Ciara and Victor led us to the remaining empty seats at the table.

The nameplate in front of the distinguished gentleman read, "Chairman, Christian D'Amico." I thought Johnny was going to fall out of his chair when Ciara leaned over and whispered, "My grandfather."

As we went around the table, each person introducing himself or herself, we learned that Victor's mother, Aurora Forte, was vice president for marketing at Maserati.

The one person who sat at the back of the room instead of at the table was Armando, who tried to suppress a smug little smile. All of a sudden, pieces of the puzzle began to fall into place. Ciara and Victor were not chosen at random for the TV show as we had all believed. Armando had engineered it. No doubt he knew everyone in the room and many of their families, so he had arranged for Silvana to call their names. I flashed Armando a knowing look, but he just reciprocated with a look that admonished me to focus on the current meeting and the business at hand.

Chairman D'Amico began by welcoming us all to Fiat and invited us to take a tour of the facilities while we were there. He confessed that he had not seen Silvana's show on Saturday night, but his granddaughter had told him what a marvelous time she had there and had insisted that he watch the recording her parents had made, which he subsequently did. On top of that, he had gotten a call from Signora Forte with a similar report from her son Victor. "It is because of their insistence that we are all here today," he conceded.

"I must tell you, young man," he said to Troy, "you are exceptionally talented and very photogenic, and you three (gesturing to Mike, Johnny, and me) are equally handsome and articulate and obviously intelligent. These are all qualities that we admire and respect here at Fiat and that could potentially benefit us.

"Signora Forte," he continued, "and our other marketing executives have been pushing us—pushing me (he smirked)—to develop new marketing campaigns aimed at younger consumers. It seems that I have a reputation around here of being somewhat old-fashioned and too conservative—" a few snickers peppered the room—"which is why I am not yet sold on this concept," he asserted. "However, I have confidence in our marketing teams, and for that reason, I am directing them to proceed with talks with the four of you to see what they can come up with. They will report back to me, and we'll see where we might go from there." And with that, he rose and left the room with the promise to meet up with us again over lunch.

"Before we get down to business," said the vice chairman, who had taken the gavel, so to speak, "I think we should all get better acquainted." On cue, caterers began bringing coffee and other refreshments into the room. Someone flipped a switch that caused an entire wall to open up to a great room resembling the lobby of a five-star resort. The other executives began mingling with us, engaging in small talk and quizzing us about the TV show and the subsequent response.

After an hour or so of this socializing, the vice chairman announced that it was time to get down to business and that Signora D'Amico would now take charge. The vice chairman and several other executives then exited the room and left us with the marketing executives from Fiat and its various subsidiaries. Mike, Maria, and Armando had all had experience with TV commercials and other forms of advertising, so they shared the lead for "our team." Johnny, Troy, and I were not mere bystanders, however. We were asked many questions, and we offered forthright answers.

After two hours of mostly brainstorming, we were met once again by Chairman D'Amico in the executive dining room for lunch, which was as good as any meal we had already enjoyed in Italy. Lunch was followed by a tour of the facilities and an account of the history of the company, including how it had come to acquire its various brands.

Johnny, Troy, and I were dying to ask, "So what about the endorsements? Are we getting contracts or not?" But Mike pulled us aside and explained that we had to be patient and let the process work its way through the system. "Corporate decisions of this magnitude," he said, "can take months—even longer. We're off to a great start," he said, "but we don't want to ruin it by pressing too hard." It was like being told that Christmas is really just around the corner when we wanted to see Santa right now. We had gotten too accustomed to instant gratification.

The next morning we gathered again for our daily briefing, which consisted mostly of everyone sharing what he thought about the meeting at Fiat. It was Wednesday, and we would be leaving on Saturday morning for our return to the States. Mike was about to discuss our plans for the remaining three days when Rob entered the room and mumbled something to him. Mike smiled and gave him a thumbs up.

"Troy," he continued, "you will continue with your language and music lessons. Maria may have some things for you to work on at the academy.

"Rick," he paused as if to figure out what to say, "you're free until we leave Saturday." And then he sighed, "And try to stay out of trouble, OK?" Troy and Johnny loved that one. "And Johnny," he continued. "Go pack your bags. You're going on a little trip with Rob."

We were all as bemused by that announcement as Johnny, who, for the first time I had ever witnessed, seemed at a loss for words. Finally, he asked, "Where am I going? Did I do something wrong?"

Mike just held his fake stern demeanor and replied, "Just go with Rob, and he will explain everything."

Johnny just sat there confused and maybe just a tad scared.

"Go!" Mike snapped. "Go with Rob. Now!"

As Johnny got up to follow Rob, the rest of us just looked at each other to see if they had any clue as to what was going on. I saw Mike throw a faint nod to Armando, who responded by getting up immediately and following Rob and Johnny.

Once the trio were out of sight and earshot, Mike and Maria lost it. They broke down laughing.

"Did you see that look on his face?"

"Poor kid. He looked like he was being exiled to Siberia."

"Or to the gas chamber."

"Mike," Troy and I kept interrupting. "What the hell is going on?"

"Relax," said Mike. "We're just messing with him a bit. Fact is, Rob has arranged for Johnny to meet with some executives at Volkswagen in Germany, so they're going up there for a couple of days. It will be very similar to the meetings we just had at Fiat, but they wanted a little more time with him. So, rather than return here, they will meet up with us at JFK in New York before we all go home together."

Aha! That's why Armando followed them. He's going to prep Johnny's wardrobe for the trip.

"Wow!" I exclaimed. "I don't know whether to be thrilled or jealous."

"Well," said Mike. "You can go with them if you want. You're free to do whatever you want from now until Saturday."

After pausing for a brief second or two, I leaped out of my chair and took off after Johnny, Rob, and Armando.

As Mike had forecast, the meetings at Volkswagen were pretty much the same as the ones at Fiat, only more extensive. They seemed to want to know everything about us right down to what kind of toothpaste we used. They might as well have asked what brand of condom we preferred.

33 Contracts

By the time we got back home to Hilldale on Sunday, we were all exhausted. Still, I was actually looking forward to getting back to my chores on the farm. Weird, huh?

I was also glad to see my teammates at football camp again. Of course, the guys all wanted to know all about our adventures...and our conquests, which we made sound as thrilling as we could without giving away too much information.

The new kid that Johnny had told us about seemed nice, if a bit rough around the edges. Though he was inexperienced in football, he had run track back in Pennsylvania and proved to be good at handling the ball, so Coach assigned him to back up Johnny as wide receiver.

Like Troy, Sam was a transplant from a big city, Philadelphia. Troy took to Sam in an instant and took him under his wing. Troy and I had agreed that we would have an open relationship, but I have to admit that I felt a slight tinge of jealousy.

That wasn't the only thing about Troy that seemed to have changed, though. He just didn't seem to have quite the passion for the game that he had demonstrated before. And I wasn't the only one who noticed. Coach had to ride him a little harder than before. We won our first few games, but they were squeakers.

Mike saw it too. Mike wasn't going to make it to Johnny's and my annual birthday bash because of his own game schedule, but the 49ers had no game the weekend before, so Mike flew in for an early celebration, and he went to our game that night. Before the kickoff, the principal announced over the loudspeaker that a distinguished alumnus was in the stadium and asked Mike to come to the press box and say a few words.

The principal asked Mike what he thought about his younger brother, and Mike answered that he was very proud, but then he also mentioned Johnny, Troy, and even Sam and talked about the importance of teamwork. "You don't win games with one or two good players," he said, "or even three or four. It takes the whole team working together."

The following week, we saw a noticeable improvement in Troy's performance. He had the passion again—and that passion was not limited to the field. Sex that night was hotter than it had been since we returned from Italy. I called Mike to thank him for what he had said since I thought that was what had lit the fuse under Troy.

"Well, maybe," said Mike, "but I suspect that most of the credit goes to Rob."

"Rob?" I asked, incredulously. "Why Rob?"

Mike explained that Rob had had a chat with Troy and reminded him of how supportive you and Johnny had been with regard to his music career. "Don't you think they deserve the same level of commitment from you when it comes to their football?" he asked Troy.

That weekend we had our joint birthday party at the Andersens' house again. It seemed like everybody in the state wanted to attend, but the Andersens drew the line. As I said, Mike couldn't be there, but Maria was there, and so was Rob, who had made so many trips to see Sarah Mazure that we teased him that he was going to have to get a Texas driver's license.

We got the usual birthday presents, and that year there were also birthday cards from Ciara, Victor, the Outlaws, Silvana, Alessandro, Ben Cohen, photographers Armando, Nic, and Claude, and even the chairmen of Fiat and Volkswagen.

When it seemed that we had opened all the presents, Rob stood up and announced that Mike had asked him to deliver his presents for him, and with that, he plopped two very thick file folders on the table, one for Johnny and one for me.

"What's that?" we asked.

"Contracts," he said. "Modeling contracts."

Flipping through the folders, we found contracts to model for wines, perfumes, men's fashions, cars (Fiat for Johnny and Volkswagen for me), and more. I suspect that Ciara had something to do with Johnny's getting the Fiat contract, and I'm glad that I decided to go with Johnny and Rob to those VW meetings.

"Now, let me emphasize," said Rob. "These are modeling contracts, not endorsement contracts." Seeing the puzzled looks on all our faces, Rob explained, "You will appear in a number of TV commercials and magazine ads as models, but you will not be pitching the products. The companies thought you would be fantastic models for their products, but your celebrity has been just a flash in the pan...so far. Once you graduate from high school and become college football standouts, it will be a different story. There was a lot of optimism that you would achieve that status, but you haven't yet. *Yet*," he emphasized.

"Now," Rob continued, "the contracts are very similar, but the ones with Fiat (he looked at Johnny) and Volkswagen (he addressed me) have a clause that the others do not. It's an options clause."

"What does that mean?" asked Mrs. Andersen.

"Well, it means that they have the option to sign you up for endorsement contracts, which will be much more lucrative, if they wish to do so any time within the next four years. If another car company offers you a contract during that time, you are not prohibited from accepting it, but you have to give them first right of refusal. If they don't want you anymore, you're a free agent, so to speak. But if they do want you, they'll have to make it worth your while...and that's when the really big bucks kick in."

"Wait a minute," interjected Dad. "I seem to recall that Mike was not allowed to accept anything but his football scholarship when he was in college...no money...no gifts...it was an NCAA rule."

"That's right," Rob agreed, "but that's why it's important that these guys sign the contracts now...if they want to do this, of course...because that NCAA rule does not apply to *prior* employment. In other words, if they agree to these contracts now (or before they sign with a college), they're home free. You could think of it as an insurance policy. You might not make a ton of money now, but if they decide to make you a star in their advertising, you can make all the money you want even if you're on a football scholarship."

"Cool," I blurted out, picking up on the word that Johnny always used when we first met. Yet, I could see the wheels turning in Johnny's head.

"Does this mean that I won't get my Maserati?"

"Oh, Johnny," chided Mrs. Andersen as she slapped her son with a seat cushion.

"Actually," said Rob. "You can. You have to be the luckiest guys in the world. I don't know how he does it, but your buddy's brother is the most amazing negotiator I have ever seen. He told those companies that you would only agree to the contracts if they included the loan of a new car each year."

"So, Rick gets a VW, and I get a Fiat?" Johnny pouted.

"You're not listening to me," said Rob. "Rick can have his choice of any car from the VW line except a Lamborghini or Bugatti, which sell for over a million dollars each. In other words, he can have any Volkswagen, Audi, Bentley, or Porsche. And you, my man, can choose any Fiat, Alfa Romeo, Chrysler, Dodge, Jeep, or Ram truck. Oh," he added, almost as an afterthought, "you can't have a Ferrari, but you can have...(pausing again for dramatic effect)...a Maserati."

At that news, Johnny flew out of his seat and mimicked a pro football player dancing in the end zone after scoring the winning touchdown at the Super Bowl.

All this time, Troy had sat quietly, though not impatiently, to hear what might be in store for him.

"Troy," Rob said with a deep breath, "your situation is different, and I'm going to let Maria tell you about that, because she had as much to do with negotiating for you as Mike did, and Armando played a significant role as well."

With that introduction, Maria reached beside the chair she was sitting in and produced a briefcase, from which she removed a very thick folder and plopped it on the table in front of Troy. "As Rob said," she began, "Rick and Johnny are not perceived as celebrities...not yet, but I am convinced that will change and quite possibly before they sign pro football contracts...but you, Troy, you are already a star. Every marketing executive we talked to whole-heartedly agreed, and they were falling all over each other to get you to be their exclusive spokesperson. The contracts in this folder, consequently, are endorsement contracts. In other words, as Rob put it, 'big bucks.'"

As Troy clenched his teeth in anticipation, Mrs. Mazure squeezed her son's arm and asked, "How much is 'big bucks'?"

"Well," Maria replied, "if Troy were to accept every single contract in this folder, we would be talking about at least ten million dollars a year—"

Everyone gasped, and Mom put her arm around Mrs. Mazure to secure her.

"...and that doesn't even include the recording contracts, which we are still negotiating. But," Maria hastened to add, "in order to do that, Troy would have to quit school immediately and devote himself full time to these requirements, and I don't recommend that and neither does Mike. As he put it, Troy should be going for the long game, not the quick win. He can do some work while he finishes high school and college, and when he graduates, he'll be worth even more, I have no doubt."

After everyone had collected their thoughts, Rob again took the floor. "Obviously, there's a lot to think about here. Before you do anything, you need to read these contracts very carefully. Make notes of any questions you may have. We'll all sit down together and go over them with a fine-tooth comb, and then we'll go from there."

In all the excitement, everyone seemed to have forgotten that we were together to celebrate two birthdays. Ordinarily, I would have celebrated in Troy's bed, but he really needed to go home and talk all of this over with his family, and Johnny and I needed to do the same with ours. I took consolation in the fact that Troy and I had fucked our brains out the night before and again that morning before the party. *If you think he's a star on stage, you should see how well he performs in bed!*

When Mom, Dad, and I got home with Maria (she stayed in the guest house), we got on the phone with Mike as soon as possible. He urged us to take our time with the contracts. "You don't have to rush any of this, and you (meaning me) remember what I've taught you: Never take your eye off the ball," which meant that I should not neglect my schoolwork or lose sight of my goal to become a writer.

Though Troy and I could not be together that night, he called, and with his sultry voice we ended up having the most incredible phone sex.

34 Commencements

When he could get away, Mike would fly home on Sundays after his games to work with us and fly back the next day. By the end of football season—ours, not his—Johnny, Troy, and I had signed several, but not all, of the contracts. When Thanksgiving break came around, we were all off to work. Troy flew to New York, where he spent one day filming a TV commercial and two days recording songs in the studio with Maria. Johnny and I flew to Mexico for a photoshoot.

Johnny and I continued to double date occasionally, but less and less as time went by. He was becoming more selective about whom he slept with, preferring quality over quantity, which just meant that he was fucking fewer girls but fucking them more often.

Of course, Troy and I continued to sleep together, but not as often as before. He was often busy studying scripts for TV commercials or going over songs he would be recording. Sam seemed to miss Troy's company too, so he and I often consoled each other.

Dad knew that I would be going away to college the following fall, so we spent a good deal of our time mentoring Carlos to take on a larger role on the farm. When I first hired him, I became aware that he had taken several college courses with an eye toward a degree in agricultural business, and without our knowledge, Mike paid for him to take further courses.

Carlos excelled at using the computer programs Mike had shown us to develop better irrigation strategies and other farming techniques. The result was greater crop yield and reduced costs. Dad was so pleased that come springtime, he gave Carlos the title of foreman, empowered him to hire two more farm-hands, and let him move from the bunkhouse to the adjacent guest suite.

The week before Christmas, Johnny, who had already been named a high school All-American, signed to play football at Stanford University. He could have picked any college in the country, but he picked Stanford because they had one of the best biomedical engineering programs in the country.

I too was offered football scholarships at a number of universities, and I decided to accept the offer from the University of Southern California (USC). I was actually tempted to pass up football scholarships and just go for an academic scholarship to focus exclusively on creative writing, but I reasoned that some notoriety as a football standout would do more to promote my modeling career and provide the financial security I would need to pursue a career as a writer. Besides, USC is known to have one of the best creative writing programs in the country.

And, of course, it was a foregone conclusion that Troy would be going to Julliard in the fall.

Spring break saw Troy back in New York filming and recording, and Johnny and I were off to Aruba and the Virgin Islands to model swimsuits with Mike.

Maria came to Troy's last spring concert at Hilldale High, but she told Ms. Garcia, the choir director, that she was only there to observe and enjoy the concert, not to sing. She did not want to distract from the real stars of the show, she said, the students. Ms. Garcia did manage to convince her, though, to introduce Troy's one and only solo.

"Rossini's 'Largo al Factotum' from *Figaro*," she told the audience, "is one of the most difficult arias in opera, not only because it requires a very broad vocal range, but also absolute precision in scales and arpeggio. It is also something of a tongue twister, even for native speakers of Italian. It is a remarkable challenge for the most experienced singers, but I can assure you that Troy Mazure is up to the challenge. Ladies and gentlemen, please welcome Troy Mazure."

Much to our surprise, Sam did not attend the spring recital, so Troy, Johnny, and I swung by his house afterward to see if he was all right. He wasn't. He was torn up inside, having just learned from his dad that his company was sending him back to Philadelphia and that he would not be able to finish school at Hilldale High. Without making any promises, we said we would see if there was anything we could do.

The next day, we called an emergency meeting of our Italian Tuxedos Club and informed our parents of Sam's dilemma. They had all become rather fond of Sam and called his parents to invite them to join us at the Andersens' house to discuss the matter. Sam's parents said they knew that Sam did not want to go back to Philadelphia, but what could they do?

To that, both the Andersens and my parents offered to let Sam live with them while he finished school. When Sam's parents objected that they could not impose on our generosity like that, Dad countered that it would not be an imposition because Sam would have to earn his room and board by helping out on the farm. And the Andersens said that Sam could stay at their house on those nights when he had football games. Sam practically jumped out of his skin at the proposal and insisted that he would work and study harder than he ever had before (and he did).

When Sam's parents moved back to Philadelphia at the end of the school year, Sam moved to our farm. Mom and Dad offered him my old room or the one I had inherited from Mike, but he insisted on living in the bunkhouse. If he was going to work with the farmhands, he reasoned, he should live with them. Of course, Troy and I suspected that there was more to Sam's offer to sleep with the farmhands than he let on, but we said nothing. We didn't have to. My parents understood.

Mom and Dad agreed to let Sam live in the bunkhouse but said that he could use one of the spare bedrooms in the house as a study whenever he wanted. Of course, Dad's insistence that Sam work off his room and board was just a ploy to convince his parents to let him stay, but Sam took it to heart and did chores with surprising vigor.

Troy was my date for the senior prom, and we capped off the night with hot sex, but it was hot mostly because we were a couple of horny teenagers with raging hormones.

At the end of the school year, Johnny was named class valedictorian, and I was named salutatorian. On the night of our graduation, we didn't really have time to celebrate. A limousine picked up the three of us and took us to the airport, where we caught a flight to New York for a few days of modeling and then to London, where Troy appeared in Ben Cohen's fundraising concert. The timing couldn't have been better because he was able to announce to a worldwide audience that his first album was now available for purchase.

After Troy sang a medley of love songs that included opera, rock, and pop and then a duet with Alessandro, Ben ushered Johnny and me onto the stage, where we made a pitch for everyone to call in their pledges to Ben's foundation. All of this was part of Maria's plan to speed up Johnny's status and mine as celebrities and not just sexy bodies.

After the concert, we joined forces with Victor, Ciara, and the Outlaws, who had flown up for the concert. Johnny had "reunion sex" with Ciara, and the rest of us had an orgy in Troy's suite along with a few fans that Troy had picked up along the way. As I lay spent and watched others fuck my lover, who never seemed to tire of one more dick up his ass, I replayed a question that had become more and more nettlesome to my mind. I had always been a top. But what was it like to be the bottom? Why did Troy (or any guy) find that more gratifying than being the one doing the pumping? It was a question that would have to wait just a bit longer for an answer.

From London, we flew to Rome, where Troy and Johnny taped separate appearances for future airings of Silvana's TV show. Johnny's appearance was the fulfillment of his promise to return for an extended discussion of the intersection of sports and the arts, and Troy, of course, sang and talked about his sudden stardom.

That fall, Johnny, Troy, and I went off to our respective colleges, Johnny to Stanford, Troy to Julliard, and me to USC. When Johnny told me of his intent to complete his degree in three years instead of four, I took it as a challenge and pledged to beat him. For a fleeting moment I even considered daring to graduate with a higher grade point average (GPA), but I quickly realized that such a gamble would be foolish.

Johnny's college football career started off much like his high school career. In high school he was put in the game when the starting wide receiver got injured. At Stanford he got put in when the starting wide receiver crapped out. The team was trailing 35-0 at the half, and even though Stanford still lost to Oregon, Johnny was able to pull his team to within 7 points, so he took over as the first-string wide receiver for the rest of the season.

At USC, our starting halfback just mysteriously disappeared halfway through the season. He later turned up at a small Baptist college back east. I never really knew what had happened, but practically every man on the team congratulated me on becoming the starting halfback. Apparently, even though the other guy was a pretty good player, for some reason he really wasn't very well liked.

With Troy out of the house that fall, Sarah Mazure, his mother, accepted a marriage proposal from Rob and moved to Switzerland with him. When she is not globe-trotting with her dashing husband, she devotes much of her time consulting with the World Health Organization, based in Geneva.

Johnny's parents and mine remained in Hilldale, but Carlos took over management of the day-to-day operations of the farm, and Sam took up residence in the bunkhouse after his parents moved back to Philadelphia. He replaced Johnny as first-string wide receiver and burnt up the field. There was talk of the Heisman Trophy and predictions that he would be the next Jerry Rice, but he hadn't even finished high school yet.

Troy was already a star in the entertainment world and was well on his way to becoming a super star. Johnny and I were not yet considered celebrities as far as the advertising and marketing worlds were concerned, but that was about to change.

Around Thanksgiving of our freshman year in college, Troy released his first album, Ben Cohen released his calendar, and Armando released his book *Men of the World* just in time for holiday gift shopping, and all of them broke sales records. Armando told me later that whenever he would travel and see his book on display, it was usually opened to my page, probably because I had "the biggest dick of all the models."

When Armando's book came out and people started realizing that two of the models were now freshmen football players at Stanford and USC, a group of fundamentalist preachers went berserk. They demanded that we be removed from our respective teams and even expelled. But when early sales of tickets for the next season's home games spiked, the presidents of Stanford and USC issued statements pointing out that their art departments often hired people to pose nude for courses in sketching, painting, and photography. They also said that they found nothing distasteful in Armando's work. Finally, they pointed out that Johnny and I were adults and fully capable of making our own decisions about our modeling careers, and they implied that we had demonstrated more maturity than the complaining preachers.

The protest from the preachers actually accelerated our drive toward celebrity status. *Sports*

Illustrated featured us on its cover with the heading "Big Men on Campus." Of course, that phrase is usually applied to college men who are deemed to be very popular and perhaps even influential, but much of the chatter on social media also suggested that the term referred to the size of our dongs, especially mine. My teammates at USC never let me hear the end of that.

The cover photo showed us in shoulder pads, but inside, they showed some of the photos that Armando and Nic tad taken of us in gyms and on the simulated Olympic medal stands.

Not to be outdone, *Cosmopolitan* featured us pictured on the cover wearing only jockstraps. Inside they actually included some of Armando's photos with us naked, but they were the ones where our genitals were obscured.

The article included interviews with our mothers as well as Maria and even some of the girls we had dated in high school and college. The editor later told us that they had to "tone down" some of the things they heard from the girls. "We do like to push the envelope," she told us, "but we can only push it so far."

Entertainment Weekly focused on our relationship with the emerging superstar Troy Mazure as well as Ben Cohen and Alessandro Del Piero. They even interviewed Silvana Serafini and included snapshots of our appearances on her show.

Our pictures also appeared on the covers of other magazines in Europe, South America, and Asia as well as the United States with stories featuring various perspectives: health and fitness, sports, the arts, religion, LGBT rights, and, of course, sex.

With our newly emerging stardom, Mike went straight to work renegotiating our modeling contracts. Volkswagen had initially intended to use me as an extra in commercials for Volkswagen and basic Audi vehicles, but after the release of *Men of the World* and our cover story in *Sports Illustrated,* they decided to feature me in ads for top-of-the-line Audi models and even Porsches.

Fiat rushed out a series of TV commercials featuring Johnny as a cowboy promoting Ram trucks. (He's from Texas, so he must be a cowboy, right?) The first series followed a basic format in four parts, what were called Work, Motion, Play, and Emotion.

Work consisted of Johnny—shirtless, of course—performing a variety of tasks on a ranch (loading or unloading hay, firewood, fence posts, or other supplies or gear).

Motion showed him driving a Ram truck over rough terrain, dirt roads, or muddy trails or hauling a horse trailer. A segue flipped between shots of another cowboy (played by Sam—also shirtless) washing down the truck and Johnny showering—with the camera focusing alternately on close-ups of Johnny's bare muscles and various features of the truck.

Play featured Johnny, now all cleaned up and dressed appropriately, picking up his beautiful date and taking her in the now-shiny truck to a line dance, the opera, a restaurant, a campground, or the beach.

Finally, *Emotion* showed Johnny retrieving a blanket from the truck and wrapping it around his date on a cold night in front of a campfire, lying in the bed of the truck looking up at the stars, or parking the truck in front of her house and kissing her goodnight on the doorsteps.

The commercials all closed with the tag line:

Whatever you want to do.
Wherever you want to go.
Whatever you want to be.
Ram!

Initially, Fiat had intended to limit Johnny to Ram and Jeep ads—especially since they already had Troy and Alessandro promoting their Alfa Romeo, Ferrari, and Maserati lines—but then Armando came up with another unique and creative idea.

In that commercial, a parking valet pulled up to the front door of an exclusive restaurant in a flashy Ferrari. When the valet stepped out of the car and held up the key, Johnny and Alessandro, approaching from different directions, reached out simultaneously for the key, which led to an argument about whose car it really was. Then the conflict turned to who was the better ball player and which food was better, Italian pasta or Texas barbecue brisket. Finally, as the two athletes debated which country had the most beautiful women, Troy walked up behind them, took the keys from the valet, and drove off in the Ferrari. That ad proved highly popular not only in Italy and the United States but went viral on the internet all over the world.

Based on the success of that ad and Johnny's appearances on Silvana's TV show as a knowledgeable person, if not an expert, on the intersection of sports and the arts, Armando created a three-part TV ad series featuring Johnny. The first ad showed Johnny pulling up to a museum at twilight in a Maserati convertible with his beautiful date in the passenger seat. The young couple sneaked into the museum after hours, and after Johnny showed his lover various paintings and sculptures of couples in the throes of romance, they began shedding their clothes. That commercial faded out on that lustful scene and closed on a shot of security guards inspecting the empty Maserati in the parking lot.

The second commercial in the series, which began airing about a month later, picked up where the first one left off, with the security guards at the museum questioning where the owner of the Maserati had disappeared to. Security cameras spotted the nearly naked couple making out on the floor behind a statue. When Johnny, now completely naked, heard the guards approaching, he urged his girlfriend to run to the Maserati and wait for him there while he distracted the guards. The camera followed her to the car and followed Johnny as he ran through the museum naked, evading the guards by hiding behind nude sculptures, Roman columns, and draperies. At the beginning of the chase, the bundle of clothes that he carried shielded his jewels from the camera, but when he accidentally dropped them and had to keep running, his junk was concealed only by the angle of his legs in motion. That scene closed with a shot of the girlfriend sitting in the Maserati and looking nervously at her watch.

The third and final commercial in the series, appearing about a month after the second one, picked up with the beautiful girl fretting in the Maserati and then more shots of Johnny running naked through the museum to escape the pursuing guards. Finally, he stormed through the exit and leaped (like a football player) into the waiting Maserati, speeding away from the scene. The series closed with the tag line, "Art Appreciation."

The series was so successful that the company decided to add a fourth commercial. It starts out the same as the third commercial, but near the end we see the beautiful young woman leaving the Maserati and re-entering the museum to look for Johnny, who is still running naked through the museum with a security guard hot on his heels. Then, the camera focuses on a marble statue of a man and a woman standing naked in a passionate embrace. As the camera pans down to the sounds of rapturous love making, we see two pairs of bare legs, one male and one female, sticking out from behind the pedestal. Finally, we see Johnny escaping in the Maserati with one of the handsome security guards, shirt unbuttoned, seated next to him, laughing and flying a pair of men's briefs in the wind. The couple making love behind the pedestal were Johnny's date and the other security guard.

By the end of our freshman year in college, Johnny and I were millionaires with more endorsement contracts than Mike had and almost as many as Troy. That summer, we could barely keep up with the demands on our time. Of course, Troy was always in demand, and we rarely got to see each other.

Between football, classes, and posing for magazine ads and making TV commercials, I found the time to write a few short stories that received critical acclaim if not much else. All of that left little time for sexual escapades, so I used my engagements with other models on photo shoots to make up for lost time.

For the rest of that summer, Troy, Johnny, and I flew separately all over Europe, posing for photos, making public appearances, and meeting with clients, potential new ones as well as those we had already signed with. Occasionally, two of us would find ourselves in the same city for one night, but never were all three of us together again that summer. Then, during our last week in Europe, Johnny and I found ourselves together on the island of Malta for a photoshoot. Since we were extras on that assignment, we had more free time than we had often gotten, and we were not as exhausted at the end of the day.

On our last night in Malta, after dinner and a few drinks, we returned to the suite we shared, propped ourselves up on the bed, and began reflecting on where we had started and how far we had come. We talked about how we had met in high school and how we had jerked off together under that oak tree in the sheep pasture. We reminisced about the Swedish college students and the high school cheerleaders and the night we lost our virginity together. Naturally, we began massaging our growing cocks through our jeans before we finally pulled them out and started stroking, not hard, but almost nostalgically.

Johnny had never been especially eager to hear the explicit details of my sexual escapades, but for some reason he began asking me to share more about my experiences, including the visit to Dante's Inferno in Milan. It felt good to be able to talk about those things so openly with him. Emboldened, I asked him, "Have you ever fucked a girl in the ass?"

"A few times," he offered, but the way he said it led me to believe that he had done it more than just "a few times." He told me about a guy he had met, a graduate student at Baylor, who liked to watch his girlfriend get fucked by another guy but would only let them fuck her in the ass. Johnny teased me that he could introduce me if I was interested.

"Did you like it? Not specifically with her," I qualified, "but fucking girls in the ass in general...as opposed to fucking them in the pussy?"

He said that he preferred the missionary position so that he could see the expressions on their faces and watch their boobs jiggle while he pumped them, but that butt-fucking was all right for a change of pace now and then. "And some girls will only take it up the ass," he assured me, "because they're afraid of getting pregnant."

"Would you ever consider fucking a *guy* in the ass?" I dared to ask.

Somewhat to my surprise, he didn't flinch but just took it as another philosophical question to ponder. "Never really thought about it," he said. But after a brief pause, he surprised me again. "Actually, that's not entirely true."

"Oh?"

"Yeah." He reminded me that on more than one occasion he had watched me fuck a guy while he was fucking a girl, and I immediately recalled those nights in Greece and Rome.

"I must admit," he continued, "that I did sometimes wonder what pleasure you could derive from that."

"Dude!" I said. (Hell, I couldn't remember the last time I had called him that, but it felt so good to be back in that groove again.) "It feels pretty much the same as fucking a pussy. It's a hole to relieve the ache in your cock and empty your balls into."

We laughed together, but then we both had to admit that it was different, not just in a physical way, but in a way that gets to the heart of what it means to be gay, straight, whatever. "With the right person, it's special," I said. "As you probably know, Troy and I have an open relationship. Both of us have sex with other guys, and I occasionally have sex with women, but it's never quite the same as it is with him."

"That's nice," Johnny sighed. "That's really nice."

I gave him a minute or so to dwell on that thought, and then I blurted out, "Would you fuck me?"

He snickered before he realized, "You're serious?"

"Yeah," I said. "You just said that when you've watched me fuck a guy, you've wondered what it was like. Well, I've never been the guy getting fucked, but sometimes when I watch a guy fucking Troy, I wonder what it's like. What is it like being the one to receive the attention, the affection, instead of the one giving it? What is it like to surrender that control to another man? But the thing is, I don't really want just anybody to show me what it's like. I want it to be somebody I trust. Somebody I can relate to. Somebody for whom it will be—or at least could be—as meaningful as it is to me. If I'm ever going to experience another man inside of me, I want it to be my best friend."

My best friend. I think that admission got to him. He had been my best friend since that first experience under the old oak tree, and he still was—my relationship with Troy notwithstanding—but it was a feeling that had always gone unspoken.

For what seemed like an eternity, he just stared at me. Then very, very slowly, he leaned over and kissed me oh-so-softly on the lips. It felt like a kiss from Troy. No, it felt like the way I imagined Troy felt when I kissed him. It was the kiss of the alpha male—gentle, but ever so much in charge.

That slow, seductive kiss evolved into a gentle probe by his tongue into my waiting mouth. Here again, it was him probing me, not the other way around. He was taking and giving at the same time, and for me it was pure delight.

He withdrew his tongue slowly but did not pull away. Instead he looked deep into my eyes as if he were seeing me for the first time. He planted butterfly kisses on my cheeks and neck. He removed my shirt with his powerful hands and kissed from my neck down to my navel, pausing to kiss and then suck on each nipple. He pulled down my jeans. My cock was already exposed, but now it was the object of his full attention. He stroked it, but not in the mechanical way he had done so many times before. He actually looked at it as if he were studying it, like it was something he had never really seen before.

Then, he did something he had never done before. He kissed my cock—first on the tip and then up and down the shaft. He tickled my balls with little flicks of his tongue and then slid his wet tongue back up the shaft. He circled the head with his tongue and then took it into his mouth. He was obviously a novice at this form of sex, so the technique left something to be desired, but the affection with which he executed the moves more than made up for his inexperience.

He rolled me over, grabbed some lube from the nightstand, and treated his cock and my ass, probing my hole with his fingers—one, then two, then three. When he started to enter me doggie-style, I stopped him and asked him to fuck me missionary style. "I really want to watch you as you take me," I said. He smiled, kissed me again, lifted my legs over his broad shoulders, and rubbed his rock-hard dick around my ass lips before entering me firmly, but lovingly.

It was so much more than just sex. It was the union of two kindred spirits.

He took my virgin ass and deflowered me in a sense for the third time in my life—yes, when I fucked a girl for the first time, then when I fucked a guy, and now as the virgin having his cherry popped.

Once he was fully inside me, he paused to give my love canal muscles time to relax. When I was ready, he swayed in slow, steady strokes, teaching me new lessons about male sexuality as he massaged my prostate. He seemed to take great delight in making me purr like a kitten. He was seeing a side of me that he had never seen before, a side that I had never experienced before. It was a great adventure for both of us, an adventure deeply rooted in fraternal love.

At times he sped up his pelvic thrusts and then slowed again as if to torture me, alternating speeds to drive me mad with carnal desire.

Every so often, he leaned against my body and kissed me or whispered lustful vulgarities in my ear. He talked to me about how I was now totally his and how he would do to me whatever he wished since I was powerless to resist, and his domination drove me absolutely fucking wild. He completely owned me, and I couldn't have been happier.

As I felt his dick throb inside me, I knew he was getting close, and he did too, of course, so he began pumping my dick until we exploded in unison. It was a multi-orgasmic experience as my prostate quaked the same time that my balls unloaded through my dick and spewed cream all over my face and body. At the same time, I felt Johnny's cock pulsate against the tender lining of my manhole and his man cream spit liquid fire deep into my gut. Together, we screamed our passion to the high heavens until

Johnny, totally spent, collapsed on top of me, our bodies fused in lust and love.

When I awoke the next morning with Johnny's naked body lying next to mine, I almost panicked. Our lovemaking had been unsurpassed. I had not realized what I had been missing all those years as a total top. Now, a whole new world had been opened to me. But I worried about Johnny. He had given me perhaps the most precious gift that any man can give to another, but it was a new experience for him as well. He had never fucked another man before, much less made love to him. How would he feel when he woke up? Would he feel good about what he had done, would he feel indifferent, or would he hate me for making him do something that he would long regret?

I didn't have to wait too long for an answer. Only a few minutes passed before Johnny opened his eyes, smiled that adorable, dimpled smile, and whispered, "Good morning, beautiful."

After we showered together and were more fully awake, we talked. I told him what an amazing feeling it was and how much I appreciated the gift he had given me. "I hope it wasn't too much of a sacrifice for you," I said. I didn't know if he was going to laugh at that comment or slug me.

"Listen, asshole...well, I guess I can really call you that now, huh? Listen, I will admit that I was unsure at first, but you are my best friend, the best friend I've ever had, my alter ego, and maybe even my soul mate. I don't know if I will ever do that again, and I'm quite sure I won't do it with anybody but you, but I have to say that it really was special. You wanted it, and I wanted to give it to you, so thank you for letting me do that."

Oh, my god! That was the most beautiful thing that anyone had ever said to me. I tried to suppress my tears of joy, but I could not. I bawled like a baby. Johnny pulled up one corner of the bed sheet to wipe my tears and held me until I was almost adult again.

35 Epilogue

The spring of Johnny's third and final year at Stanford and my final year at USC, was marked by several major announcements. Johnny was drafted in the first round by the Dallas Cowboys, but he announced that he was going to take a one-year leave to accept a Rhodes Scholarship at Oxford, where he planned to begin his pursuit of a Ph.D. in biomedical engineering.

It probably came as a surprise to everybody but those who really knew me when I announced that I would not be entering the pros but would spend the next year studying Irish literature and creative writing as a Fulbright Scholar at Trinity College in Dublin.

And most shocking of all was Mike's announcement that he was retiring from football to marry Maria, with whom he would be opening a talent agency for entertainers and athletes, and that he would be enrolling in law school at Columbia University. Mike now sits on the board of Ben Cohen's StandUp Foundation, and Maria and Troy continue to participate in fundraising activities for them as well as other organizations for gay youth.

Johnny and I both graduated from college in three years as we had committed to do. I should have bet him that I would graduate with a higher GPA because, much to my shock and amazement, I actually did. I graduated with a perfect 4.0, but Johnny fell just short because one professor gave him a B in a physics course. Many people speculated that the professor had a grudge against athletes because he had proven to be a poor one himself in his younger days, but the scuttlebutt around campus was that the professor retaliated against Johnny because Johnny refused to have sex with the man and his wife.

Our busy schedules don't allow us to get back to Hilldale very often, but when we do, we try to get together with the guys from our old team. Their girlfriends and wives know all about the underwear parties and circle jerks, but they don't seem to mind. Once, Johnny and I even had a backseat reunion with Cindy and Debbie.

During my year in Dublin, I wrote my first novel, which became a number one best seller and won several prestigious literary awards. Mike negotiated the rights to the movie, which won an Oscar for me for best screenplay and three for Troy, one as best actor in a supporting role, in which he played a sex-crazed night club singer, another one for the title song, which he wrote and sang, and for best music score, which he shared with Maria. Sam had a walk-on role and worked on the film crew.

In successive years, Troy and Johnny followed Mike on the cover of *People* magazine as the Sexiest Man Alive. When reporters asked if I felt snubbed, I replied, "Of course not. With the greatest brother and the two best friends in the whole wide world, I am the

Luckiest Man Alive, and what could be better than that?"

When Troy graduated from Julliard the following year, he and I bought a villa in Tuscany and a penthouse in Manhattan. Our homes are filled with all sorts of honors and works of art, including sculptures and paintings as well as photographs from Armando's gallery. My favorite of these is a painting that Mike commissioned for me. It depicts me as Captain America—Patrick Captain Fuckin' America Murphy.

But the one item that means the most to me, the one I will always cherish is a triple-panel box frame that hangs in my bedroom. On one side is a photograph of the old oak tree back on the farm, on the other side is that very, very special blue bandana, and in the middle rests the note that Mike left for me that remarkably memorable day: "Tie a yellow ribbon 'round the old oak tree. Your Bandana Bro."

Other Works by Brock Archer

Artbook

Brock Archer's MEN, 2022. Phoenix: Brock Archer Arts. www.brockarcher.net.

Novel

Discoveries, 2024. Phoenix: Brock Archer Arts. www.brockarcher.net.

About Brock Archer

Brock Archer has been writing homoerotic fiction for nearly two decades, but his writings have been posted mostly online, where they have received rave reviews and very high ratings from readers. *Discoveries* is his first novel to appear in print and e-book.

In addition to being an accomplished writer of gay fiction, he is also a published poet and a songwriter.

He is also an internationally recognized digital artist. His artwork has been featured in art shows in New York, California, Arizona, and Germany and online. His work has appeared in books, journals, and magazines in the United States, Germany, and Ukraine as well as his own artbook, *Brock Archer's MEN*.

Brock can be reached through his website:
www.brockarcher.net.

ES